Until the Sky Turns Silver

by Diana Faujour Skelton
and Jean Stallings

Edited by Winston Forde

Cover art by Urs Josef Kehl

© 2018

Published by SONDIATA GLOBAL MEDIA Ltd (Songlome)

ISBN: 978-1-9997878-4-4

Cover image by Urs Josef Kehl Adapted by Sondiata Global Media Ltd http://www.sondiataglobalmedia.com Songlome 36 Luna Road, Thornton Heath, Surrey CR7 8NY UK

DEDICATION

With thanks to Marie-Elisabeth Ayassamy
for support, guidance, and inspiration.

To our children:
Joline, Delora, and Tessa;
Andrea, Debra, Edgar 3rd, Melissa, and Kimberly;
and William and Eddie.

To all twenty-one of Jean's grandchildren and great-grandchildren: *How blessed to have you in my life!*

To Jean's inspiration and spiritual love, Dr. Paul Anthony Corley: *You enriched my elder years with wisdom.*

To Ignace Jeanne Ayassamy, who gave Marie-Elisabeth strength;

And to all the people who allowed Marie-Elisabeth to enter their lives, who became part of her life, and who journeyed together for a while, including:

Moya Amateau: *For being there for me when I needed it most.*

Barbara Ingram and the Children's Liberation Daycare Center: *For your dedication to early childhood education and for having helped us raise our children.*

Marie-Claire Foss: *For supporting our family and for reconnecting me with young children as a professional.*

Diana Skelton: *For having been stubborn about encouraging me to express myself.*

IN MEMORY OF

Daniel Dantzler, Karen A. Erdman, Sr. Angela Esposito,
Dick Gregory, Hélène Tombez Kehl, Harry Lennon,
Doris Newsome Lewis, Gloria Mills, Angela Price, Rosette Proost,
Camilla Roberson-Claxton, Emma Lee Williams,
and Patricia Ann Williams.
*

ACKNOWLEDGEMENTS

For critical readings or editing by: Joel Naftali Aaron, Moya Amateau, Valerie Brunner, Anne Carion, Jill Cunningham, Patricia Heyberger, Rosemarie Hoffmann, Jane Dewey Hsiao, Reachel Herbert Kayeye, Venance Francis Magombera, Anne Monnet, Salehe Mussa Seif, Julia Sick, and Emma Speaks

For inspiration or advice from: Susan Warford Ailles, Eugen Brand, Rosa Cho, Christopher Cleary, Lenore Cola, Denis Cretinon, Thomas Croft, Joshua Donchance, Hyacinth Egner, Patrice Faujour, Benzner Grimes, Connor Janes, Denis Jay, Brenda Ann Kenneally, Ruth King, Mary-Ellen Hostak, Chandra Laizeau, Tina Lindsey, Guy Malfait, Deirdre Mauss, Angela Evosevic Mendolaro, Sylvia Onder, Carol Paige, Jesse Perkins, Jacqueline Plaisir, Isabelle Pypaert-Perrin, Elijah Price, Kris Roels, Bryan Seabrooke, Ernest Sligh, Ruth Smith, Ms. Suggs, Jean Toussaint, Tony Velasquez, Ivan Williams, Raneisha Williams, and Brenda and Wanda Winslow

For archiving by: Anne Herbiet and the Joseph Wresinski Center in Baillet, France

And for transcribing by: Jessie Kaliski, Dylan S. Moglen, and Carrie Supple.

[...]
Everything we write
will be used against us
or against those we love.
These are the terms,
take them or leave them.
Poetry never stood a chance
of standing outside history.
One line typed twenty years ago
can be blazed on a wall in spraypaint
to glorify art as detachment
or torture of those we
did not love but also
did not want to kill.

We move but our words stand
become responsible
for more than we intended
and this is verbal privilege [...]

I am thinking this in a country
where words are stolen out of mouths
as bread is stolen out of mouths
where poets don't go to jail
for being poets, but for being
dark-skinned, female, poor.
I am writing this in a time
when anything we write
can be used against those we love
where the context is never given
though we try to explain, over and over
For the sake of poetry at least
I need to know these things [...]

— *Excerpted from "North American Time"*
by Adrienne Rich

Note from the authors
While none of the characters in this novel are real people, their story is documentary fiction based on our lives and those of people close to us. We have imagined their fictional story from the positions we live in.

CONTENTS

FOREWORD

My family has been in the depths of poverty. I know what it is to struggle with all your might to keep your dignity in the eyes of others.

Upper-class people might have defended people in poverty before but never actually met them in person. For them, having the possibility to get to know people personally can be important because it could help them become less judgmental. They could even become allies by helping people or sponsoring an activity.

We live in a society of expectations that grow higher and higher. Someone who does not fulfil those high expectations is judged harshly. But I think we should look for the success that poet Bessie A. Stanley describes:

> 'What is success? To laugh often and much; to win the respect of intelligent people and the affection of children; to earn the appreciation of honest critics and endure the betrayal of false friends; to appreciate the beauty; to find the best in others; to leave the world a bit better, whether by a healthy child, a garden patch or a redeemed social condition; to know even one life has breathed easier because you have lived. This is to have succeeded!'

Until the Sky Turns Silver is about people with different levels of education trying to find the best and appreciate the beauty in one another.

– Marie-Elisabeth Ayassamy

1. REACHING

When Tanita was buzzed into the speech therapist's office, her little brother Cedric had just finished with his appointment. Looking past the windowless walls and drab carpeting with the nap worn thin, Tanita focused on Ms. Adler, anxious about this initial test.

"How did it go? I know Cedric can act up sometimes, but he's a good kid —."

The busy professional waved her away, saying only, "The school will get my report." Before Tanita could say another word, Ms. Adler had brushed past her and was bestowing a warm smile on her next client. "So good to see you again, Madison."

Suddenly self-conscious about her own fraying T-shirt, Tanita looked at the white woman who must be Madison's mother. Her sleek hairstyle and well-tailored blouse gave her an air of confidence that Tanita envied.

Six-year-old Cedric bounded ahead of Tanita out of the office, finally burning the energy he had barely pent up for the past hour. Out on the sidewalk, he stopped short at a pushcart beneath two red and yellow pinwheel awnings. Smelling hot-dog water, mustard, and salt, Cedric pointed to the picture of a pretzel plastered on the side of the steel chassis. He turned a hopeful look at Tanita.

She sighed. She did have spare money for a pretzel today — but the teacher had said that Cedric might need regular sessions with this speech therapist. If she bought one on his first day, he would *always* expect a pretzel after speech therapy. That would add up to three dollars a week, which she might not be able to afford. Better to save it for a special treat. She shook her head and pointed to a newsstand instead. "What about gum? You can have gum today." Cedric's face fell, but he walked toward the newsstand to see what she was pointing at. Disappointed, he chose a pack of cinnamon-flavoured gum. He was hungry. He would rather have had the pretzel.

For so long, their family had wondered when he would learn to talk properly. Finally last spring, his kindergarten teacher had told Tanita that Cedric probably had dyslexia. "Don't worry," the teacher had said, "It's a very common learning disability."

Tanita had been furious, "What do you mean by disability? We take him to the doctor. Why didn't the doctor ever tell us that?"

It turned out that Cedric's dyslexia made it hard for him not only to learn to read, but also to remember and understand things. And today the speech therapist had tested him for "expressive language delay." It infuriated Tanita to think of all the times she had pushed herself to read to him, not realizing that somehow he couldn't quite get what she was saying. When Tanita was growing up, no one had had time to read to her. They had been moving from place to place. It had been hard enough to find matching socks to wear, let alone time to go to the library. So when Cedric was born, Tanita, then 13, had gone straight to the library. She wanted him to hear the stories she had missed. But now it sounded as though, in a way, he had missed out on them too. It felt like they had both been tricked.

Now, as Tanita steered Cedric down the crowded street toward the subway, she gave a sigh of relief to see him perk up again. Because taking trains was Cedric's favourite thing to do, he never balked at commuting. Yanking his hand free from hers, Cedric ducked under the turnstile. Still fumbling for her fare card, Tanita felt her throat swell with stress until she saw him come to a stop on the platform. When she caught up to him, she heard him chattering to himself. "Hurry up, train! Zoom!"

Looking up at Tanita as she firmly recaptured his hand, Cedric asked, "Can I drive a train?"

"Maybe someday. When you're bigger. How was it with Ms. Adler?"

"She asked too much." Cedric frowned. "Can stupid people still drive trains?"

Tanita sighed as she saw a look of defeat in his eyes. But Cedric's face lit up again as the train pounded into the station with a huge rush of air, its metal wheels screeching on the tracks. It pulled to a stop and opened its doors just where they stood.

The crowd scrambled to snatch up bags and strollers and children, and pushed past one another to find an empty seat or a handhold near the doors right under an air-conditioning vent. Tanita preferred to steer Cedric further away from the doors, where she wouldn't worry that the stampede at every stop might push him out of the train. At the very end of the car, she reached upward to grip the rigid metal rung with one hand. With the other hand, she held fast to Cedric's hand despite his sweaty fidgeting.

Straining in two directions, Tanita's worries turned inward. After interminable discussions, Pamela and the others had asked her to write a speech for the whole group. At the time, Tanita *wanted* to be chosen — but soon afterwards, she began to fear that the whole thing was a mistake. By now, Tanita was sure of it. During Cedric's appointment, she had gone to Prospect Park to try to start writing. The staid walkways and lush greenery seemed inviting. It absorbed the city's noise and stink, softening even the blare of car horns and the stench of rancid garbage. But suddenly so far removed from everyday chaos, Tanita found that, instead of being able to put pen to paper, her mind was untethered, drifting blankly from cloud to cloud.

How was she supposed to write a speech? Most of the time, working, rushing from errand to chore, looking after Cedric, her head was crowded with things she wished she *did* have time to write down. Anxious thoughts jostled and shoved one another — about rats in the vacant lot next door; friends burnt out of their home because a neighbour smoked in bed; another friend trying to hide his trips to a food pantry because he hadn't told his wife that he was out of work again; the girl upstairs who broke her leg when she tripped on uncollected garbage right outside their building.... Was any of that what she should be writing about? Tanita had no clear idea. But for the moment she had no place else to be. Holding a brand-new pen, feeling the unaccustomed luxury of time, she would try to write. The blank page in her spiral notebook overwhelmed her. Her thoughts ebbed away as she closed her eyes to enjoy the lull of the September sun on her face and the green essence of the park on the faint breeze.

"Well, of all the unmitigated gall! How could he do that to you after everything you — " A stranger's staccato voice faded away as quickly as it had punctured the bubble of stillness. Tanita opened her eyes to see a woman in a tennis skirt, already striding away, a cell phone to her ear. Tanita flipped shut her notebook, still blank, and looked at her watch. Almost time to pick up Cedric; she might as well go.

When Tanita and Cedric got home, their grandmother, Cheryl Brown, was startled out of a doze. From the shabby sofa where she had been folding laundry, she snapped, "Where have you been? School was out hours ago."

Cedric skittered across the linoleum floor to crouch by a kitchen cupboard. Pulling out a plastic cup, he began rolling it back and forth on the floor, chanting to himself, "Choo, choo!"

Tanita looked dryly at her grandmother. "Today was Cedric's test. You know, the school said to take him to a speech therapist."

Frowning, Mrs. Brown said, "You been wasting your time. You left work early again?" The only wage earner in the household, Tanita worked the phones for a survey company.

"It's not like I had a choice. You hate all those subway stairs, and Cedric gets away from you."

Shaking her head at a sock that now had two holes, Mrs. Brown said, "I don't like you working anyway. Why don't you go back to school?"

Without answering, Tanita turned away. Stepping around Cedric in the cramped kitchenette, she filled a pan with water and spooned some instant coffee into a chipped mug. She had worked hard and done well in high school. If she had started classes at the City University of New York last year, she'd be about to start her sophomore year by now. She still wondered about going to college one of these days, making something of herself — but when?

The next morning, Tanita got a phone call from Pamela. "So, how is the writing going?"

"There's just no time to write."

"That's a pity. I know how much you have to say."

Tanita didn't know how to answer that. Sometimes she had so much to say that she lay awake late into the night, with words, thoughts, memories throbbing frantically. Other times, she didn't know what to say. Like now.

Pamela was still talking in her flat British accent. "Do you think you'll have time later this week? Or would you like for us to try writing together instead?"

"No. Thanks, but... I want to start on my own." Tanita knew she sounded abrupt. Even as she spoke, she wasn't sure that what she said was true. But now that Pamela and the others had agreed that she should write the speech, how could she admit that she felt at a complete loss, just stagnating?

"Oh. Very well then." Pamela sounded chastened.

"No offence. I mean, you do help a lot when all of us write together. I just want to try on my own first."

"You're right. I know you can do it. I'll call you again soon."

Pamela

As she hung up, Pamela was twisting her hair, trying to subdue her growing stress. She was counting on Tanita to write this message for an event at the United Nations. Pamela knew how hard writing could be, and she couldn't think of a way to help Tanita. Last week, Pamela had been sure it would work out. Tanita did have something to say. When she spoke at their meetings, others would chime in: "You said it, girl. I hear you." Pamela had agreed with the group that whatever Tanita wrote would reflect their experience too. But were they asking too much? Tanita was only 19, and she was more of a talker than a writer. She had had to switch schools so many times, it was a wonder she had learned anything. And she was always so busy. She worked at a part-time job and helped her grandmother to raise Cedric. On top of that, she volunteered to help run sidewalk art workshops for children with All Together in Dignity, the group where they had all met. So when on earth could she find the time to write?

After phoning Tanita, Pamela waited for her roommate, Yun Hee, to finish rooting through the cramped closet they shared in a dilapidated third-floor walk-up apartment. Pamela had to hurry to be on time for yet another appointment with the UN official preparing the World Day event. Although Pamela had once worked in a fancy office in London, she often felt awkward dressing up now that she lived in a low-income neighbourhood of Brooklyn. She didn't want to stand out too much — but she also had to be taken seriously at the UN. So when her turn at the closet came, she rummaged past Yun Hee's flowery cotton sundresses to grab a serviceable navy blazer and slacks. The hard part was finding a white blouse that wasn't in need of mending or dry cleaning. Who had time or money for that? Finally she found a beige nylon blouse that would do, along with flat-heeled loafers that wouldn't hamper her over-scheduled day.

Varag

In midtown Manhattan, Varag and his wife, Blandine, were having breakfast together. This did not happen often. Usually Varag rose early, impatient to be out the door long before Blandine even began styling her glossy blond hair. But this morning he waited for her, calculating how best to extract a favor. In the pattern they had settled into long ago, she was the more exacting one.

The early-morning sun washed into their apartment, glinting through the glass doors of the terrace to illuminate their chess set, hand carved of sycamore and walnut, standing ready for their nightly game. Perched far above the hum of the street, Blandine was steeping a gingery beverage recommended by her acupuncturist to maintain her complexion. Varag took his coffee strong and black. With the punch of energy it gave him, he broached his subject: "You know, I had quite an interesting meeting yesterday."

Reluctantly, Blandine let her pale eyes stray from the pattern on her delicate china teapot to look at him. "Did you?"

Already, Varag regretted attempting this conversation. He was not quite sure himself just what had intrigued him about Pamela McEvoy. He had no idea how to express it, let alone how to convince Blandine to attend Pamela's meeting. But it was too late to stop now. Varag remained a determined man, even after a decade of accommodating himself to marriage with Blandine.

"I've been meeting lately with a non-governmental organization, quite a small NGO that I'd never heard of before last month. They do projects with poor children and families. What was striking about them was the way they define partnership."

"Hasn't the United Nations already defined partnership dozens of times over? Certainly you don't need an NGO for that." Now Blandine was eating celery crackers. It was amazing how daintily she could eat, as though no crumb would dare fall onto her immaculately tailored sheath dress.

"In fact, it's just the opposite. At the UN, we speak all the time of 'participation of the poor,' but without making it clear just what that might mean." Varag poured himself more coffee, and continued, "This NGO actually plans and evaluates each step of its development projects together in partnership with people who are so very poor and excluded that they would never attend a community meeting."

Blandine had finished eating and was gazing out the window as she sipped her tea. Varag knew she preferred to ease into the day without talking about work over breakfast. She said, "That makes no sense. If they don't even attend meetings, how on earth do they participate in any serious planning?"

"Their technique seems to involve a lot of individual home visits." Realizing that he didn't actually know the answer, Varag decided to get to his main point. "Listen, Blandine, I would like you to attend one of their meetings for me."

He now had her full attention. Her slender eyebrows rose as she waited, wordlessly, for him to continue.

"Maybe it could connect to your work. Doesn't your ambassador want to make a priority of development work this year?"

Blandine nodded slowly. "Yes. But what on earth does he need with any NGO? He has his programme mapped out already."

It was Varag's turn to hesitate. "Look, I'll be frank: I'm not really sure. But I'm telling you there's something unusual about this NGO and I'd like to uncover more. They talk a good game, but going to a meeting at their center is a way to find out if there's anything behind it or not."

"So why aren't you going yourself?"

"The problem is that their meeting conflicts with the General Assembly agenda point on social development. The GA is keeping our whole office extra-busy every day and night this week. So I thought maybe you would be interested. Aren't you curious?"

"Curiosity is for children. You know you ought to be a little more strategic to avoid wasting time. However — since you ask me — I will go." A graceful smile slowly lit her face. "Just as I know you will come with me to the German ambassador's reception next week, since I ask you."

Varag had often told Blandine exactly how much he hated the polite banalities of receptions where everyone was too cautiously diplomatic to ever see a debate through to the end. But he was still curious about the NGO, so he agreed to the bargain.

2. FREE-FOR-ALL

Having swept and mopped the room to prepare for the meeting, Pamela made sure to arrange several photo albums into an engaging display of the children's workshops. She had already festooned the walls with their artwork. "Be a Superhero for Peace!" proclaimed a poster. At a recent workshop, five of the children had painted it together, their hands jostling one another as they stencilled the letters before filling them in with bright polka dots and stripes. Tonight Pamela was making an extra effort to create a welcoming atmosphere for a woman who might come for the first time. Mrs. Ernestine Jones, a neighbour of Pamela's, was raising three grandchildren in a one-bedroom apartment. Usually when Pamela invited her to a meeting, Mrs. Jones would just laugh, saying, "Don't you know I'm busy enough already?"

But last week, it was Mrs. Jones who had stopped Pamela on the street one evening, just as the clouds were turning crimson in the fading sunlight. Straining her gaze to admire the slivers of sky visible between buildings, Pamela was startled to realize that Mrs. Jones' craggy voice had been calling out to her from a window: "Pamm-la! When's the next one?"

"Sorry, what?"

"Your next meetin'. You always talking about those meetings, child, so when's the next one?"

"Oh! A week from tomorrow. You mean you might come?"

"I just might. Remind me next week."

Now, as she prepared for the meeting, Pamela was glad to have the help of Tanita's grandmother, Mrs. Cheryl Brown, and another woman from their neighbourhood, Ornella Walker. The three of them were crowded into the tiny kitchen making macaroni salad and cookies. Although they hadn't cooked together before, they knew one another from the children's art workshops. Cedric had taken part for several years now, as had Ernestine Jones's grandchildren. Ornella had no children; but her husband's niece Darleen had six, and all of them participated in the workshops too.

As they worked, Mrs. Brown talked about Cedric's appointments. "I feel bad for Tanita. They got her running around like crazy to see all these different specialists and caseworkers. I just know she'd rather be picking up more hours at work. And I've always been worried about Cedric, I knew there was something wrong, but look how many years it's taken for anyone to figure out just what it might be —." She broke off to glare pointedly at Ornella. "Shouldn't you be washing that knife before you use it again?"

Raising her eyebrows, Ornella hesitated; then shrugged. Giving the knife a cursory rinse, she said, "I once nannied a girl who had dyslexia. Her mamma got an extra teacher to spend all day with her in pre-school."

Pamela was surprised, "All day long?"

"Yes, and even at home too, to give her extra learning. She was only 4 and they were getting her extra time on those tests they have for the fanciest school in the city."

Ornella began mashing sugar into butter. She continued, "If you ask me, that's too much teachin'. Children learn more from life. Back in Jamaica, if a girl can hold a spoon, she can help cook a meal." An emphatic nod of her head set her hooped earrings dangling.

Mrs. Brown frowned. "I want Cedric to get the help he needs. But we can't afford all that."

Ornella scoffed, "Well, that girl had too much. A nanny, a cook, a maid, a driver, *and* a private tutor — all at age 4! That's just no good for any child. You might as well raise them in a zoo."

Now Ornella frowned at Pamela. "What kind of macaroni salad is that, child? You need more salt and pepper, and maybe some hot chili pepper and garlic too, or no one's gonna want that. You got to bring the flavor."

Pamela sighed. She had thought the cooking would get done more quickly with the three of them. Realizing belatedly that they each had very different ideas about how things should be done in a kitchen, she remembered the saying, "Too many cooks spoil the broth." Mrs. Brown was fastidious about washing her hands frequently and washing every spoon or bowl instantly — and she looked so disappointed when Ornella and Pamela were less quick to do the same. Ornella felt strongly about adding a lot of spice to the salad, and Mrs. Brown had wanted more mayonnaise in it, but Pamela was worried about special diets for people with high blood pressure or diabetes. At the same time, she knew that her own ultra-bland salad would probably remain untouched. Should they offer a second version of the entire salad? Pamela had not the foggiest idea.

In fact, the more she thought about their different approaches, the more she wondered whether the three of them had anything in common. Would they even have made the effort to get to know one another if not for the children's attachment to the art workshops?

Anxious that time was running out, Pamela rushed as she diced another tomato. Her knife slipped, and she cut herself. Stopping short, she put her stinging finger into her mouth for a moment and then excused herself to hunt for a Band-Aid. By now, she could tell that she was slowing the other women down, her hands clumsier and less accustomed to cooking for a big group. Mrs. Brown, even with the ache of aging joints, had such highly skilled hands. Watching her cook, Pamela remembered seeing those same hands care for Cedric over the years, knowing just when to wipe his nose or to shake a stern finger at his mischief. Ornella's sturdy fingers were not only efficient in the kitchen but playful. Pamela had seen her invent games of peekaboo to coax a laugh from even the shyest child.

Deciding to leave the two of them to finish the light meal, Pamela went back to straightening the meeting room. She was just putting up a pot of coffee when the doorbell rang. Glancing at her watch, she saw that it was almost six, the time people had been invited to arrive. But the smartly-dressed woman on the doorstep was a stranger to her.

"I'm here for the meeting," announced Blandine, brushing past Pamela and into the meeting room with startlingly crisp self-assurance.

Just then, Pamela's teammate Jesse bounded into the room. "Hi, I'm Jesse Williams, one of the art workshop volunteers here. What's your name?"

A disconcerted look registered on Blandine's face as she took in this kinetic young man with a residue of aquamarine paint lodged around his fingernails. Seeing the two of them together, Pamela noticed for the first time how frayed the collar on Jesse's plaid shirt was.

"I am Blandine Dulavoir. Is this not a meeting on development and economic issues?"

"Well, if you mean ending poverty, yeah, that's the whole point of our get-togethers." As Jesse spoke, he was hoisting folding tables to move them into a square that everyone would fit around. "We meet every month or so to talk about different topics. Tonight we'll be talking about work and employment. So how did you hear about this?"

"Varag Vosgrichian of the United Nations encouraged me to come."

"Oh, do you work with him?" asked Pamela, relieved to understand Blandine's presence.

"Actually, I work at the Permanent Mission of Belgium to the United Nations. Varag is my husband. Are you the one he met?"

"Yes, I'm Pamela McEvoy. It's such a pleasure to have you join us. Would you like some coffee or tea?"

As Blandine accepted a styrofoam cup with a generic tea bag dangling in it, she politely hid her distaste and began sizing up Pamela. Strands of her mouse-brown ponytail were coming adrift. Her pale white skin looked innocent of make-up. One sleeve of her acrylic orange sweater was pushed up to her elbow, while the other had slid back to her wrist. The long sleeve bore a small, but noticeable smear of butter. Blandine had to stifle an urge to straighten up the young woman's appearance. Was this nondescript person actually the one who had so intrigued Varag? And was it even possible that Varag's interest in her NGO came more from a personal interest in Pamela herself? A silly thought, given that Varag himself had sent Blandine here; but distrust was a reflex for her.

Other people were arriving. Yun Hee, who was responsible for the art workshop programme, arrived together with a family with four children. A few minutes later, Yun Hee's boyfriend, Travis, came to help her out with the children while the adults held their meeting.

As Pamela served refreshments and made introductions, she tried to picture Varag Vosgrichian and Blandine Dulavoir as a couple. Certainly she would never have imagined them together. How could such a picture-perfect woman have chosen a husband whose shirts, expensive though they were, always seemed incorrigibly rumpled? And he had been so doggedly passionate when he spoke about using economic development to end the injustice of children begging in the streets. Pamela was sure that she herself would have no idea how to voice her own passions when she was faced with the placid Blandine.

Hearing Mrs. Ernestine Jones's heavy steps at the door, Pamela rushed to make her welcome and introduce her around. Mrs. Jones's fingers were taut against the long cross-body strap of her worn purse. Seeing a line of sweat on her forehead, Pamela offered her a cool drink and a comfortable chair.

Tanita was next to arrive, her dark hair freshly coiffed in micro-braids. Pamela made a point of sticking to small talk for a few minutes before asking about her writing. Still, "I'll be getting to it," was all Tanita would say about that.

At half past six, people were still drifting in and greeting one another casually. Sensing Blandine's unease and impatience, Pamela began the meeting abruptly. Yun Hee and Travis gathered up Cedric and the other children in the group to shepherd them into another room for a game of "I Spy."

In the meeting room, Jesse invited several of the adults to share short texts that he had helped them prepare in advance.

Too late, Pamela realized that she should have invited everyone to introduce themselves before the presentations, but Darleen Walker was already reading her piece. Pamela didn't want to interrupt, knowing that Darleen was nervous and had worked hard with Jesse to prepare. She spoke of being sent by the welfare office to stand outdoors, washing the same wall again and again. Not only was the work pointless, but the hours she was assigned conflicted with getting her children to school on time.

Then Ornella's husband, Maurice Walker, talked about his experiences looking for work and trying to bridge the disconnect between the training programmes he had enrolled in and the skills that employers actually looked for.

As the scent of baked cookies wafted into the room, Ornella rushed back to the kitchen to remove them from the oven.

When Maurice had finished talking, Helen Jansky, a teacher at a local university, began presenting the recent changes in local and national laws about workfare, welfare, and employment.

The presentation was going smoothly, when Mrs. Jones interrupted Helen, her voice loud and anxious: "What's the point of any of these laws when they don't let us raise our own kin? They say if I don't put my grandson on Ritalin, they're gonna take him away. You'd think a person would be ashamed to have ideas like that come into their head." She began coughing.

Immediately, several people began talking at once, telling their own stories of foster care or Ritalin.

As Jesse tried ineffectually to steer the meeting back on course, Pamela noticed a blank look on Blandine's face. Moving next to her, Pamela explained softly, "I don't know if you've heard of Ritalin?"

"Of course. Prescribed for hyperactivity."

"Yes, but it's often given to children in low-income families who aren't hyperactive at all. You know, if a child is having trouble keeping up with classwork in school, he may start acting up out of sheer frustration."

"And disrupting an entire class."

Pamela nodded. "Often, social workers encourage a diagnosis of hyperactivity so that the child will be put on Ritalin."

"Surely the class deserves to have the disruptions stop."

Pamela stopped talking so they could hear Mrs. Jones's objections. "I do not want Allan put on that medicine. My neighbor's son got put on that same drug. They had him on it for six years. The mother knew it was making him sick. But the doctor said he would report her if she didn't keep giving him Ritalin. And, God help him, that poor boy ended his life, jumping out a window. But the social worker says I'll lose custody of Allan if he doesn't take it."

Pamela continued whispering to Blandine: "Even if they're sure it's not what their child needs, many parents go along with it because so much pressure is put on them."

Now Darleen Walker was telling Mrs. Jones, "Don't you let that social worker push you around. You're a good grandmother; she should see that. You bust your butt taking care of all those kids."

Her uncle Maurice was nodding his head, "Those social workers want to get all up in your business."

"That's not entirely fair," Helen Jansky said. "Of course you shouldn't lose custody of your children for something like this, but I think that many caseworkers really do care about trying to keep families together."

Darleen objected, her voice strident. "They want to know everything in your life, from your toenails to the gray hair on top of your head. But don't you let them dig in for anything they can get. Once the system takes your kids away, they will be lost."

Helen argued, "They make mistakes, like all of us; but you can't imagine how heavy their caseloads have been getting in recent years. I have a friend who gets run ragged doing social work. On some days she barely has time to catch her breath, and she can hardly sleep for worrying about every family she meets."

Darleen said, "But a child taken away from his parents won't ever get over it. My sister is 24 years old, and she still talks every day to her little girl about that foster care."

By this time, several people were shouting at once. Mrs. Jones had a coughing fit and stopped talking altogether.

Blandine looked quizzically at Pamela and said, "Since you seem to have finished discussing employment, I will be heading to my next engagement."

"Oh please stay. I'm sorry we got off track —." But to Pamela's dismay, Blandine was already slipping gracefully out of the room.

Moments later, Jesse gave up entirely on trying to organize the unfolding chaos and began passing around macaroni salad dolloped onto cardboard plates. Seeing Ornella dig into it enthusiastically, Pamela guessed that the seasonings had been ramped up several notches after her exit from the kitchen.

Not feeling hungry, Pamela busied herself by passing out napkins and refilling cups. She heard a variety of discussions going on around the room — some people were giving one another advice about dealing with child protective services; others had gathered around Helen and gone back to the topic of work; still others were just chatting about life in general. Some of it sounded constructive, but she couldn't bring herself to join in any of the conversations. Blandine's evident disdain for the undisciplined discussion made Pamela wonder just what the point of the meeting had been.

As people were leaving, Pamela began sweeping up the meeting room. When it was tidy, she went to straighten the kitchen — only to find Mrs. Jones just finishing the task.

"Oh, you shouldn't have! This is the first time you've been our guest, and I know you do so much work at home."

"Cleaning settles my mind, child." She rinsed out a sponge drenched with bleach. "But I'm just so worried about Allan. What if they take him away while he's at school?"

"Do you have legal custody of him?"

"If you mean papers, no, I guess not. But I've raised him on and off since he was born. My daughter Brenda has never been up to dealing with her son."

"That must be hard for you."

Mrs. Jones sighed. "I just want what's best for Allan. But it's true that it's not easy to see my own daughter going through so much trouble. We had hard times when my children were young — and the last thing I wanted was for my children to have lives just as hard as I did. I'm just trying to help. But it's like I'm living my own life over again by raising Brenda's son."

"Where is your daughter now?"

"Usually in the South Bronx. She moves around, but we stay in touch."

"You'll probably need her to sign some papers giving formal custody to you."

"But that's not right. *She's* Allan's mother, I don't want to take custody away from my own daughter. And I do not want to put my own grandchild into the foster care system."

"Listen, I'm no expert. But I do have a friend who is a child rights lawyer. I'll ring him for some advice as soon as I get home."

When Mrs. Jones had left, Pamela cornered Jesse to take out her frustrations, "What kind of meeting was that? I thought you were going to run the discussion this time. How could you let it get so chaotic?"

"Chill out, Pamela. When people have that much trouble on their mind, they have to be able to talk about it right away. I think this is the one place where we should always respect their need to talk."

"They also need to be listened to, but by the end no one could hear what anyone else was saying." Pamela caught up the strands of hair that had escaped her ponytail, and began twisting them around her finger.

"Well then, why didn't you jump in to steer things back on course?"

"How could I? I was too busy trying to explain to Blandine what we were talking about. We must have sounded like incomprehensible numpties to her."

Jesse laughed. "Is that a British insult?"

"What do you think, you gormless prat!"

"I think that Blandine is the real reason you're upset: you think we looked bad in front of a fancy lady from the UN."

"Well, we didn't look good."

"Maybe you shouldn't have invited her in the first place. Sometimes what everyone needs is just a safe place to talk, not to 'stay on topic.' Don't be such a control freak."

Exasperated, Pamela stalked down to the cellar to wash a load of the tablecloths used during the meeting. Measuring out the detergent, Jesse's words still ringing in her ears, Pamela knew he was right. It *had* been important for Mrs. Jones to have a place to share her concerns about Allan. Pamela didn't really regret that the meeting topic had changed. But she did hate feeling so foolish in front of a person as competent as Blandine.

Blandine

During the taxi ride home from the meeting, Blandine tried to fight off a wave of melancholy. Mrs. Jones's coughing fit and the argumentative stew of voices had reminded her of the courtyard of her childhood home in Brussels. The house itself had been a haven of burnished oak, gracious manners, and bouquets of dried lavender. But when her father had a falling out over professional ethics with the head of the hospital where he worked, he quit his job and hung a shingle in his own street. The shed in their courtyard was soon converted into a consulting room for his medical practice. In pleasant weather, patients would wait their turn on benches in the courtyard itself. Blandine never forgot the agitation in their voices carrying up to her room when she was trying to concentrate on her homework. The unending procession of ill children, frail elderly people, crying babies, and worried relatives disturbed her peace of mind. The knowledge that each of them felt some kind of pain or anguish intruded on her daily life. Whenever her father was called away in the night for an emergency, she always woke as his boots thundered downstairs. Then her restless dreams would fill again with the faces from the courtyard as she wondered which patient was doing worse.

When she got home from Pamela's meeting, Varag was still working late, so she watched the news and went to bed alone.

The next morning, Blandine again found Varag waiting to have breakfast with her. Although she never ate much in the morning, he enjoyed scrambling eggs. Today, he chopped some pastrami to fold in. She knew its smoky flavour reminded him of the spicy basturma meat of his Armenian childhood.

"Well, how was it?" he asked, tucking into his meal with a hearty appetite.

"Frankly, I never saw such disorganization. It started late, everyone spoke at once, and no one stayed on topic. You would think they had never attended a meeting before. What a waste of time! Why, what's so funny?"

Varag had burst out laughing. "That's pretty much what Pamela advertised. When she spoke about building partnership with people in extreme poverty, she said that just inviting them to a meeting isn't enough. She spends months, even years, getting to know people and trying to convince them to be part of these meetings. Some of them probably *haven't* attended a meeting before."

"Well, you could have warned me."

"Would you have gone?"

"Certainly not!"

"That's why I didn't warn you. Anyway, I do appreciate your going, and I'll be going to your reception, as promised, so won't you give me a bit more detail?"

"In fact, there was something surprising." Blandine carefully poured herself a second cup of herbal tea. "Professor Helen Jansky was there. Do you know her work? She researches international labor and employment issues at New York University. Her work is quite respected. I believe she's spoken on expert panels at the UN several times now. And yet there she was, making an oversimplified presentation to people who were rudely interrupting. Really, I cannot fathom why she was wasting her time there."

"Well, maybe if you had stayed until the end of the meeting, it would have been clearer."

"Excuse me?"

"I just happen to know that you left early."

"Have you been spying on me?"

Varag grinned. "Of course not. But it seems that Pamela is an early riser. She e-mailed me this morning asking that I apologize to you for the chaos of the meeting and saying she was sorry you had to leave so quickly."

"How forward of her! She should be happy that I attended at all. In any case, my promise was to attend, not to remain until the end of a shouting match."

"I'm glad to hear it. So you won't object when I slip out of the reception early."

Blandine felt like throwing something at Varag when he teased her this way — but instead she simply flipped her gleaming hair at him as she left for work.

Tanita

Thinking over yesterday's meeting, Tanita too wondered what the point had been. It hadn't helped her feel ready to start writing a speech. Last year, it had been Ornella who was chosen to speak on behalf of the group. Tanita clearly remembered her twinge of envy as she wished that *she* had been the one to step proudly to the podium. Instead she had been stuck alone for hours preparing dozens of bologna sandwiches for their group's picnic lunch afterwards. She had been resentful. No one ever paid any attention to what she might want in life.

Now, however, she wondered how Ornella had ever found the time to prepare a speech. Tanita still hadn't even started. She was just too worried about Cedric. Again, she had had to take off from work, this time to have him evaluated by a psychologist. An evaluation had already been required before the city sent him to the speech therapist. Now for some reason, he had to be evaluated all over again. This was ridiculous. He was a perfectly normal boy except for his dyslexia. Did they think she had nothing to do all week long but take him to appointments? The really maddening thing was that this psychologist was much harsher than the first one.

After misunderstanding the address and then having to transfer across three different subway lines to get to the psychologist's office, they arrived with Cedric already fidgety and distant. Then, even though they still managed not to be late, Ms. Miller kept them waiting for almost an hour.

When finally Cedric was told to use a set of blocks to reproduce a shape shown in Ms. Miller's testing booklet, he decided instead to push three blocks into a line. Moving all three blocks ahead together, he shouted, "Choo! Choo! It's the Sooooul Train."

Ms. Miller frowned fiercely. "No. That's wrong. You didn't do what I told you to. Aren't you old enough to follow instructions yet?"

Cedric lost any shred of interest he might have had in interacting with such a grumpy lady. After clattering the blocks against the wall, he fidgeted in stony silence for the rest of the session. His refusal even to touch the blocks again made Ms. Miller doubly impatient. As she questioned Tanita about their home life — "Does he have his own bed? Who bathes him?" — Ms. Miller grew rapidly, incomprehensibly, antagonistic.

"What do you mean you sing to him after the lights are already out for bedtime? Bedtime is bedtime. He's taking advantage of you to stay up later. You're too lenient."

"What are you talking about? Lullabies *are* his bedtime; that's just how we do." Perched on the edge of a folding chair, Tanita began to feel as trapped and fidgety as Cedric.

"Look at your temper! You must be more patient if you think you're old enough to raise a child."

The entire conversation had been ridiculous. Tanita wouldn't have believed it if she hadn't been part of it. And yet, on their way home, she found herself yelling at Cedric more than usual, trying to act like the stricter adult that the psychologist urged her to become.

Now, turning the corner onto their block, Tanita stopped short. The jumbled heap of furniture out on the sidewalk could only belong to the Ramirez family, their upstairs neighbors. She had not realized that they were being evicted. It wasn't surprising, though, knowing what a hard time they had making the rent. And the landlord had never liked their four active sons stomping all over the apartment. Once he had shouted at Carmen Ramirez, "You don't belong here. You should go live at the dump."

It broke Tanita's heart to see the Ramirez's furniture heaped on the sidewalk. Would they find a place to store any of it before it was stolen? There was their ancient armchair with the plaid upholstery, threadbare and smelling of roach killer. A child's bed looked brand new, probably bought on layaway credit. Where would they be sleeping tonight? As she stared, Tanita realized that Cedric too must recognize the furniture. But did he know what it meant?

In any case, Cedric probably didn't remember living in a shelter. He had been just a baby when a fire in the apartment below theirs had sent their own family into the shelter system. At the time, they still lived with their mother, who had already tested HIV-positive. The trauma of homelessness had been hard on her health and she had died a year later.

Among Tanita's memories from their last year together was a desperate one of spending the night at the city's Prevention Assistance and Temporary Housing centre. They had tried to sleep while sitting upright on plastic bucket chairs in a crowd of other families, unable to shower away the stench of smoke and the day's heartbreak.

As they sat there, Tanita had overheard caseworkers discussing their neighbours' fire: "The kids were home alone, of course, with a cigarette lighter just lying around for them to 'play barbecue' with. Those people are just so stupid."

"Stupid or crazy. I heard the fire was started by one kid actually trying to commit suicide, can you believe it? Now just look how many clients we have to find room for."

So which was Tanita's family, stupid or crazy? Although they had never started a fire, she and Cedric were often home alone too, whenever their mother was at the health clinic. But their mother was smart. She remembered every word of the sermons they heard in church, and taught Tanita to memorize them too. That caseworker might get a higher score than her mother on a school test — but what if a preacher set a test? Tanita's mother could certainly cite chapter and verse for more Bible readings than any of their neighbours.

As that long night in the PATH waiting room wore on, Tanita had been unable to sleep at all and had thought of people she had passed sleeping on the streets. There was a weird man, his clothes filthy, always on the same block. Stretched out on flattened cardboard boxes, his head was often on a small garbage bag filled with his things. Once, when Tanita walked by him, he had been awake — and talking to Tanita's teacher, Ms. Marshall. Tanita had been scared — Ms. Marshall was old, almost retired. How could she defend herself if the man lunged at her? Tanita had stopped in case her teacher needed help.

"So you do have some family?" Ms. Marshall had been asking.

"My daughter, she ought to be in seventh grade by now — if she hasn't been left back."

"But you're not in touch with her?"

"The family she was placed with moved to Philadelphia. That's too far to visit."

"But you could write to her?"

"No, I don't want to write if I can't see her. What would I say? I don't know anything about her life now."

"That shouldn't keep you from making the effort. If you have the address, I could bring you some stamps."

"There's no point if I can't see her anymore." Tanita was startled to see tears in the man's eyes.

"Of course there's a point," Ms. Marshall said, as calmly as if she were giving a homework assignment. "I bet it would make all the difference in the world to her to hear from you. Even if she doesn't write back now, when she's older, she'll still remember that you cared enough to write to her."

At the time, Tanita had been confused. The man didn't sound crazy after all. But why on earth would anyone sleep on the streets if they weren't crazy? There were shelters that had to take you in. It was the law. Sleeping outside was disgusting. But after the fire, looking around the waiting room, Tanita started to wonder whether being in a shelter would be any less disgusting.

Already in their first few hours there, several fights had broken out. She hadn't heard the beginning of the most serious one, but it sounded like one teenage girl was blaming another for causing the fire. As they cursed and finally started hitting one another, a boyfriend and a brother jumped into the fray. It took two guards to separate them all. They scared Tanita so much that she didn't want to fall asleep in the same room with them, even if the guards were still within earshot.

As months of homelessness had dragged by, Tanita learned to sign out of the shelter and sign back in every time she so much as walked to the corner. She began to feel like she was locked behind bars.

She had to leave Ms. Marshall's class because their shelter was at the other end of the city. It would have taken ninety minutes each way to commute there. But on top of that, the school closest to the shelter took forever to allow Tanita to register. The younger children in the shelter were all enrolled in school quickly, but many of the teenagers weren't. Tanita heard that many middle schools assumed that "shelter kids" would drag down their test scores and cost them funding. And sure enough, no matter what papers Tanita's mother brought in, they would always demand still another form of ID, even after they had finally got replacements for the papers burned in the fire.

To pass the time, Tanita had started helping out in the shelter's after-school programme. Playing with little kids could be fun. But the girls her own age seemed bored and angry all the time. One in particular was always ready to pick a fight. Before the fire, Tanita would have just avoided such an angry girl — but how could you walk away from someone you were now locked in with, day after day?

Now Cedric was whining and pulling on her hand, yanking Tanita out of her memories and back to the heap of furniture in front of them. The shelter system: was that where the Ramirez family was right now?

When they walked upstairs, Tanita found the answer — of course her grandmother had made room for them. Mrs. Brown knew exactly what it meant to be thrown out of a home. She never ignored a chance to help a neighbour and she did it again this time, although the Ramirez boys got on her last nerves, even with a ceiling between them and her.

Letting their family use the living room meant that instead of having the living room sofa bed to herself, Tanita would be sleeping in the bedroom with Cedric and their grandmother. Now she would have to turn off the light as soon as they went to sleep every night, instead of sitting up to write. But maybe it was just as well. How could she have written anything if she were still imagining Carmen and Mateo Ramirez and their sons stuck at the dismal PATH waiting room?

Blandine and Sharmaine

On the day of the German ambassador's reception, Blandine decided to come home early to change. The clothes she had worn to work were perfectly appropriate; but the day was warm, and it would feel nice to freshen up. It was a Monday, the day Sharmaine came in to clean their apartment. Blandine entered to find Sharmaine standing immobile in front of the terrace doors holding a spray bottle of glass cleaner and a polishing rag. "Have you finished?"

Startled, Sharmaine tore herself away from the view of Bryant Park bathed in the late afternoon sun. "Almost, ma'am. This is the last room I do."

"Fine. It's just as well you're still here. I've been meaning to mention that you mustn't throw out the newspapers so quickly. My husband does leave them scattered about, but he keeps reading them and working on the crossword puzzles for days after they are published. Why don't you just stack them on the coffee table?"

"Oh. Sure, I can do that."

Blandine went to her bedroom to get ready for the evening. She wasn't often home when Sharmaine was there. Blandine was glad to have had a chance to surprise her. Although Sharmaine had not actually been cleaning anything when she walked in, it was reassuring not to have caught her watching a soap opera, or even snooping in a lingerie drawer, as she had caught her last cleaning lady doing. And Sharmaine did do a careful job with the housework, unlike some cleaners who confused the different polishes and ended up ruining the finish on the delicate antique furniture that Blandine loved to shop for on weekend trips to picturesque towns in Connecticut.

In the kitchen, Sharmaine rescued the newspapers from the recycling pile. Now she could return to cleaning the terrace doors. She loved saving this task for the end. Although embarrassed at being caught idle, she didn't quite regret basking in the view. In church, when the preacher spoke of the kingdom of heaven, this was exactly the view Sharmaine imagined. Far below she could make out a pair of children enjoying ice cream cones at a wrought-iron table. Several teenagers were sprawled on the grass. There was a cluster of people who each seemed to be knitting, of all things. People on their way home from work were too rushed to linger in the park, but what a beautiful commute they had when walking through it.

The buildings visible around the park did not match one another — nothing really matched in the crazy-quilt of New York — but they each had a majesty like nothing in her own neighbourhood of Bushwick in Brooklyn. Here, there was no graffiti in sight, no boarded-up windows; just soaring façades jutting into the sky. Best of all were the trees. It might be restful to stand on the ground and look up at the foliage, but Sharmaine especially loved looking down on trees, as though she were floating above it all.

Blandine

The German reception was well attended, with fifty or sixty people circulating around the main rooms of the well-appointed embassy offices. From the high windows, the UN garden was still visible in the dusk. Blandine, who always enjoyed having a glass of wine with colleagues while keeping on top of the latest chatter, often came to these events alone. But she preferred it when Varag would deign to accompany her. When she forced him to dress up, she always found his lanky form dashing. During evenings that could be much too predictable, he had a seductive way of adding sparks by challenging people's ideas.

As they made the rounds of the crowded room, Varag suddenly laid his hand on Blandine's arm. "Look, Pamela's here."

"What? Oh, so she is. Really, that girl has no sense of style whatsoever." Pamela's brown skirt and beige sweater were not inappropriate for the informal week-night reception, but they did not quite match each other, and were not particularly flattering.

"Not everyone has your leisure to pamper themselves. Stop that cattiness and come say hello."

When Pamela saw the couple, she turned to a poised young woman at her side. "Tanita, do you remember Ms. Dulavoir? She came to our meeting the other night. And this is her husband, Mr. Vosgrichian. This is Tanita Brown, who volunteers in our children's programme in Brooklyn."

Varag said, "It's nice to meet you, but please, call us Blandine and Varag. First names can be complicated enough!"

Blandine was trying to get an impression of Tanita. Her walnut-coloured micro-braids were pulled into a bun that set off her high cheekbones. Flounces on her bottle-green dress looked as though they were meant for dancing, not a staid reception among colleagues; but the dress was becoming.

The look in Tanita's eyes was guarded, although she smiled politely as she greeted Blandine. "I don't know what you must have thought of us at that meeting. Sometimes we get so full of talk we forget to listen to one another."

"It's true that I dislike shouting," Blandine said. "Perhaps it's cultural. I grew up in Belgium, but I know southern Europeans who can't say two civil words in a row to one another."

"And we Armenians, what do you think of our tempers?" Varag teased her.

"Well, I know that yours is incorrigible!" Blandine joined in his laughter and Pamela began to glimpse the couple's harmony.

A waiter proffered a tray of fried wedges flecked with red globules. Unsure what to expect, Tanita was glad she had taken a napkin when she bit into what turned out to be melted cheese with jam. The taste was not unpleasant, but she had to be careful not to get her fingers sticky.

Varag, who had polished off his own fried Camembert with a single bite, turned to Pamela. "Now that we see you again, Blandine has a serious question. She was wondering how Helen Jansky came to speak at your meeting."

"Oh, Helen has been involved with us for donkey's years now. She first got to know us when one of her graduate students interviewed us for some research on employment issues."

"Really?" asked Blandine skeptically.

"It turned out that Helen had grown up right on the same street where we run our outdoor art workshops now."

"Where is that?" Varag wanted to know.

"Bushwick," Tanita answered.

Still thinking of Helen, Pamela continued, "Even though Helen has moved a few neighbourhoods away to Cobble Hill, she felt quite strongly about getting involved. It's been a real godsend to be able to count on her for so long. Tanita, you worked with her last spring, didn't you?"

"That's right. My neighbour Carmen was having a real bad time with her boss, but she was afraid to complain because even though she's legal, her husband's not."

Pamela said, "Carmen was too nervous to go to an office, even to ask about her rights."

"The professor came all the way out to our neighbourhood," Tanita continued. "She just chatted with Carmen like a friend, letting her know what the law says about sexual harassment and what she could do without getting her family in trouble. Carmen thinks she's just wonderful."

A waitress passing by refilled Blandine's glass of white wine.

"And was the situation with her employer resolved?" Blandine asked.

"Well, things got a little better," Tanita said. "I think he got the wind up when he realized she'd been studying up on sexual harassment law. But the problem now is that she got evicted. Just looking for a new place to live is taking her so much time that she might lose her job anyway."

"You didn't tell me they'd been evicted," Pamela blurted, frowning. "Is the family in a shelter?"

"Actually, no, they're in our living room," Tanita said with a smile.

"That must be awfully crowded." Pamela began twirling a few strands of her hair between her fingers.

"Sure, but you know Grandma. How could she let them go to a shelter? Mateo wouldn't be allowed to stay there. And Cedric is best friends with Carmen's younger boys."

"I know. Well, finding housing is awfully hard these days, but you must let us know if we can help somehow."

Just then a beefy man began talking to Blandine in rapid French. She slipped away from the conversation with Pamela and Tanita, murmuring, "Nice seeing you again."

Varag sighed. "This is why I hate receptions. You're not actually meant to have a substantive conversation, just to buzz around the room like a mosquito. And the waiters are passing around more wine than hors d'oeuvres. That's never a healthy sign."

"No, it's not my cup of tea either," agreed Pamela. "But it was kind of the ambassador to invite us. I think he appreciated the paper we submitted on social development, so I felt I should come. But I was glad to talk Tanita into keeping me company. And now we need to be getting home."

"Already?"

"I'm afraid so," said Tanita, "My grandmother won't get any sleep if I don't make sure all the kids are settled down. But it was nice to meet you."

Pamela and Tanita

As they walked toward the subway, Pamela again asked Tanita, "How has the writing been going? Have you been able to find time for it? It must be much harder with all the Ramirez boys underfoot."

"Oh, they used to come over a lot anyway, so it's not *that* different. Just from overhead to underfoot." Pamela laughed.

"But I have a question for you," Tanita continued. "Is what I write supposed to be just about my personal experience? Or can I write about things all of us go through, even people who don't come to our meetings?"

"It's up to you, but I think it's especially important to write about what a lot of different people face, and how they face it."

"That's not what Ornella did in her speech last year." Tanita kept her eyes on the sidewalk, careful not to catch the heel of her shoe in the subway grating. "The whole thing was all about her and her husband. I bet everyone was bored out of their minds."

"That's not fair. Didn't you see how well received her speech was?"

"No, you made me prepare the picnic for afterwards. I only read her speech after she gave it."

"Oh, I'm so sorry, I'd forgotten that." Pausing to rummage through the calamitous mess in her purse for her subway card,

Pamela thought back to last year. "I do remember that you were annoyed when she was invited to speak."

"Well, it's just the way she talks, on and on. I can't even listen to her." Tanita swiped through the turnstile and strode to the subway platform.

When Pamela had caught up with her, she said, "This time round Ornella will be the one listening to you. That's why it's high time you got serious about preparing."

Tanita looked down the train tracks into the empty tunnel.

Pamela continued, "You know, at the United Nations, they have started, more and more, inviting people who live in poverty or in a war zone to come and speak personally, to give a kind of first-person testimonial."

"That's good."

"Yes, it could be. But what drives me round the bend is that the people invited that way are expected just to unveil their most personal experience of suffering — and then to leave the room while the policymakers debate what should be done about it."

"It's not fair to expect people to say so much personal stuff, like they're on trial."

"Exactly! I once heard a young man speak at the UN about how hard it was for him to escape the war-torn country he'd grown up in." Pamela paused for a moment as an express train screeched to a stop. At this hour, the train was only half full, so it was easy for Pamela and Tanita to find seats together. "The first question a diplomat asked him was why he hadn't tried harder to help his sister get out. I think the young man already felt terrible about his sister's death. He was the one who spoke of her in the first place."

"So that question just twisted the knife."

Pamela tried to ignore the vague odour of rot coming from somewhere in the subway car. Soon they reached 14th Street and got out to transfer to the L train. After a concrete corridor and several flights of stairs, they waited on a platform and looked at the miniature bronze figures around them. One six-inch figure, on a low tile wall, depicted a stout man in a suit and bowler hat. In front of him was a girl so tiny that she seemed to be of a different species, standing barely an inch high. The girl's outreached arms were trying to grasp a gigantic penny that the man held out to her. The coin was only one of a half dozen pennies spilling out of the man's arms onto the tile wall.

Reaching out to touch the smooth bronze of the girl's tiny head, Pamela took up her train of thought again. "Diplomats speak at the United Nations every day. But they are never asked to speak in such a personal way. Let's say a man begging in the street asks Blandine for help: how does she respond?"

Looking at the bronze figures, Tanita's mouth twisted sarcastically. "Good luck with that."

"Even if she doesn't give money, what goes through her mind? What does she feel? Diplomats don't tell us that. But they expect someone who's been chronically unemployed to speak about how awful they feel."

Tanita walked around a pillar to discover another bronze figure. This one was a policewoman holding a truncheon and a gun. She stood firmly planted atop the sack of money she was guarding, her frown permanent.

Following Tanita, Pamela continued, "A diplomat's never going to speak into a microphone about his most embarrassing failure, or a speech he messed up, or a cultural blunder he made."

"If it's that bad, why does anyone ever agree to go speak at the UN?"

"But it's *not* that bad for everyone. Let's take labor union leaders. It's *expected* that they speak on behalf of many thousands of people. It's also expected that they speak not only about suffering but also about proposed solutions."

"No one asks them personal questions?"

"Right. If they talk about difficulties on a factory assembly line or underground in a mine, they're talking from a collective point of view. But when you introduce a speaker who lives in poverty, the expectation shifts. People want to hear something deeply personal about the past, and nothing at all about how to change the future together."

"So that's why you think I should be speaking for a lot of other people?"

"Indeed, it is. And in fact, that's how you already speak at our meetings. So even if you're having a hard time starting to write, I'm sure that you can change the way some people listen."

Tanita sighed. "We'll see." Looking for more statues, she called, "Hey, look at this one." On another low tile wall, the rich man in the suit and bowler hat was lying helplessly on top of his coins. His ample stomach had become a cushion for a woman in a sleeveless dress who was engrossed in a gigantic book.

Pamela grinned, "Cool. What would you name this one?"

"Books Beat Cash. But having cash is good too."

3. HAVOC AND REMEMBRANCE

That night, Pamela changed into sweatpants and hung her brown skirt in the cluttered closet, noting how drab it was next to Yun Hee's cheerful wardrobe. Regretting the reception wine that was starting to give her a headache, she made a cup of tea. She sat on the couch and called her friend Bill, whom she'd got to know at the UN's weekly briefings for non-governmental organizations. As the representative of the International Association of Lawyers, perhaps he would have advice for Mrs. Jones about Allan.

"Bill at the Big Snapple here," was his growled greeting.

"Bill? This is Pamela McEvoy.

"Did you see the mayor just sold this city to Snapple?"

"What?"

"Yup. For only $166 mill, New York now has an official soft drink."

"Wow! That's a lot of money."

"And in exchange, every school and official office in the city will install only Snapple machines."

"Oh dear. That's a lot of sugar being pushed at kids. But, Bill, listen. I actually called because I've got a quick legal question."

"Shoot."

"A woman I know is raising her grandson, but she doesn't have legal custody of him and is afraid of him being taken away to foster care."

When she had told Bill the whole story, he said, "I hate to say it, but she's right to be worried."

"But she's so responsible and takes very good care of him."

"With the boy's mother not living with them, he could easily be removed. You should help your friend get legal custody."

Pamela's next phone call was to Mrs. Jones. Although Pamela explained what Bill had said, Mrs. Jones did not sound enthusiastic about taking legal custody away from her daughter.

But after continued urging from Pamela, she agreed to go with her up to the Bronx to talk to Allan's mother about the situation.

A few days later, when Pamela had got the forms that Bill specified, she knocked on Mrs. Jones's door. "All set to go?"

"What's that, child?" Mrs. Jones was still wearing a robe, her hair hidden under a scarf.

Wasn't she usually an early riser? Pamela thought she looked disoriented. "Have you forgotten? We must visit your daughter Brenda with the custody papers for Allan."

"Is that today? I'm sorry, I just don't feel up to it. Allan's cousin, Little Willy, had an asthma attack last night. I need to sit tight here and keep an eye on him."

From her vantage point in the doorway, Pamela could see the boy asleep on the sofa, his breathing raspy. "What about your other daughter? Couldn't she stay with him?"

"No, she's already left for work. Why don't you go without me?"

"What?" Pamela was taken aback. "But I've never even met Brenda."

"I told her all about it on the phone. And if there's any problem, you just call me. I'll be right here."

Frustrated and unsure, Pamela nevertheless set out alone for the long subway trip to the Bronx. As she passed the newsstand, she noticed solemn headlines and her mood worsened. It was September 11, the second anniversary of the terrorist attack on the World Trade Center. Her thoughts flashed back two years. Bill had been the one who phoned and told her to look out the window. She had been so busily working that she failed to take in the import of what he was saying. Of course any airplane crash was tragic; but crashes happened so often in one part of the world or another. Moments later, however, stepping outside, she had seen billows of smoke farther downtown. Like crematorium smokestacks.

As that infamous day had worn on, things had grown more and more incomprehensible — a second airplane shattering the concrete and glass of the Twin Towers — the dawning realization that this was terrorism — one skyscraper giving way and collapsing — and then the other as well.

With cell phone lines jammed and pay phones out of order, it was impossible to get information about friends further downtown. You could see television coverage in the storefronts where electronics were sold, but as Pamela understood only days later, the coverage they saw in New York was limited. The destruction of all the antennas on the World Trade Center left the city for weeks with only one local channel. There was no national or international news — unless you had cable, which she and Yun Hee could never afford. Emotionally hollowed out and bleary, Pamela had felt herself slipping into the isolation of a pre-telecommunications past. Wasn't the distant past of world wars also where such vengeful carnage belonged?

On that fateful 9/11, unsure what to do, Pamela had headed for the nearest hospital to give blood. Waiting on a long line with scores of other donors, she watched New Yorkers flee uptown on foot, away from the gigantic crime scene. Some had been given gauze masks to prevent them choking on the stench of burning fuel. Some had stopped along their escape route to buy good walking shoes. Others simply walked as they were, women in high heels and men in suits, all covered with ash. They hurried north with purpose, as though they could escape survivors' trauma even while breathing in the smoke that was burning the bodies of thousands.

Over the days that followed, Pamela had been dazed by the deluge of information on their one local news channel. Talking to her neighbours, she realized that some people were even more overwhelmed, having now started watching the news for the first time in their lives. Although many fumbled for the "right" words, everyone reeled from fear, hurt, and anger. In a city usually marked by stark divisions between rich and poor, Pamela had the feeling that the terrorist attacks erased those differences. Strangers reached out to one another on the streets, their feelings reflected in one another's eyes: common shock and anxiety; and a common sense of humanity.

In the west of Manhattan, the Javits Convention Center quickly became an improvised staging centre for people volunteering to help. In the early hours and days, when there was still hope of being able to dig tunnels to help survivors out of the rubble, Pamela had been moved to see streams of labourers arriving. There were iron workers, and men trained in construction or demolition. Unskilled labourers had come too, all hoping for a chance to help. Some carried their own tools — shovels, hard hats, pick-axes. Many had walked to New York from New Jersey across bridges now closed to traffic.

One man told Pamela he had hitch-hiked all the way from Colorado, hoping to help. Pamela, who had no manual labor skills, soon joined those who distributed sandwiches and drinks to the crowd. She had been particularly touched by one older man holding an improvised cardboard sign that read, "Please, pick me to help. I need to help." She felt humbled at witnessing the best of what humanity had to offer.

As trucks arrived with donated supplies to be unloaded, Pamela had joined a young man who leaped to help unload. As they formed a chain passing boxes, he had told her, "My name is Hassan. I am from Morocco, but I am not a terrorist. I run a shoe store in the Bronx. That is why I am helping. People must know that we are not terrorists."

"Surely people *do* understand," Pamela said. "There are terrorists of every ethnicity and religion. It would be stupid to think there's anything about being Arab that promotes such unimaginable violence."

"I'm afraid people may not understand that," Hassan had said. "As soon as this happened, police came to stand outside our mosque, round the clock."

"Why?"

"They say we are now targets for revenge, even though we are mourning for all those murdered, just as everyone else is." Just then a convoy of dump trucks from ground zero rumbled past, with firefighters standing on the rubble, thickly covered in dust. Along with everyone else nearby, Hassan and Pamela began applauding and cheering for all they were worth.

Now, traveling to the Bronx exactly two years later, Pamela thought of her brief encounter with Hassan. Was his shoe store anywhere near Brenda's apartment? And had he managed to stay in business all this time? So many small businesses had closed when tourists began avoiding New York. Had anyone in his neighbourhood thought of him as a target for revenge?

Tanita

When Tanita's alarm went off, she felt a weight on her face. Slowly forcing her eyes open, she saw Cedric's limp arm there. For a moment, she enjoyed feeling his baby breath on her cheek and admiring the gentle swoop of his closed eyelashes. Even damp with sweat, he was adorable. Then she slipped out from under his arm without waking him and pulled on a pair of jeans and a fresh T-shirt, letting her grandmother have first use of the shower.

In the living room, most of the Ramirez family were still sleeping, three in the sofa bed and two on the floor. Only 9-year-old Johnny was awake. He already had the television on. But he found no cartoons today. Most channels were broadcasting coverage of the anniversary at ground zero, as relatives of the victims gathered to read the long roster of their names. Tanita brushed her teeth at the metal kitchen sink and then knelt on the floor for a moment to join Johnny in watching.

When Tanita thought back to those long days in September 2001, she remembered worrying about Susana. They had grown up together in Brooklyn, but then Susana had moved to Chinatown in Manhattan. She lived with her boyfriend and his son, Alonzo, who was a year older than Cedric. Their apartment was not *too* close to the World Trade Center site. But when Tanita had tried phoning them in the days following the attack, there had never been an answer. Increasingly concerned, she finally made time to pay a visit. The elevator in the building was not functioning, so Tanita and then 4-year-old Cedric had a sweaty walk up seven flights of stairs. When they reached the apartment, it was a huge relief to have Susana open the door and throw her arms around them in welcome. With her windows shut tight against the smoke and debris still in the air, the apartment was particularly hot and airless.

As the two boys began racing around the apartment together, Tanita and Susana chatted over glasses of soda that had lost its fizz. "Why haven't you been answering the phone?"

"Sorry, I turned it off. I unplugged the TV and radio too. I just don't want 'Lonzo seeing those horrible images on TV and hearing about it all the time."

"Wow. I don't think I could protect Cedric like that. I need to know what's going on."

"It's true, I guess I don't really know the news myself this week. Are schools open yet?"

"You mean Alonzo hasn't been back to kindergarten yet? I bet they're worried about him. In most of the city, schools were only closed for a day. The schools around here did stay closed for a few more days, but they're open again now."

"Oh. I guess he should go back tomorrow then. It's just felt safer staying right here."

Now Johnny Ramirez's eyes were glued to the reading of the names. "Will that happen again?" he asked Tanita.

"I don't know, honey — " Catching sight of his tense face, she corrected herself, "but it won't happen here. There's so much more security that this city is the safest place on earth now."

Remembering that Johnny was still dealing with his own family's eviction trauma, Tanita did not want to add to his worries, already too adult for his 9 years. But neither did she believe it was possible to protect such a huge city from every terrorist in the world. Not wanting to continue saying what she knew was false, she set water to boil for instant coffee, and then emptied the bucket from under the sink, where there had been a persistent leak for months now. Despite her efforts to disinfect, she could smell mildew winning out.

Soon Mrs. Brown was done with the shower, and Carmen got up to take her turn.

Once Carmen had showered, as she was fixing her hair at the bathroom mirror, she called through the open door, "Hey, Tanita, you got that professor lady's phone number? Maybe she'll have some ideas about where we could move to."

"On the wall," Tanita answered, pointing toward the door where she had taped a list of phone numbers.

Helen

When the phone rang, Helen Jansky was measuring organic molasses into the ingredients for pumpernickel bread while listening to the reading of the names of 9/11 victims. Now, hearing about Carmen's struggle to find an affordable place to live, Helen felt herself getting angrier and angrier.

"This is unfair. Of course you can't find a new home, because our country's priorities are such a backwards mess." She began kneading her dough fiercely, while cradling the phone against her shoulder. "Look how many people died on 9/11, and here our government has used it as an excuse to start not one but two wars. We're just giving ammunition to people who want to spread hatred." Pummelling her righteous indignation into the dough, Helen said, "We're killing innocent people over there. On top of that, the soldiers we send to risk their lives are too often from families who can't even afford a decent home here."

"Well, no one likes war." Carmen shot back, "But we got to get Saddam Hussein. He destroyed the Twin Towers."

"He's been a cruel leader, but he's not Osama bin Laden. The tragedy is that our country has twisted 9/11. It's been made all about vengeance in a world of good and evil. Most of us aren't perfectly good or perfectly evil." Helen paused, trying to find the right words. "To me the powerful thing about September 11th was that we got a chance to see the heroism of ordinary New Yorkers. Do you know how people in the rest of this country usually think of New Yorkers?"

"Sure: loud and proud!"

"Yep. They also think we're rude and uncaring, arrogant and unfriendly. And okay, sometimes we are. This is a big city, and we have to shout to make ourselves heard. We can forget to take time for one another. But remember those weeks after 9/11? There was such an outpouring of volunteering and of sacrifice."

"We'll never forget," Carmen answered. "Everything we thought was safe was gone. But all those police and firemen ran straight into the towers."

"And after the buildings collapsed, so many rescue workers and metalworkers ruined their health by searching through poison to look for human remains. So many others went down there to bring them coffee, and had to force them to stop long enough to eat occasionally or even just to rinse the smoke out of their eyes. They didn't want to waste a second."

Carmen cast a glance at her son Johnny who was hopping from one foot to the other while waiting for a turn in the bathroom.

Helen was still talking about 9/11: "And everywhere in the city, people were looking each other in the eyes and sharing emotions: people in three-piece suits, people wearing rags, people who never spoke to each other before, all coming together for candlelight vigils."

"I wouldn't know about that. We don't see people in suits out here."

Barely registering Carmen's skepticism, Helen continued. "We were changed by that. But how can we show that everyday heroism in another way? How can we mobilize New Yorkers around a cause like low-income housing to make sure that you and your children can have a decent home? But here I am, going off on a rant when you called me with an urgent problem. Can you meet me at one o'clock? I have a friend who knows a lot about the housing market. Let's pick her brain and see what we can figure out."

"Finally," Carmen thought to herself as she thanked Helen.

Blandine

Good with dates, Blandine knew exactly what day it was. She had scheduled no meetings for today and planned to stay home. Varag had left for work by the time she got up. Although she did not usually watch much television, she turned on a European cable channel. As she had thought, the Europeans did not dwell on the anniversary, but gave it just a brief mention before turning to current affairs around the world. She listened attentively to a report on the safety of seafood in Japan, and then one on the slow progress of women's rights in Mongolia. But when an update on Israel and the Palestinian territories came on screen, Blandine flashed back to the memories she had been avoiding.

Two years ago, on September 11, 2001, she had in fact been on her way to the Gaza Strip as part of an observer mission verifying the situation on the ground during the second intifada uprising. When they heard about the attacks, not knowing whether they, themselves, were in danger, her delegation had immediately returned to their hotel in Jerusalem. In the bar there, strangers were watching the news together, hearing estimates that as many as 10,000 people might have been killed. Flight schedules were in complete disarray, and it would take days before they could fly home. Those had been eerie days, the streets quiet and completely barren of tourists, even at the most magnificent historical sites.

For Blandine, it had been horrifying to hear news of the attack on New York, the vibrant city she lived in and loved, and of the chaotic evacuation of the UN buildings. Israelis around her, however, seemed almost unshaken by the news. They expressed sympathy and friendship — and some wondered aloud whether the world might now better understand their own struggle fighting terrorism. Beneath their words, Blandine had the impression that they were already so shell-shocked by the frequent bus bombings around them that this far-off attack, despite its scale, made scarcely a dent in their weathered emotional armour.

It had taken twenty-four hours before Blandine could confirm that Varag was unharmed, and another day before she could reach him by telephone. That was when Varag told her that their dear friend Mira Pérez was among those missing and presumed dead. Mira! Blandine had known Mira for years, ever since they began university together in London. A gifted mathematician from Argentina, Mira had managed stock portfolio analysis for an investment company based in the World Trade Center. Nine employees from her company were "missing." Mira's daughter was 12 and her son, 8. With Mira's partner, Octavia, the family had often joined Varag and Blandine for a dinner at home, or sprawled on a picnic blanket to listen to a concert in Central Park. Their families were always teasing one another and making jokes.

In the days that dragged by while Blandine waited at the sumptuous King David Hotel for a flight home, she felt maddened from inaction. She couldn't bear any more small talk with the others in her delegation. It felt particularly deadening to talk to Jean-Christian Roche-Fontaine, a Frenchman who had gone to all the right schools and generally considered himself in line to receive a higher political appointment at any moment — even though his current mid-level embassy work was not distinguished. Beginning on September 11, he had launched into a long tirade about how the US had been asking for just such an attack with its high-handed foreign policy, to say nothing of its cultural imperialism. It was possible that he had a valid point or two; but because he never listened to anyone but himself, his monologue tended to twist quickly back on itself without ever sharpening into a constructive argument. By the third day of their wait, the mere glimpse of him at the other end of the hotel atrium had sent Blandine racing outdoors for fresh air.

As she walked, Blandine found herself remembering her last year at university. Over their years there together, she and Mira had shared a flat and pretty much everything else. They often took the same classes, dated young men from the same sports teams, and drank too many piña coladas at the same parties. Blandine, who struggled to assert controversial opinions and preferred fading into the shadows, was entranced by having such a vibrant and exciting friend.

Mira had no fear of embroiling herself in an argument with a respected professor. She could jump on a table and dance for a crowd, just as she would spring in front of a microphone to protest injustices on the other side of the globe. In addition to dating men, Mira had dated quite a few women as well. She loved telling people how liberating bisexuality was: "Imagine being able to love everyone!" It was at the beginning of their final year of classes that Mira had taken Blandine out to dinner at a new Thai restaurant — and told her that she had fallen in love with her.

The idea stunned Blandine, who admired and cared for Mira enormously but had never even considered a physical relationship with another woman.

"But you know I'm dating Martin," she had answered.

"Martin! You must be joking. He drinks too much; he belittles you in front of his friends; and you never even stand up to him. What kind of relationship is that? Don't you care at all about yourself?"

It was true that Blandine was not happy with Martin Fielding. She had started seeing him because the intensity of his gaze made her feel special — but by now she had realized that he focused the same nearsighted scrutiny on every pretty girl he met. Still, she felt invested in the relationship. She wasn't sure if she was in love with him, because she wasn't sure if she had ever been in love, or just what that might be like. But his gaze could still stir her emotions; so most of the time she convinced herself that she was in love.

To Mira, she answered, "Martin loves me. I'm not breaking up with him. But that doesn't have to change anything between you and me. We'll always be friends."

Mira had fled the restaurant overwrought and furious, off to spend the night at another friend's home. By the next day, however, everything seemed back to normal. They had continued to live together, throw dinner parties for their friends, and quiz each other before exams. Their conversation in the restaurant never again came up — until two months after they had graduated, when Mira had already begun working on Wall Street with challenging analytical assignments along with great pay and benefits. Blandine was back in Brussels, living with her parents, and doing repetitive statistical work for the European Union.

Blandine was excited when she received a fat letter with a US stamp on it. True to form, Mira had even illustrated her missive, with clouds and tree branches snaking along the margins. But as Blandine began to read the 14-page tirade scrawled in purple ink, she dissolved into tears.

"...I can't believe how long it's taken me to tell
you how I really feel. You always say I'm brave, but

you are so horrifically placid that I don't know how ANYONE could exert enough willpower to tell you the truth about passion. Maybe someday you'll fall in love for real and begin to understand....

"How could you tell me, 'This doesn't have to change anything between us'? How could you just sweep MY feelings onto the floor as though your unhealthy and oh-so-forgettable relationship with that robotic Martin and his self-imposed norms was the only thing that mattered?

"Of course I could understand a rejection from you, it's only what I'd expected. But what I just can't BEAR is the way you systematically undervalue yourself, your worth, your true emotions, your friendships. What a cop-out! Are you addicted to self-abasement and martyrdom? Sticking meekly with Martin for as many months as you did was real proof of how little self-esteem you have. When will you outgrow the 'people-pleasing' behaviour ingrained in you? Blandine, you have to stop deluding yourself and realize that you will never discover true passion until you learn to respect yourself...

"I've fallen in love with someone else now, an amazing woman named Octavia. She is a singing waitress in a theme restaurant here, and you should hear her belt out Edith Piaf songs standing on the fire escape at 2 am in nothing but her bra and panties! I'm at a high emotional pitch, on the edge, but it's worth it. We may both be too opinionated for our own good, but being with her is like running through a thunderstorm holding hands. The danger of lightning doesn't matter as long as we're both going in the same direction. That's what I wish for you — that you learn how to love yourself, stop being so very practical, and finally unleash your own passion.

"I have no idea how you'll react to this letter. But as you know I'm not the type to let go of a friendship I value just because there's trouble. I'd rather fight to keep our friendship and go through the pain of making it whole again. It's really the only thing I can do."

With an ocean between them, it had not been easy to rebuild their friendship. But after Blandine was hired by the Belgian foreign ministry and had a posting to its consulate in Quebec, she and Mira could visit one another more frequently. The scar tissue that now bound them together made their relationship feel ever stronger than before.

In 2001, with the news that Mira had not escaped the World Trade Center, Blandine was devastated. The turmoil she felt at remembering Mira's letter was punctured by the tentative voice of a boy, no more than 4 or 5, asking in broken English, "Money, give money." Jarred, Blandine realized that her aimless walk had taken her into the Arab zone of East Jerusalem, where the streets smelled clogged with misery. As she hunted in her purse for something to give the disheveled boy, a young man came up to her.

"Lost? You pay me, I take you back."

Handing a few coins to the boy, she tried to size up the person in front of her. He was probably about 17 or 18 and he towered over her. A hardened look in his eyes frightened her, and she hated the idea of admitting she needed help. But if she refused to buy his protection, would he simply grab her purse or body the moment she turned away? Theoretically, she could summon Belgian embassy security on her pager. However, she had a feeling that if she actually needed it, she wouldn't be able to wait the time it would take them to send someone — particularly given that she had no idea how to tell them where to find her. Kicking herself for having wandered so far from the hotel, she nodded in agreement, and the young man took her elbow and steered her firmly through the streets.

As they walked, he continued speaking. "My sister have baby soon. She sick, need doctor. We live all in tiny room, twelve of us. How much you give me?"

With fear as her ruling emotion, Blandine emptied her wallet, giving him $30 and glad she had left the rest of her cash and her passport in the hotel safe. Would he keep his word now that he knew her purse was empty? But he could have simply stolen the money if he didn't actually want to be helpful. They continued walking and soon enough she saw the walls of the Old City ahead. The young man at her side said, "What happened was bad. I don't hate the American people."

Startled again, Blandine slowly realized that he was speaking about the terrorist attacks. Not waiting for her to respond, the young man gave a nod toward the Israeli guards now in sight and said, "I leave now. You okay."

"Yes, thank you." Before the words were spoken, he had slipped into an alleyway and disappeared.

Days later, when Blandine's flight finally reached JFK Airport, her adopted city seemed so eerie that she almost felt she was still in Israel. Varag convinced her to take a walk with him downtown, toward ground zero. Although they did not go south of the improvised checkpoints at 14th Street, they were breathing in smoke from fires still smouldering at the site a couple of miles away. Blandine couldn't help wondering if she was breathing in the ash that was once Mira, joining their bodies in some twisted way. They walked past many impromptu memorials of flowers, candles, and messages in parks and on the sidewalks in front of fire houses. Everywhere, walls were covered with notices describing missing loved ones. When she read one describing a pregnant newlywed, just 22, she insisted to Varag that it was time to go home for a drink.

Pamela

The subway trip toward Mrs. Jones's daughter Brenda in the Bronx was a long one. Pamela had time to read through several short stories in a collection by Nadine Gordimer. Soon her head began to ache from reading violent plots woven around barbed wire and security fences. Finally, she got out at the stop Mrs.

Jones had named. The South Bronx was certainly not a South African township; but with Gordimer's images in mind, at first Pamela saw only grime and decay. She wondered which of the pockmarks on the buildings were left by stray bullets. Perhaps the urban decay in the Bronx was not dissimilar to that in her own part of Brooklyn; but as a stranger here, she saw blight instead of neighbours to greet.

She had trouble finding the street address and had to ask directions several times. The building in fact had no visible number at all, and no working doorbell. Pamela had to shout up at the windows, "Brenda!" She felt funny using the first name of a woman she had never met; but feared that no one would respond if she called out in her British accent, "Is Ms. Brenda Jones there?" After her third shout, a frazzled-looking woman stuck her head out a third-floor window.

"Who're you?" The voice was hoarse and guarded.

"Are you Brenda? I'm a friend of your mother's. She sent me here."

There were a few moments of silence as Brenda sized up Pamela. "Yeah, I guess she mentioned someone might drop by."

"May I come up for a few minutes?"

"I guess. It's not locked." The wooden front door of the building, its dark green paint chipping off, had a few splinters in the place where it must have once held a lock. On the ground floor, Pamela saw a syringe in a corner, and then passed a door bearing a scotch-taped sign announcing, "Crack kills."

She wondered whether children could grow up here without knowing someone who ended up in jail or in drug rehab. As she started up the stairs, she noted the distinct smell of urine. A door on the second floor had a different sign, in Spanish this time: "We're Catholic and we love our religion so don't ask us to change." Just how many proselytizers plied this neighbourhood? Were there as many evangelists as drug dealers? On the third-floor landing, Pamela hesitated. She was disoriented trying to figure out which was the left-hand apartment, now that the stairwell had her turned her away from her view on the sidewalk. Seeing an Arabic bumper sticker on one door, she guessed it wasn't Brenda's apartment and knocked on the opposite door.

Brenda opened the door silently, stepping back so that Pamela could enter the room. She was not invited to sit. Just as well, thought Pamela, seeing that there was very little furniture. Springs pierced through the small sofa, and almost every surface had a few roaches scurrying across it. Brenda was wearing a stained Bob Marley T-shirt and a pair of cut-off shorts. Her short, bleached hair showed dark roots.

"What do you want?" Brenda asked.

"Well, it's about Allan."

"Is he in trouble again? You people are always going on about him."

"No, no, he hasn't done anything wrong."

"If his teachers knew what they were doing, he'd be better behaved."

"Your son is such an inventive boy. I think he's great fun to have around. But his teacher is worried that he's hyperactive. And when your mother disagreed with the teacher about how to help Allan, the teacher threatened to have him put in foster care."

"That's crazy!"

"I agree, it's unfair."

"He has a family, and we don't abuse him."

"Having to leave your family would be a hardship for him." Pamela had known children in foster care to feel completely deserted and unloved by everyone, even when their foster family was warm and welcoming. "But because your mother does not have legal custody of Allan, she's in a difficult position. So these are some forms you could sign, stating that you wish her to have custody of him."

Again, Brenda was silent for a few moments, frowning. "He's my son, not hers. If the teacher is making so much trouble, he could just come here and change schools."

Now it was Pamela's turn to hesitate. Mrs. Jones had told her that Brenda was addicted to drugs. "Of course he's your son. But he's lived with your mother for so long that he might be unhappy about moving so far away from her and changing schools."

In changed circumstances, Brenda might be a wonderful parent; but her life was clearly in disarray right now. Pamela continued, "Allan has good friends on our block too. Signing these papers won't mean that you're no longer his mother. It would just help your mother to be able to continue raising him for the moment."

"'For the moment?' Like hell! I know how these things work. Once they take your kids away, you never get them back. And I'm in a rehab programme right now, so I *could* take him back."

Pamela smiled, "That's great that you're in rehab. It must be very hard work, and I know your family will be proud of you. About custody though, the risk of never getting a child back is greater once they enter the system to live in a group home. Signing these papers is a way to make sure he remains *with* your family. It doesn't mean he would never live with you again."

"Look, I got to think about this. You can come back next week."

"But I'm not sure I'll have time to come all this way, and your mother needs you to sign the papers as soon as possible. What if we ring her up now to talk it over?"

Brenda hesitated. "I guess. You got a phone?"

Seeing a phone in the room, Pamela wondered if the service had been cut off. She fished her cell phone out of her purse and handed it to Brenda, who then left the room to phone her mother. Pamela balanced herself gingerly on the edge of a metal folding chair and looked away from the roaches. Twisting her hair, she tried to imagine herself on a beautiful mountaintop. But instead the images that filled her mind were Nadine Gordimer's stories of lives torn asunder by apartheid and revolution.

Brenda and Ernestine

The apartment had just one room, so Brenda took the cell phone into the bathroom for some privacy. Her mother picked up on the third ring.

"Ma, it's me Brenda." Brenda leaned against the cold sink basin for support. "Some white lady is here about Allan."

"I know honey; she's doing us a favour. You know how hard it is for me to make that long trip, and Lord knows you almost never make it here either."

"But what the freak are the papers she's waving at me?" Transferring the phone to her left hand, Brenda used her right hand to grope in her back pocket. Finding a package with one cigarette left, she lit it. "I'm still Allan's mother."

"Didn't say you wasn't. But as long as Allan's living with me, I look like a blind fool with his teachers if I don't have legal custody of him."

Brenda was silent, so Ernestine Jones continued. "Are you really picking today to give me trouble? Don't you remember what day this is?" Brenda searched her mind for the date. She was still groping when her mother continued, "It's 9/11, Brenda. Has your electricity been cut off again? If you had the TV on, you'd know what day it is."

"Oh shit. I didn't realize, Ma."

Ernestine's second husband, Joe, had been killed in the World Trade Center. A cook, he had been out of work for almost a year when he went on the morning of September 11 to apply for a job at the Windows on the World restaurant. There had been no survivors from the uppermost floors, and the restaurant was at the very top. Today Ernestine listened to other widows reading names on television at the site. She was not asked to attend because she had not registered on any of the lists of survivors.

She remembered Joe with every fiber of her being, and that memory of him was the important thing. At the time, Ernestine had the impression that for most widows the point of registering was the hope that insurance would replace their husband's lost potential income. In her case, she was afraid that asking for benefits would come down to a discussion of the fact that Joe had not been earning any income for so long before his death. That judgment would have been an unfair way to remember the man who had fallen in love with her when she felt long past her prime, the man who had played such a strong and caring role in the lives of her children and grandchildren, as well as with his own.

Ernestine supposed that she could ask to become part of this group of bereaved families. But she was pretty sure she would not feel at home among them. She certainly did not want to go on television to try to read some of those unpronounceable names. Last year, she had found a personal way to mark the first anniversary of his death. She figured that at least some of Joe's ashes must have blown into the East River, so she had gone to the wharf below the Brooklyn Bridge. Feeling the spray of water as a motorboat went by, she had tossed a can of Budweiser and one of Joe's darts into the river for him. Wherever he was, she hoped he could still enjoy a beer and a game of darts.

Brenda, thinking back two years, remembered the city-wide panic. At the time, she and Allan had been staying with friends near JFK Airport. The neighbourhood had quickly filled with police and the national guard, while military planes circled overhead. When she first heard the news, she had run faster than ever in her life, all the way to Allan's school to make sure he wasn't hurt. The friend hosting them had also taken her children home immediately. Despite the apartment having two bedrooms, they had decided to sleep in one room all week long because otherwise the children were too scared to fall asleep. They kept the television on day and night for warning in case of another attack.

Brenda remembered watching a television interview of the head of the Cantor Fitzgerald finance company, a man who had lost almost seven hundred people from his company. His own brother had been killed too. Brenda was surprised and moved to hear a man talking so frankly about his own loss and devastation. In tears, he spoke about the obligation he felt to support all seven hundred families who had lost someone, sobbing "too many people, too many names, too many people that I loved...." As Brenda and her mother realized that Joe too had been killed, Brenda wished that he could have had a boss like that man, one who really seemed to care about the people he employed.

Now, still standing in the bathroom and talking into Pamela's cell phone, Brenda asked, "Ma, do you want me to come over and stay with you today?"

"No, baby, I'm okay. Just make sure you'll sign the papers for me. And don't mention anything about Joe to Pamela. It'll just upset her."

"You mean she doesn't know?"

"No, I only met her last year. She never got to meet him."

Pamela

When Brenda came out, she told Pamela, "I'm going to visit Ma tomorrow. I'll talk to her about the papers then." Sighing, Pamela wondered whether Brenda really would make the trip to Brooklyn, and whether the papers would ever get signed.

"By the way," Pamela said as she was leaving. "Would you like to come to an event my organization is holding at the United Nations in a few weeks?" She began fishing in her bag for an invitation. "You'd be very welcome to join us. Your mother and Allan will both be there too."

"The United Nations? Are you shitting me?"

"Not at all. It's the World Day for Overcoming Poverty. People who want to end poverty come together to share testimonies and to encourage one another."

"What do you mean, like some prayer circle?"

"Well, it isn't religious, but it's about people building solidarity with one another to try to end something unfair. I guess that's what many prayer circles do too."

"Huh. I don't know. Maybe."

"Well, I hope you do join us. I enjoyed meeting you. And please do visit your mother to sign the papers with her. I think you can really help Allan."

Pamela headed downstairs and began the long subway trip to the Lower East Side of Manhattan.

When she got to the All Together in Dignity centre, Jesse was typing a report. He and Yun Hee kept meticulous records of which children attended their art workshops or were missing.

Noting each child's reactions to the activities they proposed helped them evaluate and plan.

"Want some iced tea?" Pamela asked, opening the fridge.

"Sure. You look beat. What happened with the custody papers?"

"A dead end, at least for the moment. Mrs. Jones couldn't come with me, so I went alone."

"Seriously?"

"Well, they talked to each other on the phone while I was there. But in the end Brenda just said she'd visit her mother tomorrow and sign then — *if* she remembers." Pamela was pouring iced tea into two glasses.

"You didn't seriously think she'd sign papers that important, just with you? You're a total stranger to her. I don't even think you should have gone there without Mrs. Jones."

"Well, I had to do something." Hot and tired, Pamela began losing her temper. "Mrs. Jones was up most of the night with another grandson who had an asthma attack. She works so hard taking care of those children. She just wasn't up to making that long trip."

"Maybe she didn't really want to go after all, and just couldn't face telling you that."

"What? But she's being bullied by the school. It's not fair that they push her into putting Allan on medication that she doesn't want for him. Allan's mother says she's in rehab, and she seems like a nice person; but I'm not convinced that she's actually about to visit her mother. I wish she'd signed the papers today."

"But once she signs them, Mrs. Jones will be the one in charge of her son. And what if the mother completes the rehab and wants to be the one raising Allan again? I think she should have that conversation with her mother before she starts signing papers that are so important." Shaking his head, Jesse added, "You were a little crazy to go all that way today. Besides, I'm not sure that just a signature would even be enough. Some grandparents have to go to court to get custody of their grandchildren."

As quickly as it had flared, Pamela's surge of anger deflated into limp discouragement. Collapsing into a chair, she fanned herself with a piece of construction paper left over from the game Yun Hee and Travis had organized for the children the other evening. "Court! But that would be awful for all of them."

"Yes, it would," Jesse agreed. "When I was a teenager, our neighbour asked for legal custody of her granddaughter. She wasn't happy about going to court, but she really thought it was the best thing for the kid."

"Maybe it was." Pamela began twisting her hair.

"But when they got to the courtroom, the girl, who was only about 8, was taken into a separate room away from all her relatives. They questioned her to make sure she wasn't being influenced against her parents."

"Poor kid!"

"Our neighbour did get legal custody, but she hadn't expected they would be separated in court. She was just devastated at having put her granddaughter through that. That's why I don't think you should have gone to the Bronx without Mrs. Jones. This must be so painful for her."

Defensive again, Pamela said, "Well, my plan was for Mrs. Jones and me to go together. When I planned it though, I'd totally forgotten it would be September 11."

"What difference does that make?"

"It's such a sad anniversary. I should have stayed in bed all day instead."

"Yeah, right!" Jesse said sarcastically. "I can't picture that. You'd be bored and impatient."

"What were you doing on 9/11? Weren't you still living in Tanzania?"

"Yeah. I didn't even know anything had happened for a few days."

"That must have been so strange."

"Well, it felt pretty far away, and we didn't get much news in general, so I don't know if it was strange. But it did make me decide to come live in New York."

"Oh, so that's how we got saddled with you?" Pamela smiled at him.

As Pamela sat down to check her e-mail, Jesse's thoughts drifted back two years.

Jesse

As an African-American, Jesse had always dreamed of going to volunteer in Africa — but after moving to Tanzania, he felt more American than ever before.

He didn't miss the suburban townhouse he had grown up in, on a dead-end street of green lawns where life felt sanitized from over-scheduling. But in Tanzania, he was shocked to discover homes where people had to crouch in low huts cobbled together from scraps of cardboard and plastic sheeting.

He met people working in a stone quarry, where men perched on hillsides to smash off hunks of rock that women and children then bashed into gravel. In the dust-choked air, their bare hands swinging heavy mallets were vulnerable to frequent accidents. A boulder tumbling down could crush their fingers, limbs, or whole bodies.

From his first week in Africa, Jesse began to fantasize about the families he met getting a chance at the so-called American dream — or at the very least a chance to live in a *real* home, where you could stand upright during the day and have room for everyone to stretch out and sleep at night, with protection from rats, dust storms, and flash floods.

Jesse remembered his revulsion at the way other foreigners from rich countries often looked down on Tanzanians. One retired British businessman he met had announced, "I came here because life is cheap. You can hire a well-trained cook and chauffeur for a pittance. But our presence here is a daily reminder to Africans that they're incapable of running their own countries. Just look at the sanitation disaster! And you're better off not touching the cash at all. Those filthy bills pass through so many hands that they'll give you a skin disease." Disgusted, Jesse had done his best to give rich expatriates a wide berth from then on.

Avoiding foreigners and living in a district with no electricity, Jesse was cut off from news most of the time despite being in a large city. Even when he started to hear occasional reports about 9/11, they were sketchy:

"There was a big fire in your country."

"Important hotel buildings fell down."

As the rumours multiplied, one Tanzanian friend, Ahmed, kept asking, "Is your family okay? You have to get news from your family." So the two of them finally made the trek to a neighbourhood with a cybercafé.

Having stumbled often during his first days in the city, Jesse had learned to keep his eyes on the road as he walked. Many paths were studded with jutting stones and pocked with deep holes. It made Jesse smile to remember how annoying even one small pothole at home was to his father. So as he walked with Ahmed, he kept his gaze on his own feet, well protected in his leather sandals, following his friend's more calloused feet in a worn pair of plastic flip-flops.

Jesse was beginning to recognize the different smells they passed: sizzling oil from a stand where a teenage girl sold fried potatoes and cassava; a heap of rubber tires steeping in the sun; precious gasoline being funnelled into a plastic jerry can; a donkey hauling a load of maize; sweat from a man whose bicycle cart was loaded with lumber; the charcoal brazier of an older lady selling fish and rice.

The "cybercafé" Ahmed led him to was a simple wooden kiosk between a busy road and a sewage canal. Although its appearance — and the chicken clucking in the doorway — made Jesse dubious, inside it did indeed have electricity, functioning computers, and a large photocopy machine. In between power cuts, Jesse was able to exchange news with his parents in Maryland, and to read a few headlines on websites that didn't take too long to load.

As the news sunk in for them both, Ahmed, on the wooden stool next to Jesse's, put his head in his hands. "I don't believe this. So many dead! This is terrible for America."

Jesse agreed, but found it hard to take in. The United States had never seemed further away. Frowning, he turned to face Ahmed. "It's true, this is a tragedy. But so many other people die around the world without the news saying much about it. A mudslide in Central America or an earthquake in South Asia can wipe out thousands of people, and it barely gets mentioned on the news in our country."

"But people say America is everything. If things like this can happen, even there, is there anywhere on the planet where people can live in peace?"

Ahmed had a point. His question reminded Jesse of how worried his parents had been when he left home. They were sure he was going to a more dangerous place than the United States. But if such attacks could reach New York City, did it make sense to think of any place as safe?

In the months that followed, Jesse kept thinking about all the world news that Americans ignored. So many places in the world did not even have the resources to let others know about catastrophes. A friend of Jesse's serving in the Peace Corps had told him about a cyclone destroying thousands of homes in one area of Madagascar — while people elsewhere in the country had scarcely heard any news about it at all. Even those who did have electricity and televisions couldn't see what had never been filmed. There were simply no journalists in that part of the country to interview the newly homeless.

Now, every time Jesse saw another American news report about people whose homes had been damaged in a disaster, he had to force himself to relate to their hardships. He knew that they were going through something tragic and traumatizing — but they also had at least a chance of getting insurance, federal assistance, and private donations that most of the world could never even imagine. Could Americans imagine whole countries where hospitals lacked the most basic supplies like sheets and disinfectants?

Even after 9/11, although nothing would ever make up for the loss of lives, Jesse had heard that New York City was deluged with letters of friendship from schools around the world, shipments of teddy bears from Japan, braided bracelets from Indiana Girl Scout troops, and other donations of all kinds. What had families bereaved by the genocide in Rwanda received to show that *they* could have friends somewhere in the world?

Jesse's decision to move to New York had not been to help a city under attack. Instead, his hope was to tap into the grief that all New Yorkers had undergone and to mobilize them to help people in even greater need around the world.

So far, however, he wasn't sure he was making much of a dent toward this goal. He found the 9/11 anniversaries particularly galling. So many merchants displayed American flags in their stores. Flags were fine; but the fact that most of the merchants and taxi drivers displaying these flags were not born in America made Jesse suspect that, even if they sincerely loved their adopted country, the flags were probably also meant as proof of allegiance and loyalty. Maybe the flags were really there to safeguard against the bigotry and harassment that blamed terrorism on all Muslims or simply on anyone who "looked foreign," whatever that meant.

By now, the flags jabbed at Jesse's heart, making him wish he were back in Tanzania rather than Brooklyn — but he did love working at the housing project in Bushwick. One of the teenagers in Bushwick, Darleen Walker's son Dauntay, disliked American flags as much as Jesse did. His reasons were different though. When he saw his mother marking the anniversary of 9/11 by cutting out a flag from a newspaper and taping it to their window, he objected, "That's embarrassing, Mom. What did this country ever do for us?"

But Darleen would not be swayed. "Have some respect for this flag. You should appreciate living in a country where young kids aren't thrown in jail with adults. You should appreciate that all those girls you like to look at don't have to wear burkas here."

Jesse had begun getting to know the Walker family last year, the first time he helped run an art workshop. Their neighbour Tanita had been the one to show him around. Just 18 at the time, she had participated in these art workshops as a child and had been helping Yun Hee to run them whenever she could.

The neighbourhood had amazed Jesse: ornate newel posts on top of wrought-iron railings along the stoops of homes that were elegant a century ago; graffiti-covered walls, pock-marked by bullets; corner stores with overpriced junk food and not a fresh vegetable in sight; vacant lots filled with every kind of debris and with the rubble of buildings that had been torn down. Jesse was most taken aback to discover that a few homes were wrapped cellar to rooftop in metal bars to fend off intruders. What must it be like for children growing up inside these oddly caged buildings? What must it be like for the children outside, growing up as the ones the bars are meant to keep out?

Tanita had led Jesse to the block where the Walker family had just moved in. Burnt out of their last apartment, the Walkers had spent more than a year in several shelters before finding this apartment. Yun Hee, who had known them for six years now, moved the art workshop to their block to help them settle into their new home. So, on the sidewalk in front of the building the Walkers lived in, they spread a blanket for children to sit on, despite the litter nearby. Among other things, a broken toilet leaned precariously on a heap of debris just a yard from the blanket. Jesse wondered how the pervasive filth might affect the drawings that the children would make. While Tanita and Yun Hee went inside to let children know the workshop was about to begin, Jesse set up some art books and materials for drawing.

On that day, the first of the Walker children to come outside had been 6-year-old Lissa. She had walked slowly, her gait just slightly pigeon-toed. At first, Jesse hadn't been sure whether she was a girl or a boy. Her hair was cropped close to her head, and she wore unisex T-shirt and shorts. There were stains on the T-shirt and a hole in the leg of the shorts. Not knowing Jesse, she had stopped several yards short of the blanket he had spread out. Despite his attempts to engage her in an activity, she stayed silent and immobile until Yun Hee and Tanita returned with Lissa's sisters and brothers, and a dozen other children from their building.

Following Yun Hee's lead, Jesse soon set Lissa and several other children to work making drawings that they would paint at the next session. But no sooner had Lissa begun in earnest to try drawing a tree than she stopped in frustration. Before Jesse could stop her, she had torn up her paper and begun walking away. Jesse followed her a few steps away from the others.

"Lissa, why did you tear that up? You were doing fine."

"You angry? I don't care. Drawing is stupid."

"I'm not angry at all. Look, if you want to start over, there's more paper."

Lissa was silent for a moment, watching the others draw. "I wanna go home." She continued walking toward her building. Just then, two other children began arguing over a red pencil, so Jesse reluctantly let Lissa go.

He remembered that it had taken another two months of regular workshops before his encouragement helped Lissa to succeed with a drawing that she liked enough to show to her mother.

"Hey, I like that," said Darleen Walker. "Nothing can stop you now, girl!"

4. MOTIVES

Tanita was getting nowhere with her writing. She knew exactly what the Ramirez family was going through. She knew many other people stuck in unfair situations too. But how could she write a speech to give at the United Nations? She had no idea who might actually listen to it. There were plenty of fine-looking people in suits at the German reception. What on earth did they know about poverty? She couldn't imagine any of them being able to relate to Mrs. Jones's dilemma with her grandson. That snooty Belgian woman had actually walked out of their meeting while Mrs. Jones was talking about it.

Finally Tanita gave in and called Pamela to ask for advice. Instead of being upset that Tanita hadn't written a word yet — or, worse, deciding that Ornella should do the speech instead — Pamela just said, "You're right. You deserve to know who you'll be talking to. Why don't we go to meet with someone at the UN, one-on-one, to get to know each other better?" So here Tanita was, in her sharpest blouse and slacks, smoking a cigarette and waiting for Pamela on the corner of Second Avenue and 42nd Street. Her high heels pinched her feet, and she hoped Pamela would hurry up, although she knew she, herself, had arrived much too early.

Two cigarettes later, Pamela arrived at the planned time. She was weighed down by a fraying shoulder bag that she couldn't quite zip closed around something bulky. "Look, I brought our photo album, so you can show Varag some of our projects if you want."

They were walking together toward the main UN building. "You said Varag is the one from the reception who's married to that tight-ass lady?"

Pamela laughed. "Well, yes, that's him; but I think he's much more open-minded than she is. And in fact his work relates to what we do more than hers does. So I thought he'd be a good person to start with."

"Start with! You think I got time to do this every week? I've been thinking, I'm not sure I even have the time to prepare this speech. Maybe you should just ask someone else to do it. As long as it's not Ornella again."

"No, please don't give up too fast. Let's talk to Varag first, and we'll see how you feel after that, okay?" Before Tanita could answer, they were stopped by a police officer on the street.

"ID?"

Pamela showed him a laminated card issued to non-governmental organizations.

"Sorry, you can't cross the street right now — UN staff only."

Sighing, Pamela drew Tanita back a few yards to explain, "There's probably some head of state visiting whose security they're particularly worried about. Let me ring up Varag so he can come outside to meet us."

"Man, we might as well be in Bushwick. Lucky the guard didn't want to frisk us for drugs or weapons."

Varag, Pamela, and Tanita

Incredulous that NGOs were not being allowed in the building, Varag joined the women. Five minutes later they had walked two blocks away, where they settled at a small table in the back of a deli. The odours from the all-day hot buffet were distinctly unappetizing. A dull neon light reflected on the shabby linoleum floor and made Pamela regret that she had no fancier place to offer Tanita, who didn't often come to midtown Manhattan.

"So?" asked Varag, pushing hair out of his eyes. Remembering that Blandine kept nagging him to go to the barber, he wondered whether Pamela was the type to nag. "What's this about?"

Taking a sip of tepid coffee, Pamela gathered her thoughts. Looking at the array of pens in Varag's shirt pocket, she noticed ink stains on his fingers. She *did* consider him an open-minded person — but he was also a busy and impatient one. Hoping to make the most of both his time and Tanita's, Pamela plunged into her topic. "You know that we're preparing a speech for the World Day for Overcoming Poverty. Tanita has things to say about people she knows and how they fight against poverty. But she'd like to know more about the audience. How will people at the UN understand what she has to say?"

"I guess that depends what it is you say," Varag answered carefully, turning reluctantly away from Pamela to look at Tanita. "We know all the facts and figures already, at least from the countries where data has been properly collected. But, despite the number crunching, we haven't yet put an end to poverty. So if you have new ideas, or if you can inspire the UN to work harder, I think people will listen."

"But I don't even know who you are!" Tanita burst out. "People in poverty don't have a lot of privacy. They may not get a chance to speak their mind very often, but if you live on the street, everyone knows your business. Reporters think they can say anything they want about your neighbourhood, your school, your people.... I'm just saying, I think there should be a little give in the other direction. What can *you* tell people about yourself? *Why* do you want to fight poverty? Isn't it just your job, or do you really care?"

Varag was taken aback by the onslaught of questions from this teenager asking him to justify himself. At the same time, it occurred to him that she had a point. God only knew, too many UN resolutions had no effect whatsoever on ordinary people's lives. Recovering himself, he asked, "Have you ever heard of Armenia?"

Tanita shook her head.

"It's near Iran, isn't it?" Pamela asked.

"Just north of Iran, east of Turkey, west of Azerbaijan. None of them have been good neighbours. Armenia is where I grew up. Did you know that the Armenians were the victims of the first genocide of the twentieth century?"

"Genocide?" Tanita was unsettled.

"By the Turks in 1915 — and partly in reaction to do-gooder American missionaries at the time who were aggravating religious differences. The Turks thought we were getting too uppity, so they used the cover of World War I to execute Armenians serving in the Turkish army and then to try to deport the whole population of Armenia to the deserts of Syria and Mesopotamia. When heat and hunger didn't kill people fast enough, some were even buried alive, and many of the women were kidnapped. One and a half million Armenians were killed."

"That's terrible!" Tanita was trying to imagine a whole country forced to march into a desert.

"But the Turks lost World War I," Pamela remembered. "Did Armenia become independent then?"

"Sure — for two whole years. Then we were taken over by the Soviets for seventy years. You can imagine the repression and poverty."

"Are you a Muslim?" Tanita asked.

"Armenia is not a Muslim country. That's partly why Muslim countries have mistrusted us. Actually, Armenia was the very first country in the world to make Christianity its official religion, even before the Roman Empire. My father's family is Christian. My mother's family is Jewish. Jews have been in Armenia even longer than the Christians, although they're not nearly as numerous. At this point, most Jews have left Armenia, but when I was born in 1955, there were still thousands."

Tanita wondered if Varag was insulted that she had asked if he was Muslim. Feeling anxious, she wished smoking were allowed inside the deli.

Pamela wanted to know, "So how did you get from Armenia to the UN?"

"Our whole history is one of poverty and oppression. So I studied economics because I wanted to find a way out for my people. The more I read and studied, the more I learned of the tragedies of other peoples — colonialism, slavery, apartheid, the Holocaust. Hatred and racism helped cause these injustices, but so did economics. Slavery helped make agriculture profitable. Holocaust victims were murdered, but also looted for anything they possessed. Apartheid and colonialism systematically stole people's labor, land, and resources. I'm not saying that economics alone can overcome evil, but what we need today is more sustainable economic policies — fair trade, microcredit, anything that helps people take charge of their own destiny instead of laboring to enrich others."

"What do you mean, 'slavery made agriculture profitable'?" Tanita burst out. "You make slavery sound like a business strategy."

"I didn't mean that it *should* be one; of course slavery is evil. But unfortunately, today it still remains an unscrupulous business strategy in many places. Forcing other human beings to work for free — or for starvation wages in a factory compound that they are never allowed to leave — well, that's how certain unethical people and businesses continue to make great fortunes."

The smell of wet pavement as a customer swung the glass door open drew Tanita's eyes to the sidewalk, now being pummeled by rain. Passers-by had quickened their pace and were popping open their umbrellas.

Thinking about the great fortunes of the few reminded Tanita of the fortune she wished she had. Tuition at the City University of New York was no longer free. Although the cost remained far less expensive than most colleges, full-time students there were charged $4,000 a year for a four-year degree. How on earth could she earn $16,000 that wouldn't be needed for her family? And if she were earning that much extra money, when would she find time to take classes and study? She fired questions at Varag: "Well, what kind of family did you grow up in? You've got such a fancy education, where did the money for that come from?"

"In fact," Varag answered, "many countries don't expect students to be able to pay any tuition at all. And my family certainly wasn't rich. My father was a shopkeeper and my mother was a homemaker. But it's true that I benefited from parents who always encouraged me in my studies and who could afford to have me continue living at home while I finished my degrees." Now Varag laughed. "My father encouraged me to study because he saw that I wasn't much good at anything else. I always lost to the other boys at wrestling, and I was never any good at fixing things. I much preferred to do crossword puzzles or read poetry. So father would just shake his head and say, 'God didn't spoil you with muscles; let's hope at least that you have a brain.'"

"What kind of poetry?" asked Pamela.

Varag was silent for a moment, his gaze fixing hers, before he recited a few lines:

"...Only what I gave away,
extraordinary, only that;
what went to others returned sweetened and
strengthened to rest with me eternally."

He added, "That's from a poem by one of our Armenian poets, Vahan Tekeyan, writing about what he received from life — only what he gave away."

They fell silent, and the sounds around them seemed to sharpen: the squelching of shoes on rubber matting in the aisles; the thudding of refrigerator doors being swung shut; the soft or shrill voices ordering sandwiches.

Pamela had another question. "You said that Armenia's poverty led you to economics, and that led you to the UN. But the connections are hard for us to see. Can you tell us more about economics and your work at the UN?"

Again, Varag looked at Pamela, wondering just what it was about her that had caught his interest. "I suppose I could give you an example." He waved toward the rainy sidewalk. "Let's take water. Too many people around the world lack clean drinking water, or can't afford to pay for it. So one way a government can address that problem is to subsidize it, paying for water to be purified and provided cheaply in different parts of the country. Now, when a government has very little money to begin with, subsidizing water means spending more than it has. Some people call this bad economics. They want poor governments to collect more tax money before anything else. But one of the things economists can prove is that it's actually more expensive in the long term to ignore the lack of clean water. When poor people can't afford water, diseases spread, even to middle-class populations. This means fewer people are healthy enough to work, and fewer customers can buy whatever businesses are selling. Many companies flee places in this situation — so in fact even if it does cost money to subsidize clean water, we can show that it's a smart economic strategy in the long run."

Tanita was frowning. "You have to convince governments that everyone needs water? Don't they know that already?"

Varag sighed. "I suppose they *do* know it, in theory. But plenty of other things that everyone needs also cost a lot of money. And the question of who will pay for what, and how dynamic a country's businesses and tax base can be — all of that is economics."

"So your job is convincing governments to pay for what people need?"

"No, not exactly. I work for the United Nations, which is made up of governments. It's governments that contribute all the money that allows the UN to function, and it's governments that make all the decisions. Our job in the UN Secretariat is to do the research and policy work that enables governments to make careful decisions and then to be vigilant about following through on them. To continue the example of clean water: despite what I said, it isn't necessarily governments that must pay for things everyone needs. Some people think it should be the private sector — that is to say, businesses — that should contribute money toward the common good."

"What does that mean? That those bottled water companies would give away their bottles for free to people who can't afford to buy them?"

"I don't think that's the best approach, if only because manufacturing so many plastic bottles wastes too many of our planet's resources." As Varag's long arm swung out to indicate the many shelves of bottled drinks in the deli, Tanita wondered if she was supposed to feel guilty for sipping her soda from a plastic bottle.

He continued, "But many businesses, in addition to selling products, also run charitable foundations. They could donate the know-how for tasks like digging and maintaining clean water wells if they were convinced that providing clean water would also help their business to make a profit."

"Making a buck, that's all most people care about," Tanita said. "A business that won't clean polluted water should have to explain why by talking to families who are sick from their pollution."

"I think so too. But we in the UN Secretariat don't get to make the decisions."

"Then what do you do?"

"We conduct research and publish reports about things the UN either is considering doing in the future or has done in the past."

"So you're just like ... reporters?"

"We hope this helps governments to make smart choices — and businesses too. Although when it comes to businesses, the UN has its work cut out for it to try to convince them. But when we see businesses acting unethically, we can point it out to the public."

"Reporters, like I said."

He laughed. "We can also tell businesses how we think they could contribute to economic development."

Only half-listening now, Pamela was watching a young man restock the buffet. He had removed an almost empty platter of chow mein when he slipped in a puddle spreading from the soaked umbrella of a lady behind him. The man managed to catch his balance, but not quickly enough to hold onto the platter. It clattered loudly on the floor, spattering sauce and a few scraps of noodles. After glaring at the employee, the lady looked anxiously down at her skirt, and then hurried away, relieved not to find any stains. As the employee began mopping up the mess, Pamela sighed.

Turning back to Varag, she said, "You've been speaking about the UN Secretariat here at headquarters, but in developing countries, the UN also runs its own programmes through UNICEF and the UN Development Programme."

"Yes, of course. In many countries, UN agencies do get directly involved on the ground."

"How?" Tanita wanted to know.

"By running programmes to vaccinate children against disease, or by creating microcredit opportunities for poor women to start small businesses, for example."

"School enrolment too," Pamela put in. "UNICEF tries to make sure that all children get a chance to go to school."

"But the principle is the same," Varag added. "Decisions are made by the governments that run the UN, while UN staff runs programmes and does the research to plan and evaluate. And often the work is done in partnership with NGOs like yours."

"What?" asked Tanita.

"NGO means non-governmental organization," Pamela explained. "Non-profit groups can apply to the UN to be recognized as NGOs because of work we do to promote the well-being of people and communities."

Then Pamela turned back to Varag. "Earlier, you were saying you think it was economics that caused colonialism, slavery, apartheid, the Holocaust. Is that what was taught under communism?"

Varag grinned. "You'd be surprised just what can be learned in a communist country. Not everything is taught in universities of course, but there were always people to learn from, even during the communist era."

"When did you leave Armenia?" Pamela asked.

His face darkened. "The earthquakes in 1988 in Armenia were very severe, and my family lived in the wrong place. My parents were killed outright. Several of our relatives died from their injuries in the days afterward."

Taken aback, Pamela murmured, "I'm so sorry."

"Emergency aid sent by the Russians got blocked and never reached us. So I did not see much reason to stay. When the borders became easier to cross in 1990, I moved to New York."

"That's awful," Tanita exclaimed. "But do you get homesick? Do you still feel like your roots are there?"

Quiet for a moment, Varag remembered his mother's knotted hands kneading dough to make flatbread. His father had been forever hammering to add new shelves to his tiny store. "I suppose every immigrant keeps some feeling of roots, even linked to a place he might not want to return to."

"Of course," Pamela nodded.

Varag continued, "What you have to watch out for is not homesickness, but rootlessness. Moving to another continent is destabilizing, no matter why you move."

"Yes, moving to another continent, or I think also even when you're going back and forth between two communities," Pamela said. "I remember an interview of Bernice Johnson Reagon."

"Who?" Tanita asked.

"A wonderful composer and singer from the south of the U.S. She's still singing, but I think she was more famous in the 1960s when she sang for the civil rights movement."

"What did you mean about two communities?" Varag asked.

"She said that joining the civil rights movement was her first experience of distancing herself from the culture she had grown up in. She found herself choosing parts of the civil rights culture, reorganizing that culture and then bringing it back to her home community in a new way."

"I wonder if she felt she belonged to both communities," Varag said. "Some people may not feel they belong anywhere at all."

"Now you're talking like my great-grandmother," Tanita said. "That's just how she used to talk about the end of slavery. She said that even after slaves were freed at the end of the Civil War, they didn't move away."

Pamela frowned. "That doesn't make sense."

"Well, they did eventually. But it wasn't until a whole generation later that their children started moving up north."

"Why did they stay?" Pamela wanted to know.

"Maybe the older generation went through too much, you know?"

"Do you think maybe they were afraid they wouldn't belong up north?" Varag asked.

Tanita hesitated. "Maybe, yeah. Even when they finally did move, my great-grandmother said she felt out of place because she hadn't been to school much. And she had a southern accent. Up here, southerners felt like other people looked down on them."

Varag said, "I've known immigrants to end up feeling lost and aimless with no balance in their lives."

"That's so sad," Pamela said.

"To be part of the world, you need to build a base of trust somewhere, whether it's in the place you were born or not."

Tanita considered Varag's words, thinking of the Ramirez children. Where was their base of trust? "Do you have children?" she asked.

Varag frowned. He had long wished for children, but Blandine never seemed to feel ready for motherhood. He felt it would be wrong of him to interfere with her career. To Tanita, he said, "I think I've had enough of satisfying your interrogation. Maybe you'll be sharing your own story in your speech, Tanita, but now why don't we question Pamela for a change? You must have things to ask her too."

"Hey, that's true! I've known you for years, Pamela, but you don't talk a lot about yourself. How did you decide to get involved in fighting poverty?"

"What, me?"

"I know you used to work at a magazine back in England, right? How did you get from there to here?"

Pamela smiled, "I did love that job. I worked on layout."

"What did you like about it?" Varag asked.

"Designing a layout is brilliant fun. You want to intrigue the reader, create some glossy razzmatazz that catches the eye. Maybe I should go back to that; it was so much less complicated."

"But you quit that job to join All Together in Dignity," Tanita said. "Why?"

"Hmm... I guess my detour was because of Rez. He was a boy I met at university. We were still dating a few years later."

"Never heard you mention this guy before. You still seeing him?" Tanita asked.

"No, not for a while now. Don't worry, I haven't been hiding anyone in a closet. Now do you want to hear this or not?"

"Go on."

"His father was really keen on genealogy and he wanted research done in Hungary, where he was born. But the father was in poor health, and his doctor advised against such a long trip. He was gutted, but he asked Rez to go for him. Rez didn't want to go alone, so I went along for the ride."

"Following a man!" Tanita smiled. "And you pretend to be so independent."

Pamela smiled. "Touché. Anyway, I just learned so much in Hungary. We stayed with Rez's Uncle Sandor in Budapest. Sandor is a social worker."

"So he worked with people in poverty?" Tanita asked.

"It was more complicated than that. Under communism, the official theory was that there *was* no more poverty left. So Sandor was meant to work only with alcoholics and drug addicts. And of course he also got to know people who didn't fit into those categories but were still having a hard time, or even living on the streets."

"So it wasn't true that no one was poor?"

"Not really, no. And when he met people like that, he often ended up bringing them home to stay in his kids' room until he could help them get back on their feet. I thought Sandor was amazing."

"You were there during Communism?" Varag asked.

"No, our trip was several years after it ended. But this was how he'd worked for most of his life."

"So why did you change jobs?"

"Well at one point, Sandor sent us to visit a small town populated mainly with Travellers."

"Like tourists?" Tanita asked.

"No, not at all. You Americans still think of them as "Gypsies,' but in the UK and Ireland, they prefer to call themselves Travellers."

"I've heard of Gypsy fortune tellers," Tanita said, "but I thought they were from a long time ago, kind of like knights in shining armour."

"In both Eastern and Western Europe, there are plenty of Travellers. But they don't have a good reputation. Even buying the train ticket to get to that town was a challenge. The ticket seller kept insisting, 'No, no, you don't want to go there. It's a dodgy den of thieves; you have no idea.'"

"Wow! Were you scared to go?"

"No, that was rubbish. He just couldn't imagine us nice British tourists going to a place where he wouldn't set foot himself. It's like here. A tourist might be told he's mistaken if he wants to go to the South Bronx."

"Or to Bushwick," Tanita said with a wry smile.

"Sadly, yes. Once we did get to this town, a friend of Sandor's made us very welcome. But it was still a shock to see the poor living conditions. The families' income depended mostly on scavenging and sorting scrap metal."

"What do you mean? Like collecting tin cans for the rebate?"

"Sort of, but they would hunt for any kind of metal — old bits of machinery, or old nails they could wrench out of a piece of wood, or anything really. But if it didn't bring a good price, they were stuck. I remember a teenager with a toothache who pulled his own tooth out with pliers."

"Pliers? Ouch! How could he do that?" Tanita wanted to know.

"He was a tough kid, not scared of pain."

"Why didn't he go to a dentist?" Varag asked. "If the Communists were good at one thing, it was free health care."

"True. But I think he just wanted to avoid having to go to a dentist's office where he knew that people would look down on him."

"People like the ticket-seller who didn't want you to go there?" Tanita asked.

"Right. He wasn't the only one who thought the place was a den of thieves, and this boy knew it."

Varag shook his head sadly.

Pamela continued. "I remember a mother there too. While we were talking, I wanted to show her a postcard of London to describe where I lived. I was rummaging for it in my bag, when a crumpled scrap of notepaper fell out."

Tanita laughed. "Your bags are always a mess."

Pamela smiled sheepishly. "Well, I never know what I might need. But the scrap that fell was unimportant. I would have discarded it if I'd been more organized — but the woman picked it up so carefully from the mud and returned it to me like it was a piece of treasure."

"How come?"

Pamela hesitated. "I can't be sure. But I don't think paper was something she ever had used much herself."

Varag suggested, "Maybe it was her way of showing respect to you."

Pamela nodded. "Yes, maybe. And her family lived in a broken trailer up on cinder blocks, way down at the end of a path. That path was so muddy that it was hard to walk without slipping."

"They call themselves Travellers but can't afford to replace the wheels on their trailer," Varag observed.

"Exactly. I know that most of the world copes without plumbing or electricity, but after the splendours of Budapest, this village was quite a contrast."

"No electricity at all?" asked Tanita. "So they don't have any light at night, or any TV?"

"The more dynamic families do make their own electricity from rigging up homemade generators, and others have candles or battery-operated radios."

"That's good."

"Yes, but with or without generators, they all seemed to be stuck with the damp. The winter there gets so cold and muddy, it seemed like the laundry was never able to dry properly."

Tanita wrinkled her nose. "So, mildew?"

"Right. Even though I saw those mothers constantly scrubbing, their children had to leave for school in the morning with that awful odour of damp."

"That certainly doesn't help when you already have people who are so prejudiced against Travellers," Varag said.

Tanita was pensive. "I never imagined real-life Gypsies getting such a raw deal out of life."

Pamela nodded. "You mentioned hearing stories about fortune tellers. I grew up hearing lots of stories about children being 'stolen by Gypsies.'"

"Old wives' tales," scoffed Varag.

"Repeated by plenty of men too," Pamela said pointedly. "You don't get to blame women for gossip."

"Point taken," Varag said, smiling at Pamela's feminist indignation.

"How do you think lies like that get started?" Tanita wondered.

Varag answered, "A few generations ago, most people spent their whole lives in the same village, never traveling anywhere.

So perhaps lots of children dreamed of being able to run away and live outdoors with dancing and music."

"Like running away to join the circus," Tanita said. "I remember wishing I could do that."

"Exactly," said Pamela. "Running away may be a child's fantasy, but that made parents extra suspicious of people who went from place to place."

"They got in the habit of blaming them for anything bad," Varag said.

"So much so that it became part of the English language. That's why people say they've been 'gypped' when someone cheats them."

"Wow, I never thought of that," Tanita said.

"That's how the word 'Gypsy' became an insult. Travellers like the ones I met are sure that outsiders will disrespect them. I remember going up to a woman because I wanted to talk to her. I had barely opened my mouth when she started picking up her things to move aside. She assumed I wanted her to move out of my way."

"What year was this?" Varag wanted to know. "You said several years after the end of Communism?"

"I was 25 at the time, so it would have been 1995."

"That's six years of a new regime. Didn't you see signs that life was improving for people?"

"Well, I saw change, yes. The country was in the midst of huge upheaval."

"I'm guessing that Sandor no longer had to hide his work with people in poverty."

"True, that had changed. But as for improvement, it's hard to say."

"Wasn't the country as a whole getting much wealthier, very quickly?"

"I guess it was. But I don't think anyone wanted to share that progress with Travellers or with unskilled Hungarian labourers living at the sharp end of poverty. One woman said to me, 'Before, at least the government talked about everyone having a home and a job. Now, no one cared when I lost my job. Our country now is for those who are fast and independent. No one else is needed.'"

With a crackling buzz, the neon light above their table sputtered out. Twirling strands of her hair around her finger, Pamela continued, "Hearing that woman made me think of people in Britain."

"Why?" asked Tanita.

"In the town where I grew up, after the textile factory closed, some people never found steady work again."

"Harsh."

"I believe in the democracy and free speech that arrived in Hungary with the end of Communism; but I'm not so sure about free-wheeling capitalism. That Hungarian woman had a point. Anyone who isn't fast enough gets left completely behind."

"So you quit your magazine job?" Tanita asked.

"Well, not right away. But after we got back home, it seemed like poverty in London kept jumping out at me."

"What do you mean?"

"When I first moved to the city, some years before our trip to Hungary, I tried to get used to seeing homeless people. After our trip to Hungary, I decided that wasn't something I *should* 'get used to.' But at the same time, I would see a young woman my age who lived in the streets and have no idea what to say to her."

"And maybe she didn't want to talk to you," Tanita suggested.

"Maybe not. So when I found an opportunity to do anti-poverty work with All Together in Dignity, that was what I wanted. And gradually I've discovered that I *do* have things in common with people like that young woman, whose background is completely different from mine. I feel like I learn so much from people I would never have imagined being able to talk to."

"Like what?" Varag asked.

"Sheer gumption, for one thing. It's amazing what some people put up with, and yet they just keep going, day after day. Oh, and I have to say that Sandor really inspired me."

"Oh yeah?" said Tanita.

"At one point, it looked like there wouldn't be any more funding for his job as a social worker. But he said that wouldn't stop him at all."

"He has gumption too," commented Varag.

"I remember Sandor pounding on the table and shouting, 'Fighting poverty isn't a job that stops at 6 p.m. If I stopped, I'd be letting down my own children's future. You sit home and cry, or you get up and do something.' So I decided that I needed to do something too."

"And what became of Rez?" Varag was the one asking this time.

"His father was pleased with our research." Pamela looked up at Varag, suspecting that his question had been meant more personally. "I'm done being interrogated too. We should start grilling Tanita now."

"Look at the time! I got to get to work." Tanita laughed. "Anyway, I'm the one who has to make a speech, so it's only fair I got a chance to ask some questions."

Pamela

Back on the street, Tanita headed for the Grand Central subway station and Varag back to his First Avenue office. As they left, Pamela realized that she had forgotten to even open the photo album still in her bag. It didn't matter, since they had found plenty to talk about. She decided to walk downtown to the All Together in Dignity centre. Often she took the bus, but she had good walking shoes on today. At meetings in midtown she often felt out of place for not trying to be stylish. When she had been in her 20s, she used to wear high heels all the time; but she also frittered much of her salary away on taxis. Now that she had chosen to earn less, she appreciated sensible shoes that worked for the subway or long walks. Today the weather was inviting. Now that the short thunderstorm was over, the air felt refreshed. Autumn sunlight filtered through the smog, and breezes from the East River reached Second Avenue.

Tanita had been right; Pamela never talked about Rez. It had been strange mentioning his name in such a tangential way, as though his one role in her life had been to accompany her to Hungary, where she had discovered the kind of injustice that she had avoided examining in her own backyard. But Rez had never been tangential. Their first conversations had sparked an intensity of emotions that neither had experienced before. They had fallen in love quickly — and they fought constantly. Looking back, Pamela wondered if some of their arguments were simply misunderstandings. They had grown up with such different frames of reference that words had different meanings for each of them. To Pamela, "feminism" was a political movement, while to Rez it represented the force that had shattered his parents' marriage.

It was shortly after their return from Hungary that Rez had proposed to her. In a way, it was high time. They had been dating for six years; but Pamela hadn't really thought about marriage before he asked. He made the proposal ceremoniously, holding out a ring in the middle of a romantic walk through Grosvenor Square, one of their favourite places. And yet she couldn't just go with the moment and say yes. She needed time to think it over. Rez asked her to wear the ring while she thought it over, and she agreed. How could she quash the proposal he had planned so carefully without even letting him slide the ring onto her finger? But in the following days, while Pamela tried to imagine them married, for better or for worse, the ring felt heavy and awkward on her finger. She was never able to explain to herself just why she didn't feel ready to get married. She and Rez loved each other, and she had nothing against marriage in general. But they had been a couple for so long that she was starting to wonder who she was outside of her relationship with him. So after a week she returned his ring. She thought they would be able to keep dating, but Rez felt rejected and ended things abruptly. When a promotion took him to Canada a few months later, they fell out of touch for good.

Pamela didn't even know his current phone number. However, she had started googling his name every now and then, just to see what he might be up to. From his company's press releases, she could tell that his career was on track; but there was nothing to indicate whether he was in love, or married, or had children. The few friends they had socialized with as a couple were also people Pamela had gradually fallen out of touch with.

Now, eight years later, more time had gone by than during their entire relationship. Pamela didn't regret her decision. Still, she was sad to think that the two of them, who had once intuited each other's moods through and through, would probably never again speak.

Varag and Blandine

Over dinner that night, Varag played a recording of Charlie Parker's bebop jazz. As they ate, he recounted to Blandine his conversation with Tanita and Pamela. Ending with Pamela's description of the changes in Hungary following the fall of the Berlin Wall, he said, "She argued that capitalism is no better than communism because it's the early birds who get all the worms while others are out of luck."

Blandine objected. "But that's foolish," she said. "More people were left behind under communism. A planned economy always ends up with someone completely incompetent barking out impractical orders. And without a free market, creative entrepreneurs have no room to develop new technologies and better business models."

"Are you seriously arguing for a completely free market? It's obvious that without a socialistic approach to health care and education, a society is doomed to failure." As "Summertime" started playing, he closed his eyes to better appreciate the seductive harmonies.

"Are *you* actually the one defending communism for once?" Blandine smiled. "You know perfectly well that you would wither away in misery without the freedom to bellow your opinions from the rooftops on every occasion."

"Touché!" Varag laughed. "In any case, it was interesting that Tanita's goal was to find out what motivates both Pamela and me to care about poverty."

Thinking this over, Blandine felt increasingly vexed. She wondered just how much time her husband had spent with Pamela over the past month. "I suppose your life sounded quite romantic and noble to them?"

"Can I help it if I had to give them a lesson in modern history?"

"In your usual condescending style, I suppose. Don't they know that your main motivation in life has nothing at all to do with poverty?"

Varag frowned. "What do you mean?"

"Oh, I know exactly what drives you forward — it's your fixation on winning every possible argument."

He laughed, as Blandine added, "Here's something you can't argue about: it's your turn to clear away the dishes."

Ahmed

In Tanzania, Ahmed had news. After reading a new email from Jesse in the cybercafé, he headed back to his own part of town to tell his mother. When he passed an 8-year-old girl in ragged clothes struggling to carry two heavy buckets of water, he made a detour to carry them home for her. But finally he arrived in the courtyard where his mother was bent over a bucket, scrubbing laundry for several neighbours who employed her.

"Mother, I got another letter from Jesse."

"I am glad to hear it," said Ambata, looking up without slowing her work. When the sun had dried the brightly patterned khanga garments, she would put a heavy iron on her tiny coal stove to heat it. Her meticulous washing and ironing left the cotton fresher than if it were new from a store. "Are he and his family well?"

"Yes, they are fine — and you can't imagine what else he has written. It's about All Together in Dignity, but over there in America. Jesse and the others have invited me to go there for the World Day for Overcoming Poverty."

"You — to America?" Amazed, Ambata let her busy hands fell momentarily idle. Listening carefully now, she asked, "What in heaven's name for?"

"It's not forever, I would go only for about ten days, returning before Ramadan begins. For their event at the United Nations, they will have people speaking about their work fighting poverty in different countries. They want me to speak about the work we do here with Kafeel and the others."

"Ten days in America?"

"Jesse says they have received a grant that will pay for the air fare, and I would stay at Jesse's home."

"So you're going to see Jesse again? I can hardly believe it. But won't you need papers?"

"The passport I got when Jesse and I visited Madagascar is still valid. And he's sending me papers for a visa application, so hopefully it will be okay. But is it fine with you that I go? I can ask Kafeel to visit you while I'm gone, in case you need help with anything."

Ambata sighed, "Of course it's good. I would never ask you to miss a chance like this. Jesse is someone we all trust. And we know that this World Day is special because it is about fighting poverty. Maybe this can become a chance for many people in poverty. I might have known that even at a distance Jesse would keep on surprising us."

5. "THE GREATEST MISFORTUNE"

Tanita, arriving home, was startled to find Carmen and Mateo Ramirez stuffing their belongings into plastic garbage bags. "What on earth are you doing?"

"We're going to a shelter."

"You can't do that — they won't let Mateo stay with you."

"I'll figure something out," Mateo said. "But you know the landlord won't like us being in your place. You could get in trouble. And the main thing is that if Carmen and the boys go to PATH, they'll have a better shot at getting a real apartment later."

Tanita's heart sank. The Prevention Assistance and Temporary Housing centre never had room for the thousands of parents and children who passed through, spending nights crowded into the waiting room or the hallways. It was the kind of place where everyone was on edge and tempers flared more easily than anywhere else. But Mateo was right that her own family was taking a risk by housing his family. Overcrowding was illegal, and the landlord could throw them all out. On top of that, Tanita's apartment had become a mess, with too many boys constantly wrestling, and all of them putting up with long waits for a turn in the bathroom. Mateo's oldest son, Montrell, often talked back to his father. When Mateo began losing his temper, Carmen would interject, "Let it go. You'll only make things worse." Then Carmen and Mateo would end up arguing with each other late into the night. Even when they switched to Spanish, which she didn't understand, their sharp tones put Tanita on edge.

Still, she knew only too well how hard it would be for them at the PATH. "What about school? You'll be so far away from here."

"Well, we can't change them to a new school until we get into some kind of temporary shelter," Carmen explained. "But Montrell is 12 now; he can bring the others back here every day."

"That means taking at least two trains each way. And maybe the bus too."

"What else are we gonna do?"

"What about Professor Helen? Wasn't she trying to help you?"

"She still is. But to get into a housing project eventually, we got to prove we were evicted, and so we got to go to PATH. You mind if we leave some of our stuff here?"

"Not as long as you make sure we hear from you. You know my number. And you better call Pamela too. She was upset that she didn't even know you'd been evicted. She and Jesse and Yun Hee will want to know where to visit you."

Almost as soon as the Ramirez family had said good-bye, Cedric started shrieking. Tanita knew he would miss all the boys. Cedric was now going regularly to the speech therapist, but his teacher had told Tanita that it would take a long time for his language development to catch up. How could she have a conversation with him about when he would next see the boys? And anyway, what could she tell him? She was angry about their homelessness too.

Later, when Yun Hee knocked on their door, Cedric had quieted down, but was still sulking. "Hey, it's time for the art workshop. Wanna come help me invite some other kids? And where's Johnny and his brothers?"

Cedric grabbed at Yun Hee's backpack, trying to see what materials she had brought this week. It smelled of crayons.

Tanita filled Yun Hee in on the Ramirez family's departure.

"Oh no! Hey, do you think Darleen Walker will have some advice for the Ramirez family? Hasn't her family been through the whole shelter system?"

"Yes, every which way. You're right; I'll ask her while you're setting up the workshop."

By the time Yun Hee and Jesse had set up pastel and charcoal drawing chalk on the sidewalk in front of the Walkers' apartment building, a dozen children had come to join them, as well as a few teenagers who helped distribute paper to the younger children.

Darleen, from the stoop of the building, was reminding the children to take turns with the different coloured pastels. She greeted Tanita: "Hey girl, how you doing?"

"I've just had it up to here with Cedric. He keeps throwing tantrums and he hates his new teacher in school — already. It's only been two weeks. How 'bout Lissa, does she like school this year?"

"Oh, she ain't started yet. The school say she need a vaccine first, and they too crowded anyway. Besides, you can't believe how much it cost to get school supplies for the older ones, so I can't get her things yet. She can start in October."

"Really? Won't you get in trouble if you don't send her soon?"

"Shoot, they the ones say the school's too crowded. Anyway sometimes it's the school that makes our kids start late. Remember a few years back, summer was finally over, I couldn't wait to get the kids outta the house — and then they go and announce our school's gonna open two weeks late because of the lead paint?"

"Oh, I do remember that. Cedric wasn't in school yet, but I was so angry; I was trying to take college prep classes and they just kept us waiting. Just let them try to pull something like that out in those fancy neighbourhoods on Long Island."

"You said it. No one there would stand for it. But here they just do what they want and we have to take it."

"Listen, Darleen, I actually wanted to ask you about the Ramirez family. You know Carmen from my building? They're over at PATH now and I thought you might have some advice for them."

Darleen shivered, "Only advice I got's: don't be homeless. I remember one of them guards at PATH, he was so rude, getting too familiar with me."

"Oh no!"

"Yeah, I was afraid my husband was gonna kill him."

"But you didn't have to stay there too long, did you? What about after that?"

"Weren't you in the shelter system too?"

"Sure, but I was younger, so I don't remember that much about how my mother coped with it all."

"Well, PATH is just at first, see? You get stuck in a room with 50 or 60 people."

"Yeah, that's scary."

"I was always afraid there; you never know what's going to happen. And at first they'll send you places you can only stay one night at a time, so you keep going back to PATH again and again, and your older kids don't sleep anywhere near you."

"They don't?"

"Well, not boys. The rooms for big boys are away from the moms and the little kids. You just have to do what you're told, so you can hurry up and get out of there. Then you can get in a Tier 1 shelter."

"That's better, right?"

"You do get a whole room for the family. But it's like being on probation, the way they sign you all in and out every time you set foot out the door, and the social worker always looking over your shoulder to tell you how to raise your children."

"Really? I wonder if my mom felt like they were bossing her that way."

"My oldest, Dauntay, he just stopped minding me in that shelter. 'Cause I wasn't in charge of nothing there, so why would he listen to me?"

"You must have been so frustrated."

"It's like for the enrichment programme. The social worker made me send him there. But half the time, it was just kids throwing checkers at your head. That teen kid running it didn't have one clue how to 'enrich' my kids."

"That's awful."

"But I had no choice. They watching you all the time in the shelter. I was even afraid to correct my children. I was so scared they might get taken away into foster care. So I stopped punishing them."

"Oh no."

"And all that time, Dauntay couldn't go to school neither. We really tried. We kept going to the high school to register him but they said they was crowded and he should keep going to his old school."

"But he didn't?"

"It was all the way across the city, a school that didn't want him neither. Schools really just don't want shelter kids. That's what my kids got called all the time, 'shelter kids' like it's a contagious disease or something."

Tanita shook her head thinking about the worries her mother must have had.

Darleen continued, "That's when Dauntay got mixed up with a bad crowd. There wasn't much choice for him in the shelter neither. If you don't wanna see somebody, where you gonna hide?"

"Man, I remember that part," said Tanita. "This one girl in our shelter was always looking to pick a fight. I really wanted a door to slam in her face."

"Well, I don't even know if Dauntay wanted to slam that door. And even now we have our own place, Dauntay didn't suddenly start minding me again. He's stayed with that kind of crowd. They wanna be players. I'm worried sick about what trouble they gonna get into. You can lay down the law for your kids, but they can still go astray the wrong way."

Lissa was pulling on her mother's sleeve. "Look, Mom! I made a new picture."

Barely glancing down, Darleen said, "What'd I tell you about interrupting? Go on back and do some more."

Crestfallen, Lissa returned to the group as Darleen continued her outpour. "It ain't just Dauntay. I worry about the younger ones too."

"Why?"

"Well, take Lissa." They both looked at her climbing onto Yun Hee's lap. "When we was in the shelter, Lissa used to wet her bed there all the time. And she got so used to us all crowded together to sleep, she's scared to use the other rooms we have now. The girls still all sleep together cause they got so used to it."

"Well, maybe that's cozy? But it's too bad she still feels scared."

"In the shelter, the kids just had no place to play. They were always in the street in the front of the building. They could've got hit by a car. And Shaniqua was only 3 then. She could have just picked up a used drug needle anywhere, so I never let her out of my sight, not ever, even if she was with her big sisters."

"Yeah, 3 is the age when they can get into the worst trouble with no clue what they're doing." Tanita remembered how Cedric had started trying to run off as soon as he could.

"There was a shooting on that block too, a 14-year-old boy shot dead by a grown man — grown! I don't know how a grown man could do such a thing."

"Oh my God!"

"My kids got so scared they didn't even wanna walk to the store. They were scared to go to school, and Shaniqua used to hide under the bed. Even when the man went to jail, my kids were still scared he'd come back."

Tanita looked over at Shaniqua. Crouched down on the sidewalk, she was ignoring the artwork and picking at a scab on her knee.

Darleen was still talking. "The shelter affected all of 'em. Makayla has been giving me back talk ever since we landed there, and now that she's in puberty, it keeps getting worse."

"Well, that's the age for it," Tanita said, laughing. "I wasn't so easy to deal with either a few years ago."

"A shelter just isn't a home. You need an apartment to raise your family. Now we're more close, we start to feel like a real family again."

"That's good."

"Like yesterday, Tyrone told me he's being picked on in school. In the shelter, we just weren't close; he wouldn't even have told me. Being in the shelters with a family, you meet people with problems, people who don't know how to behave. You get caught up and you got no choice. It's scary. No, all I can say is, don't be homeless."

"But Carmen's family is homeless," sighed Tanita. "I just wish there was something I could do about it."

"There is. I'm real glad that you're staying in touch with her. When we first went in the shelter system and then I heard that Yun Hee came looking for us, it made me cry because someone was still thinking about us. She told me to call her anytime, just to talk. That makes a big difference."

Later that evening, Tanita made her way back to All Together in Dignity, where people were arriving for another meeting. Although she had left Cedric at home with their grandmother, who didn't feel up to coming this time, several parents had brought their children along. Yun Hee had a new activity to propose: using only cotton swabs to make pictures out of tiny dots of paint.

Tanita was surprised to see Susana Montoya arrive. "Hey, Susana! It's been ages, how you doing?"

"Good, I'm good."

"We haven't seen you lately, what have you been up to?"

"I got tired of coming alone, and it took me all this time to finally convince Luis to come with me."

Tanita tried to size up Susana's boyfriend, Luis, but his cool gaze couldn't tell her what kind of mood he was in today. Just then, Pamela called them to join the group so she could get the discussion underway.

"Hello everyone. Before we get started, you should know that Carmen and Mateo won't be able to join us tonight. They're busy trying to sort out a new place to live, but we all want to keep in touch with them wherever they end up. I have a greeting card here if any of you want to write a message to them or their children, and we'll take it to them. Also, we want to welcome Luis Marquez, who's here for the first time. Luis is Susana's partner, and we're glad you're both here."

Luis, a man in his mid-thirties with a skull tattooed on the side of his neck, squirmed with embarrassment at being singled out.

Pamela continued: "In fact, we're very pleased that all of you could come tonight because, as you know, very soon it will be 17 October, the World Day for Overcoming Poverty. So we need to prepare together. When we met back in August, you remember we all agreed we wanted Tanita to write a message on our behalf, so she's been working hard. And tonight we can continue sharing with her things that we think are important to tell everyone."

"October 17? That's the day when we go to the UN?" Darleen Walker asked.

"That's right. The UN made October 17 the official day against poverty back in 1996. It was already a day that lots of people in low-income communities around the world had been observing since 1987, many of them with our teams, and also others who heard about it. There are a lot of official international days, but I believe that this is the only one that was created by ordinary people, not by a diplomat or policymaker who just came round to the idea in a meeting."

No longer listening, Tanita wondered if there might be a way to get one of the others to prepare a speech for her.

Pamela continued, "So the day belongs first of all to everyone whose daily life is taken up with struggling against poverty. And it's important that the UN makes us welcome for this event, because people there try to work against poverty too, in their way. For instance, you remember Blandine Dulavoir. She was the guest who came here last time for our meeting about working conditions and finding jobs. She works with the UN on those same questions about how people can have decent working conditions —"

"She looked like a real phony to me," Darleen blurted out. "She came here in a fancy taxi, but she ain't gonna come to Brooklyn and walk around our neighborhood. She looked at us like she knew all about us before we opened our mouths."

"Now Darleen," Helen said calmly, "You need to give Blandine a break."

Darleen ignored her. "Things going on is too serious to waste time. There's too much trouble in our lives. That lady should come to my house, come and stay all day, to see how we live. But she don't care. She just sat here like she was looking at some kind of show-and-tell."

"Yes," Helen nodded. "She probably did think she knew all about poverty and employment issues before she came here, but I think it was quite a surprise for her once we opened our mouths. Half the time we were all talking at once, which can be challenging enough for someone new. And she also heard some things she didn't expect to hear. I don't think she knew what to say to us at the time, but maybe we'll see her again on October 17, and maybe there are things we could learn from her too."

"I just don't think her heart was in it," Darleen continued. "What's the point in talking to those fancy UN people anyway? Are they going to invite Carmen's family to live with them, like Mrs. Brown did?"

Helen answered, "I think it would take a lot more time for someone like Blandine to begin to understand Carmen's situation. It's not that her heart isn't in it; it's because the things people go through in extreme poverty can be unimaginable to others. Like, for instance, last year there was bad wiring in Carmen's bathroom. Her family was getting electric shocks whenever they went to wash; it was dangerous."

"That's true," Tanita confirmed. "And the cord for their refrigerator wasn't a heavy-duty one. It was as thin as a lamp cord, so mice chewed through it."

"But the landlord didn't even believe Carmen about any of this." Helen shook her head. "He assumed she was lying. So many of us just can't imagine what's going on in other people's lives. Like eating caterpillars."

"Say what?" Darleen asked.

"I've heard that's a special delicacy to people in Central Africa," Helen said, "but to me it's unimaginable. I can't even picture it, so I might just assume that it can't be true."

Jesse objected. "I don't know, Helen. I think Darleen has a good point. Nadine Gordimer once said about the rich that poverty lets them be 'bountiful.' Like poverty exists to boost their self-esteem."

"That's awful," said Pamela, grimacing at both his words and the thought of the caterpillars. Beginning to twist a lock of her hair, she turned to Darleen. "You're right that people at the UN do have office jobs and, yes, they can afford taxis. But actually many of them make less money at the UN than they would if they worked for private businesses. They *choose* to work for lower salaries at the UN because they believe in what the UN is trying to do: to build a world where everyone can live decently. Not many people in the world make a choice to earn less money than they could."

"Ain't that the truth," Tanita said. "The other day, I was taking Cedric to another appointment and when we were waiting for the elevator, these two men in suits were talking about the entry-level salaries their company was paying. One of them thought the entry-level workers needed more than the minimum wage so they would spend more and stimulate the economy; but the other one said, 'No, if they earned more, there'd be no money left for me to get a raise.' The first man was saying, 'But we already earn ten times as much as they do. Where's your compassion?' But the other one just didn't care."

"Like that UN lady," Darleen said. "She didn't care one bit about anything we said."

Pamela responded, "I think Helen is right. Many people, like Blandine Dulavoir, who haven't experienced it, just can't imagine what it's like to be treated disrespectfully your entire life. So it's hard for us to communicate with them. But I still think it's worth trying. Most of them joined the United Nations because they are idealistic. Blandine's husband was actually very skeptical when I first talked to him about coming to our meeting."

Tanita did a double take. "Well, then, maybe we should just leave him alone and forget all about going to the UN."

"But you saw how much time he spent with us the other day. If he was skeptical, it's not because he doesn't care about fighting poverty. On the contrary, I think it's because he cares deeply. He's so worried about the urgency of ending poverty that he's in a rush not to waste time. So he's skeptical of us because we do have a slow way of working. To some extent, our slowness is deliberate, because changing relationships and stereotypes requires a lot of time and care —"

"And because sometimes we're just not as organized as you always want us to be," Jesse put in, tipping backwards on the legs of his chair.

Ignoring him, Pamela continued, "— but I respect his feeling of urgency too. We all want change *now*. The UN charter talks about 'we the peoples of the United Nations.' Well, that's all of us. Not just our presidents and ambassadors, but all people from every country. So it's important for us to make the effort to get to know people like Blandine Dulavoir, her husband, and others who will be at the October 17 event. Both we and they *are* the 'peoples of the United Nations' — despite that smirk on Jesse's face — and we all have to work together toward that goal of a world where everyone can live decently."

Ernestine Jones nodded in agreement. "That's right. All people from every country. I got a neighbor who don't talk English that well. He's Chinese. And his wife's an invalid. I see how much he does to take care of her. He's a man like anybody else, no matter how he talks. I like those words about all people from every country. If we all stuck together for a change, the world would be a better place."

"I hear you," Susana Montoya answered. "But there's so much to do. You got people out there who got newspapers for sheets, and shoes for a pillow. How we gonna get governments to open up their brains and acknowledge what's going on? The world don't make no kind of sense, and look at us — just two dozen people. How is what we say gonna change anything?"

More serious now, Jesse sat up straight in his chair to respond. "We might be only two dozen people in this room, but every one of us knows other people, people like Carmen and Mateo who are struggling every day." He looked around the room and continued, "And people like Helen's colleagues at the university, who also want to fight poverty somehow. And there are also people like us in countries around the world who are preparing for October 17. Actually one of them just wrote me a letter I was meaning to read to you. His name is Ahmed, and he's a young man I got to know when I lived in Tanzania."

"That's in Africa, right?" It was Darleen's son, 17-year-old Dauntay Walker who was asking, although he hadn't even seemed to be listening. He was leaning against the open back door, smoking a cigarette.

"Dauntay is correct," said Pamela. Picking up a globe, she spun it to the southeast coast of Africa to point out Tanzania.

Jesse said, "I wrote to Ahmed about how we're preparing for October 17. They're preparing there too, with a whole group of people who are planning to perform songs, messages, and poems. Here's what he wrote back: 'I was so glad to get your news and to hear what everyone in your group has been doing. How is the little boy you mentioned, Allan? I find it very hard to believe that the government might tell his own grandmother that she should not be raising him as she sees fit. Please give her my respectful regards.' "

"What a sweet young man," Mrs. Jones observed. "They ought to hire someone like *him* to work at child services."

Jesse continued: "There's more in the letter. Ahmed writes about how they are preparing for October 17: 'Together, we have been thinking about how important it is for everyone to have links to other people. One of the others who works in the fish market here, Samueli, told us how he first started living in the streets when he was 15, many years ago. At the time, he had no contact with his family. Samueli says, "When I lived in the streets, I didn't care about family or uncles. I never went back home, not even once a year. But it was not fine, and I feared that a bad thing could happen in my life."'"

"He *should* be scared," Darleen put in. "You got a lot of kids out here today walking the streets, just going astray. If they ain't gonna get it by a cop, they gonna get it by somebody's gun. It don't make no kind of sense." Darleen's oldest daughter, Makayla, shot her mother a disdainful look, and left the room.

Jesse continued reading Ahmed's letter: "'Then Samueli joined our group. He came with us when we went to help at the school for blind children by painting their classrooms and dormitories.' Here, Dauntay, do you want to read what Samueli says now?"

Looking at the letter Jesse held out to him, Dauntay read, "This experience was important for me because I discovered that, even though I have a very tough life, I'm able to support people living in harder conditions than myself. Now I'm again part of my family and I feel responsible for my relatives."

Taking the letter back, Jesse continued reading Ahmed's words, "Not only does Samueli help his family, but he keeps looking for more ways to help others. Two years ago, he started supporting a very poor woman who has five children. This lady is helped by her church community and by the group of HIV-infected people that she is part of, but she was very dependent on them for everything. Samueli's family has loaned her a place for growing plants and bananas, so now she is able to feed her family on her own."

Dauntay said, "That's like here. We don't want no welfare, we want jobs."

"Jobs are indeed important," Pamela said, "but I also like what Ahmed said earlier in his letter: how important it is for everyone to have links to other people. When Samueli was on his own in the streets, he was afraid. But once he started helping other people, he felt ready to get back in touch with his family. Sometimes at the UN, there are discussions about the difference between poverty and extreme poverty. I think poverty becomes extreme when people get stuck without family and friends on their side."

"That's right," said Ernestine Jones. "That's exactly why I worry about losing Allan. Once children go into foster care, who can tell them that their family still loves them?"

"When kids think no one's on their side, that's when they do stupid things and get in trouble," added Susana.

"Not just kids," added Helen. "A neighbour of mine is in his 70s, and sometimes he waits for months to get a visit from a relative. When he doesn't have visits, he gets depressed and his health gets worse."

"For some people, there are even worse things than not being visited," said Jesse. "I remember how some people in Tanzania were insulted or even attacked by others, either because of a sickness they had, like leprosy, or because they were suspected of witchcraft."

"People can be so wicked," said Mrs. Jones. "I've seen that kind of wickedness here in New York too. I've seen storekeepers pour bleach on the food they throw out, to make sure the homeless won't spend time in their back alley. I've seen people spit on a homeless man sleeping on the sidewalk. How can people treat one another that way?"

Luis Marquez spoke up, "Easy. When you're on the streets, the dirtier you get, the more people move away and stop listening."

"It's a form of segregation," said Helen. "We thought we made progress by moving away from supposedly 'separate but equal' schools; but we still keep some people separate and unequal."

"Sometimes whole families are on the street," Luis continued. "I met a family living in their car under a bridge last year. They were catching some fish in the river. But it's filthy there, and their kids were always running around, so their mother worried that they might fall in the river. And shelters don't help. I've seen beds get flipped over in the shelter, people robbed at knifepoint for a pair of sneakers because there's only a few security guards for two thousand men."

"You put desperate men together and that's what happens," Helen said. "But sleeping outside isn't safe either. Every year, people die when the temperature drops too low, or someone attacks a homeless person."

"The programmes for the homeless," said Luis, "are all for people with problems — people on drugs or crazy. But what if being homeless is your only problem? When you work, they take out taxes; it's supposed to be a safety net. But when you need it, there's no net and you keep falling. You might as well be high because there's no safety net."

Susana reacted, "The ones who spit on the homeless think that whatever they, themselves, are going through is the worst thing that's ever happened. They forget about anyone else. I look at everything and say it could be a thousand times worse maybe. People's excuse is 'I wanna get myself together first,' but let's be real: how many women blame their children for their lives and are still nowhere now that their kids are grown?"

"We should have a little more pride instead of blaming everyone else and spitting on the homeless," said Darleen.

"Like when people talk about you behind your back," Susana said. "They talk if you're doing badly, and they'd talk if they think you're doing too well. But let 'em talk! If I can occupy that much time in their head, let 'em talk; it don't make no difference. They got that much time to spend on me, let 'em talk."

Pamela reached for a binder full of speeches and began turning the pages. "Our conversation is reminding me of something once said by Joseph Wresinski, the man who first started this World Day back in 1987. Here it is:

"The very poor tell us over and over again that a human being's greatest misfortune is not to be hungry or unable to read, or even to be without work. The greatest misfortune of

all is to know that you count for nothing, to the point where even your suffering is ignored.... The greatest misfortune of extreme poverty is that for your entire existence you are like someone already dead.'"

"That's what we have to tell that fancy lady," said Darleen. "Them at the UN, they're the ones running the world. The money is going to them. And they're not stupid. They see on TV what's happening in Africa and all those other places, so they've got to know something about poverty. But I don't see where she did nothing about it yet."

"Well, she did come here to meet us," Pamela said. "She could have said, 'Oh I can't, I'm busy.' Maybe she hasn't done a lot yet, but making the trip all the way here and trying to figure out what we're talking about is not nothing. And yes, people see things on the news about poverty, in Africa and here in New York too. But no one can know what it feels like to be homeless just from watching the news. It's people who've gone through it who really know what it's like to have others look away and pretend you don't exist, or even spit on you. And people who've gone through it need to share that, from one person to another."

Jesse said, "That's what October 17 is about: that chance to share from person to person what things are really like. So in fact, Pamela and I are hoping that my friend Ahmed can travel here to join us for the event at the UN. Just like Tanita will tell other people what it's like to cope with poverty here in the US, Ahmed can help people understand what things are like in East Africa."

Tanita sighed. This speech she was supposed to be writing was getting more challenging week after week. Then she looked at Dauntay. He too had said very little, but she could tell he had things on his mind. Maybe she should have a talk with him.

6. KINSHIP

When Tanita emerged from the subway, Jesse and Dauntay were waiting for her on the street. Looking around, Tanita saw a part of Brooklyn unfamiliar to her. Instead of storefronts for off-track betting, graffiti-covered walls, and windows protected by iron bars, she saw century-old trees and what looked like very expensive boutiques. "Where on earth are we going?"

"It's just down this block," said Jesse. "We're going to Helen's apartment. I think both Dauntay and Helen can help you prepare your speech."

"You didn't tell me that. I thought we were just meeting Dauntay. I got nothing against Helen, but this is getting more and more complicated."

Helen Jansky let them into a beautiful brownstone building. In her living room, Helen settled them onto her couch and arm chair. Books overflowed the shelves and were piled on every surface. She poured hot coffee into hand-painted earthenware mugs and passed around thick slices of raspberry cheesecake. The coffee had a deliciously roasted aroma, nothing like the watery coffee from a corner deli.

By the time Helen sat down in a rocking chair, Tanita was feeling more and more uncomfortable. Everyone was going to so much trouble about this speech. She had wanted to give it, and she still wanted to do a good job — but she didn't even know where to start yet, and time was running out.

"Look, Tanita," said Jesse after he had polished off his cake with gusto and started helping himself from a bowl of nuts and fruit, "Helen has spoken at the UN before. Maybe she can help you figure out who you'll be talking to and what they're like."

"I thought you worked at a college."

"Yes," said Helen, "I do teach, but on several occasions I've been asked to be part of panel discussions at the UN."

"So you talk to people from all those different countries? How do they even understand one another?"

"Well, of course there are headphones and translation in most of the meetings — even though most participants speak very good English. And sometimes they do have misunderstandings. There are plenty of times when they don't agree on a given policy. But I think that most of the time, the reason they do understand one another is that they have more in common than you might think. In the panel discussions, for instance, they're very careful about making as diverse a panel as possible. They'll invite half women and half men, and have speakers from all different continents. But then they'll introduce us by giving our biographical details — and almost every time, the people on this diverse-*looking* panel turn out to have studied in many of the same universities here in the US."

Tanita's heart sank. "Are there ever speakers who haven't been to college at all?" she asked.

"Hardly ever. And our backgrounds might be different, but it's rare to hear any speaker who grew up struggling with extreme poverty. So even though the speakers do have different experiences and politics, I think that all of us tend to have the same frames of reference. But you saw what it was like when Blandine Dulavoir came to our meeting. She didn't have the same frame of reference as many of the people in the room, so she often had no idea what we were talking about. Pamela had to keep explaining to her what was behind people's words."

"So when we talk to people from the UN, we really have to explain things."

"Definitely. They do *want* to understand, you know. It used to be that the only people besides government diplomats and UN staff who set foot in that building were rich ladies supposedly running charities. They were there in the name of the whole non-profit world — but I think that a lot of them were simply the wives of very rich men. Some wore the biggest, longest fur coats you've ever seen. I remember them sitting in the front row — but never saying one word in the discussions. Well, you have to give the UN credit, because they changed that. They opened up the rules for NGOs — I mean non-governmental organizations — so that much smaller and less well-connected groups could apply. That way, they finally opened the door to people doing real grassroots work. And around the same time, UN reports began insisting on the 'participation of people living in poverty' or on hearing the 'voices of the poor'."

"Participation? In what?" asked Dauntay. "Do they have jobs programmes or something?"

"Well, that's a tricky question," said Helen. "The UN does support some initiatives for people to start businesses with microcredit loans, or to make sure that working conditions are decent in factories — but that's only in developing countries, not here in the US, where they expect it to be the local government fighting unemployment. And when they say 'participation' at the UN, they usually mean making people's voices heard. But to tell you the truth, I have the impression that they have no idea just what conditions they should create to make it possible to hear the voices of people who are never asked what they think about anything and who have to be convinced that they have something to say. And I also think that at the UN they don't expect to really engage and think together with people living in poverty. They'd be happy to hear about first-hand experience of difficulties — you know, someone just listing all their problems — but they don't realize that people who have seen plenty of anti-poverty programmes come and go actually know something about what works and what doesn't."

Jesse said, "Helen, when Tanita met with Pamela and that man from the UN, she asked why he cared about fighting poverty, and also how Pamela first got involved in this kind of work. I want to ask you the same questions." As he spoke, Jesse helped himself to a second slice of cheesecake.

"Hmm. Why do I care?" Helen thought for a moment. "Well, to begin with, I feel a kind of kinship with people who live in poverty. I have never known, and I hope I never will know, what it means to have to sleep in a shelter or go hungry. Still, I feel a kinship. When my parents first came to this country from Russia, they had to struggle for a long time. It was very hard for them to make a living and to make sure their children would have more schooling than they did. But we got help too. There was one lady who gave me a scholarship. She helped a lot of young people."

Helen began refilling her guests' coffee mugs. "I remember once that lady came out to the housing projects where I grew up. She didn't want to come upstairs though; she just stayed outside with her son and pointed up at our window. 'Look,' she told him. 'You see how nice the Janskys' curtains are? Even though they're poor, they keep their curtains washed and ironed. They make an effort, so you can tell they're worth helping.' It's true that both my parents worked hard. But in the window next door to ours, my friend Mary's family didn't even have curtains hung. Her mother died when she was young, and her father had a drinking problem, so it was hard for him to hold down a job. That wasn't Mary's fault, but she never got a scholarship and she's had a hard time all her life. You hear people say, 'My grandfather first came to this country without a dime in his pocket and he pulled himself up by his own bootstraps, just like anyone else can do if they work hard enough.' But I don't think it's fair to compare. Situations can be so different."

"That's true," Tanita said. "You never really know what it's like to walk in anyone else's shoes."

"Exactly." Helen rocked back and forth thoughtfully. "Even if at one point my parents didn't have a dime and came from a village where everyone was poor, they did have other resources. They both grew up with a sense of community. They were confident that they could work hard and be good parents and neighbours. I'm not sure that Mary's father ever had that. He grew up in orphanages, and I think he was later in a juvenile detention centre. I wonder whether anyone ever told him once in his life that they expected good things from him. He didn't have the training or skills to earn much money, so he knew he couldn't do much for Mary or her brothers. Maybe that's partly why he drank."

"You mean he felt humiliated because he didn't have a steady job?" Jesse asked.

"Yes, I think he did. That's why I was so glad to help Carmen when you all first contacted me. And then eventually, I was glad to get involved in everything you're doing together. Plenty of charities talk about 'the deserving poor' in such a patronizing way. They mean the ones who iron their curtains. But who are we to judge? What do any of us really know about one another, even our closest neighbours? I don't want to judge who's deserving or not. I think it's more important that we find ways to believe in one another, so that children don't go through life without ever hearing that someone expects them to do great things."

"My brother, Tyrone, never hears that," Dauntay said. "He's 10 now, and I don't think he's had a single teacher yet who didn't hate him."

"Teachers can't say they hate a child," Jesse put in.

"Maybe not straight out, but you can tell, just from the way they look at you. They're sure you're a trouble-maker. They wish you was in someone else's class. A teacher will tell you that you're never gonna amount to anything and that you're gonna be a loser on the street. They'll say that right out in front of the whole class. You can tell when they think you're stupid."

"True enough," Tanita said. "You can tell when a boss thinks that too, when he just feels you're wasting his time by even asking for a job." She sighed. "Dauntay, what do you think we should say for the day against poverty?"

Dauntay thought for a moment. Then he turned to Helen. "What you said about Mary's father."

Helen looked blank for a moment. "Which part do you mean?"

"You said he drank. But you also said why he drank."

"Why is that important to you?"

"Well, life's about stepping up, getting money for your family." Dauntay hesitated. "But if you can't find a job, you can't provide the way you want to. And people treat you like you're trash."

Jesse put in, "You mean like when judges call kids 'unmanageable' and send them upstate to a detention centre?"

"Yeah. And cops stop and frisk you all the time. They'll throw you up against a wall and treat you like trash just for walking down the street. Guns drawn and pointed at you: 'Don't move or you're dead.' And drug deals go down, right in front of little kids. Stray bullets going by them too. My friend's in jail right now."

Helen frowned. "What was your friend involved in?"

"It was nothing," Dauntay sprang to his feet to respond. "Caleb wasn't even part of anything. It was just that he heard shooting, and he was scared 'cause he's been shot before, and he knows people get shot all the time. One kid just had an orange plastic water gun and he got shot sixteen times by the police. They could'a shot once in the air to warn him, but not sixteen bullets when he didn't do nothing."

"But your friend Caleb didn't get shot sixteen times."

"Well, see, he heard shooting and got scared, so he went outside shooting too — but it turned out the shooting he heard was the cops on a drug raid next door. Only Caleb didn't know they were cops when he got out his gun. And even though he barely scratched the cop, I don't know when he's gonna get out of jail." His voice unsteady, Dauntay stopped talking and sat down.

Helen was shaking her head sadly. "If he injured a police officer, even superficially, you're right, they're going to keep him in prison as long as they can."

"It's messed up," said Tanita. "I just wish no one had guns, not dealers, not the cops — and not your friend either. What was that boy thinking?" She too shook her head.

Then she turned to Jesse, "What about you? You got the three of us to meet today. Why did you get involved in the art workshops?"

Jesse stood to stretch his legs. Pacing in front of a bookshelf, he began to talk. "Fine arts is actually what I studied in school. I always loved painting. I used to work painting backdrops for a theatre show."

"That's cool," Tanita said.

"Sometimes it is. You can't just paint whatever you want in that kind of job, but it was exciting to be part of something, building a performance, and creating a fantasy so people will believe they're somewhere else. But other times the shows I was working on weren't very good, so I got bored with that. I'd always wanted to go to Africa, so a few years after I joined All Together in Dignity, I finally had the chance to join our team in Tanzania."

Jesse paused, remembering the streets in Dar-es-Salaam, perpetually thronged with trundling "dala dala" mini-buses, bikes, motorcycles, and people of all ages, walking everywhere in flip-flops. Women and young girls walked with babies on their backs, sacks of rice or vegetables balanced on their heads, or eggs for sale held aloft. If they stopped walking, it might be to chat while fixing a friend's hair. Men and boys were often hawking phone credits, or inventing new ways to repair old carts or motors. People might be carrying soapstone, or carving it, the dust etching patterns into every crevice of their worn hands. Even in the intense midday heat when people working since dawn needed a rest, they often napped out in the open: labourers dozing on the roof of an unfinished building, porters asleep inside the wooden carts they pulled, fabric vendors drifting off on top of the bolts they displayed in the marketplace.... So much life, all lived outdoors. It was what Jesse had thirsted for, after a suburban childhood segmented into age-appropriate activities, blocked off by air-conditioned houses into the loneliness of private spaces.

But he soon discovered that upper-class Tanzanians lived apart too, warning their children away from life in the streets. Aloud, he said, "Daily life there is completely different from here. But in both places there are these invisible walls between the rich and the poor."

"What do you mean?" Tanita asked.

"Well, Tanzanian society is based on solidarity, and I guess most people are really close to their extended family and their neighbours — but even there, you have some kids living on their own and getting looked down on by other people."

"How old are they?" asked Tanita.

"Teens, mostly, but some are really still kids. They might be only 8 or 10. And they're just trying to survive in the streets."

"Quite young indeed," commented Helen.

"They have to hide from the police because you're not supposed to sleep outdoors. It used to be mainly boys, but now there's more girls too."

"Why are they on their own?" Tanita wanted to know.

"They might have left home for all kinds of reasons. Maybe their parents got sick, or sometimes they just heard that you could get rich in the city."

"Like most immigrants to America," Helen said.

"They leave their village sure they'll return someday with presents for everyone. But once they leave home, there's shame and blame."

"Why shame?" Tanita asked.

"The village might criticize their parents for not having been able to keep them at home. And if the kids do manage to visit home, people suspect they might have done bad things to survive. That would make their family ashamed of them."

"That happens here too," said Dauntay.

"True. There are runaway kids, or adults who lose their homes and end up on the streets. And no one else wants to go near them."

Leaning forward in her rocking chair, Helen thumped down her coffee mug and said, "Every one of our societies ends up banishing some people. We forget that they are the very people we might need. Long ago, in the Bible, King Saul banished the soothsayers and witches. But as soon as he had trouble of his own, it turned out that what he most wanted was advice from one of the very soothsayers he had driven into hiding, the Witch of Endor. Suddenly he had to look at her differently than he had before."

"I didn't know there was a witch in the Bible," Jesse said, laughing. "But that is what I mean: people turn away from the homeless without realizing that we all need one another."

The room fell silent for a moment. Looking at Jesse, Helen said thoughtfully, "So, do you regret not becoming a painter?"

"Hey, he paints with the kids all the time," objected Tanita.

"That's not quite the same," Helen said. "I want to know how you connect art with your concern about solidarity."

Jesse thought for a moment before answering, "I guess I got to thinking about the way people look at each other. It's so hard to change those ideas we all grow up with about what supposedly makes us different from one another. And that's the thing about art. I think that art can change the way we look at each other."

"What do you mean?" Tanita asked.

"Well.... I think someone can fall in love with a painting before they even realize that the person who made it is someone they might feel scared of if they passed each other on the street. And art even changes the way we each see ourselves." Jesse's voice trailed away as he gazed out the window at a pair of sparrows balanced on a tree branch.

"Go on," urged Helen.

"Maybe it's like your sister, Dauntay — when we first started, Lissa just didn't believe she could make anything. She didn't even dare try. But after a while, she found out that she *could* make something she felt proud of. She did it all on her own, and it was so cool."

"I remember that," said Tanita. "The first time she made a picture she really loved, she started jumping up and down."

"She was so excited, it was like she was bouncing on a trampoline. So there you go, that's why I paint with the kids."

7. DIRECTIONS

"In a few weeks, I want you to speak on a panel discussion about women and the Millennium Development Goals," Varag told Pamela.

"Me? But — I don't have much experience with that kind of thing. Who else will be speaking?" Nervously, Pamela looked around Varag's office. Surely no one could find anything in the heaps of papers and reports jumbled every which way, bursting with population statistics and rates of employment growth.

"We wanted the French ambassador to speak about a women's microcredit programme they're funding in West Africa, but he has a scheduling conflict, so I think he's sending Jean-Christian Roche-Fontaine to speak. Mai Trong Pham will speak about her non-profit work against human trafficking in Southeast Asia. And hopefully we'll also have the Under-Secretary-General for Economic and Social Affairs to give the panel some visibility. So you see, we need a second NGO voice, and we definitely need another woman. Imagine a panel on the status of women with only one female speaker! I'd be run out of town. But in fact I'm also asking you because I think that All Together in Dignity might have something unique to add. I have the impression that your approach to the MDGs is different."

"I'll say! To hear the UN, the Millennium Development Goals are like a new religion that we must all worship devoutly — but they were an enormous disappointment to us."

"Now hold on a minute. The Millennium Declaration starts by vowing to eradicate extreme poverty — exactly what you call for. And it was something of a miracle to have 189 heads of state sign it. I wouldn't have bet they could agree that the sky is blue, let alone make a priority of an issue that had been languishing for years, far behind sustainable development and the environment."

"The vow to eradicate extreme poverty is crucial, I agree. But practically in the next sentence, the MDGs set the target of reducing extreme poverty by 50 percent over fifteen years."

"You've got to start somewhere."

"Sure, but not only is that the wrong starting point; it also makes a mockery of human rights. When you say from the outset that you're going to focus on only *half* of the people living in poverty, what those people hear is that it certainly won't be their half. People in the worst situations, the ones who always end up getting left behind, know very well that the MDGs have nothing to do with them and bring them no hope —"

The jangle of the telephone on Varag's desk cut Pamela off. As he answered the phone, she gave a quizzical look, gesturing toward the door. Varag shook his head at her, indicating that she should stay put. With a few sentences, he dispatched the phone call and turned back to Pamela. "You were criticizing the MDGs?"

"Well, on the policy end, once you set that target of 50 percent, it's in government's' interests to focus on people who are easier to reach, the ones just below the threshold of what they define as 'poverty.' So in fact, new MDG programmes tend to widen the gap between those who were born into generational poverty and those who just faced temporary set-backs. Some people can easily take advantage of a microcredit loan to get ahead, while others, even if they do somehow qualify for the loan, may get stuck and need the loan to repay another debt or to cope with a family emergency —"

"What on earth does that have to do with human rights violations?"

"If the MDGs used a human rights-based approach, they would have to take every single person into account, not some percentage of people. And I don't think that the MDG approach is even pragmatic either. It might seem straightforward to start with those who are the easiest to reach, but that means ignoring the knowledge and experience of the unreached people. It also means that even if that 50 percent target is met, there will be that much more distance between people who are still stuck in the worst situations of poverty and others who are doing a little better. And policymakers still won't have learned anything new about how to think together with people living in extreme poverty."

"Well, you see then? You certainly do have a different approach to the question. I think you'll make our panel interesting."

Pamela hesitated again, gazing out the window past the East River toward Queens. From this distance, you couldn't make out the energy of the neighbourhoods across the river, energy that came from having so many recent immigrants from almost every part of the world, getting jobs, starting businesses, and looking out for their neighbours. Instead she saw only sooty buildings, relics of the past. "You said the panel is about women and the MDGs. But what about gender? The situation of men is important too."

"Men have been getting ahead in the world for thousands of years now. It's women and children who are mired in extreme poverty."

"It's true that most men have all the rules of the game in their favour. But men who've lived their whole lives in extreme poverty aren't the ones who make the rules. Here in the US, for example, starting in the 1960s policies began offering welfare support to single mothers with children. Of course this was meant to help. But it also meant that a father who had no training and no job knew that his family would get more financial support if he weren't around. He would see his presence in the family as almost harming them, because support isn't available to two-parent families. For a long time, you had some fathers who stayed in touch with their family and cared about them, but who were hiding so that their children would have more income or so that the rest of the family could get access to housing. One of our members told me that, when he was growing up, the social worker would always stop by unannounced and go through his family's closets and drawers to look for proof that his father still kept his things there sometimes. And the social workers would be asking the children, 'Doesn't your father like visiting you?' trying to trap them into getting the whole family in trouble. It was demeaning to all of them. How could that boy grow up respecting his own father?"

Barely pausing to catch her breath, Pamela continued, "They did finally change that policy, but there are still policies that help women with children but not the whole family. We know another father whose family lost their housing. He was actually told by a police officer, 'The best thing for you to do is to beat your wife and I guarantee she will have a shelter to stay in. You'll go to jail, but she and the kids'll be okay.' Imagine how awful that father felt, to think that the only way he could find housing for his family was to pretend he beat his wife. And some men do end up in jail, for so many reasons. Their wives might look to an outsider like single mothers, but those women will spend long hours traveling with their children in the middle of the night on expensive bus trips to visit these men. The mothers aren't 'single,' but their family life is stuck in noisy, crowded visiting rooms."

Varag caught whiffs of Pamela's citrusy perfume as she waved her arms theatrically. Objectively, he knew, she was not as attractive as Blandine. And she was certainly much less polished. What was it about her way of talking that made him enjoy arguing with her?

She continued, "And then there are fathers who might do a lot to take care of their children — to earn money off the books with odd jobs, for example — but their income doesn't exist in official statistics and so policymakers assume they are 'deadbeats.' There are also some fathers who end up so humiliated by the situation that they leave for good. They might have many reasons to leave, but I think that one reason is an unintended consequence of a policy that assumes two-parent families don't need any support. And in developing countries, now you have microcredit programmes that will fund only the work of women. Again, it's great that women get that support — but if at the same time it ends up humiliating and driving away men who do the least skilled work, then it's as though we're punishing the men and their entire family for all the worst results of capitalism. Multinational corporations can still get away with treating workers no better than the industrial robber-barons of the nineteenth century."

Varag burst out laughing, "Look how dramatic you are! You *have* to join our panel discussion. But don't you agree it's important to give special attention to the status of women?"

"I do, but I think that NGOs and the UN in particular have already begun doing just that for years now. And when you get to know women living in extreme poverty, in the UK, in Tanzania, and everywhere else, they're just as concerned about their sons and husbands as they are about their daughters and mothers. For instance, one of our members here is terribly worried about her teenage son. She says that their time in the shelter system pushed him away from her. He was kept out of school for months because high schools threw up administrative hurdles to keep him out, as they do for many other teenagers, suspecting they would lower the school's test scores. And that pushed him to spend too much time in the streets. I'm worried too. I know how often he and his friends are frisked by the police, so roughly. Even if he never went near a gang, he knows that he's not trusted, and that the taller he grows, the more other people are scared of him. He says he really wants to find a job, but if he doesn't manage to find one soon, I'm afraid he'll lose the courage to look."

As Pamela trailed off, consumed with frustration, Varag was silent for a long moment. Then, closing his eyes, he began to recite:

> "...*cradled guns that hold you under cover*
> *and everything is pure interrogation*
> *until a rifle motions and you move*
> *with guarded unconcerned acceleration —*
> *a little emptier, a little spent*
> *as always by that quiver in the self,*
> *subjugated, yes, and obedient.*"

After a minute, Pamela said, "Yes. It's awful, and I imagine that's how Dauntay might feel every time he gets frisked. Where is that from?"

Varag stretched his lanky arm toward a heap of books on a shelf behind him, unerringly plucking out just the one he had quoted, despite the clutter. He opened the well-worn book, a hardcover without its dust jacket, and held it out towards Pamela. "It's from a poem by Seamus Heaney. He's an Irishman from a family of farmers and mill workers who won the Nobel Prize a few years back."

"And you know his work by heart," Pamela smiled. "May I borrow this? I'd like to show it to Dauntay."

"Go ahead. And you do have a point about what men in poverty go through. So if we change the title of the panel to make it about gender and the MDGs, will you join us there?"

"Actually, could it be someone else from my organization? There's a woman in Canada who would be quite a good speaker on this topic."

Varag frowned. "Well, I don't know her. And there'd be no funding to pay for her trip here. But if you're sure, send me her CV and we'll see."

Blandine

A few blocks away, Blandine remained in her office during the lunch hour as usual. Her schedule and Varag's did not mesh well, so they rarely had time to meet in the middle of the day. Once she had finished her edamame and wheat-berry salad, she often used the time to read. Before 9/11 however, lunch had often been the time when she and Mira could chat by phone. Neither had time to get away from work to meet in person, so phone calls were perfect. Somehow, Blandine had not made other friends like Mira. Her colleagues were mainly men — and of course there was no one quite like Mira in any case. But with the end of those electrifying conversations, Blandine felt her thoughts now caught in a maze, stumbling aimlessly up and down the same paths. Without exactly deciding to, today she found herself beginning to type an email:

> *Dear Mira,*
>
> *I miss you. Obviously, who wouldn't?*
>
> *I know how much Octavia and your children miss you, and compared to their immeasurable loss, mine seems so small and petty. After all, I have Varag. But I don't talk to him the way I used to talk to you. I'm not even sure my life makes sense any more without your voice telling me when I'm off-*

track. Remember how right you were about Martin Fielding? Oh, I haven't thought about him in ages, but he <u>was</u> completely wrong for me, and you saw that in instant, in a way I couldn't. And I think sometimes that I'm still oblivious, that others see things that I can't.

I told you about Jean-Christian Roche-Fontaine. He still infuriates me. What a sense of entitlement! I sometimes think he has no scruples at all when it comes to advancing his career. But I'm afraid I bow to his sense of entitlement as much as anyone else does. When he lobbied to get himself named to the bureau of the social commission, I was more qualified; but I just stepped back and watched. Why do I <u>do</u> that? Am I too polite? Too feminine?

I'm probably not feminine <u>enough</u> for Varag. I know he hopes we'll have children someday, and I suppose the "someday" ought to be soon, given my age now. But I'm just not sure. It's not the same for a woman to have children and continue her career. Oh, I know you managed it flawlessly — but you did have Octavia stepping up behind the scenes. Now of course she's stuck managing without you, but ever since she became a teacher, her job just <u>fits</u> with motherhood better than yours or mine would. So: will I in fact decide that I'd rather have a career than children? And wouldn't that be ridiculous when I don't even dare step out of my comfort zone to advance my career by competing with someone like Jean-Christian?

Well, you know me; I haven't decided anything at all, of course. You're the decisive one. Who knows, perhaps you'll have time to give me a sign, even as you keep busy watching over your family? In fact, I think that...

Blandine was startled by the rattle of her cell phone vibrating against the desk — and even more startled to see that the caller was Octavia. With an effort, she refocused her mind on the present and answered. Typically, Octavia began their conversation with a rush of words tumbling out:

"How've you been doing? We leave it too long between getting together. But I'm sure you're in a rush now, so I'll get right to the point. Do you remember Mira's sister, Sasha? Her son needs to travel up to New York for some college interviews. This just isn't a good time for him to stay with us because the kids got so stressed out after the 9/11 anniversary and I think I just need to focus on them. So I hoped that Alejo could stay with you and Varag. Okay? He flies in from DC next week, but it's only for a few days."

Blandine barely got a word in edgewise before Octavia hung up. Should she have tried to beg off? Varag certainly would not mind the company. He liked to say that homes should always have a door open to the unknown. Blandine, however, was more dubious. She had never met this teenage nephew of Mira's, and barely remembered Sasha, whose husband was posted at the Argentinian Embassy in Washington. But it was no easier now to refuse Octavia's requests than it had ever been with Mira's.

Pamela

That evening on her way to Brooklyn, Pamela already regretted agreeing to provide a speaker for the panel discussion. Although Varag was right that All Together in Dignity did have things to say, when would she even have time to prepare? She would have to contact their team in Quebec to make sure Florence Grenier would be free for the event. Pamela knew that Florence had no CV prepared. Her expertise came from living in poverty, and she did have some experience with speaking out in the name of others. But it would be a challenge to frame that experience in a way that the UN could understand and respect. Pamela had her work cut out for her. If it worked, then there would be the matter of making Florence welcome in New York and facilitating her preparations.

But there was still so much to do before the World Day for Overcoming Poverty. She knew that Tanita was nervous about writing — maybe Pamela should insist that they sit down to work on it together? And so much else still had to be done. Yun Hee and Jesse were preparing some of the children to perform a skit during the event, and Pamela had plenty of other tasks. She had to make sure that invitations went out. Because the event would be outdoors, she needed to organize the logistics of renting a sound system and folding chairs that would not damage the UN lawn or pose any security hazards. She had to put together a programme that described the history and meaning of the day. And the guest list had to be coordinated with UN security to ensure that everyone would be allowed into the UN garden.

Fearing that she was forgetting a dozen other urgent tasks on her to-do list, she was jostled by rush-hour crowds while she transferred from a bus to the subway train that would carry her under the East River. Should she tell Varag she had changed her mind?

As her thoughts drifted back to her conversation with Tanita and Varag, she felt strange about how much she had spoken of Rez. Was he someone she missed using as a sounding board for this kind of question? Perhaps not, Pamela thought, realizing that, in any case, she had not often had this kind of conversation with him. Reserved by nature, she liked making her own choices most of the time. But should she ask Yun Hee or Jesse's opinion? As teammates, the three of them ought to be able to figure things out together. She didn't want to ask Jesse, though. She had felt stupid when he reproached her for expecting Brenda to sign custody papers without even seeing her mother in person. He was right — but she hated being in the wrong. As for Yun Hee, she was already so anxious about the children's skit that Pamela didn't think it would be helpful to try talking things over with her.

When Pamela finally got to Dauntay's block, she found Tanita, Yun Hee, and Jesse running the art workshop on the sidewalk together. Makayla, hands on her hips, was announcing to Yun Hee: "This is stupid. You never bring the right stuff." Before Yun

Hee could respond, Makayla had turned and disappeared around the corner.

Looking at Yun Hee's stricken face, Pamela wanted to give her a hug. But Yun Hee had already turned back to the other children, most of whom had barely glanced up at Makayla's dramatic exit. Seeing Dauntay halfway down the block, Pamela called him over to show him Varag's book.

"Tanita, you should hear this poem too," Pamela added. "It's about being stopped by the police in Northern Ireland, where the poet is from; but it's also about how hard it is to write." While Dauntay and Pamela waited for Tanita to finish rinsing Lissa's paintbrush, Pamela glanced around the neighbourhood, wondering if it had anything in common with Northern Ireland. While Pamela could see that one or two people were growing plants on their window ledges, it was painfully obvious that the absentee landlords repaired nothing. Broken windows remained that way for months, with only packing tape holding them together. Few people in the neighbourhood were white, and almost none were dressed for office work, as Pamela was. She had been asked more than once whether she was lost, even though her own home was just around the corner.

When Tanita joined Pamela and Dauntay, the three of them stood to the side of the workshop. Pamela held Varag's worn book in her hands and read aloud:

From The Frontier Of Writing
The tightness and the nilness round that space
when the car stops in the road, the troops inspect
its make and number and, as one bends his face

towards your window, you catch sight of more
on a hill beyond, eyeing with intent
down cradled guns that hold you under cover

and everything is pure interrogation
until a rifle motions and you move
with guarded unconcerned acceleration—

a little emptier, a little spent
as always by that quiver in the self,
subjugated, yes, and obedient.

So you drive on to the frontier of writing
where it happens again. The guns on tripods;
the sergeant with his on-off mike repeating

data about you, waiting for the squawk
of clearance; the marksman training down
out of the sun upon you like a hawk.

And suddenly you're through, arraigned yet freed,
as if you'd passed from behind a waterfall
on the black current of a tarmac road

past armour-plated vehicles, out between
the posted soldiers flowing and receding
like tree shadows into the polished windscreen.

"Why'd they keep stopping his car?" Dauntay asked.

"The poet is from Northern Ireland. The rest of Ireland is one country, mainly Catholic, but the northern part of the island is part of the United Kingdom, with a population that's mainly Protestant. There was a long history of the Irish suffering under the British Empire, and for many decades since then, there was violence around the question of which country Northern Ireland should be part of. Thousands of people were killed in bombings. So there were lots of searches by the military."

"Man, it happens everywhere. 'Repeating data about you.' Like you're just a number! Ain't there a place where a guy can get through a day without getting searched?"

Then Tanita asked, "What's it have to do with writing? What frontier is he talking about?"

"Well," Pamela answered, "a frontier is a place no one has gone before. For example, like the 'frontier of outer space.' And here in the United States, you used to talk about the 'western frontier,' because European-Americans hadn't gone west yet, even though of course Native Americans had lived there for a long time. So I think that maybe the frontier of writing is where a poet stands whenever he's trying to make his writing go somewhere no one's ever gone before. And a frontier can also be a border between two countries where you have to show your papers and perhaps will be searched."

"So he feels like he's getting frisked whenever he tries to write? And feeling — " Tanita broke off to take the book from Pamela and look at the poem. "Feeling 'that quiver in the self'?"

"I think so. I know I've felt that quiver when I try to write something I'm not sure about. I'm feeling it now because I was just asked to help prepare for a panel discussion on a topic I needed to challenge and with people I'm intimidated by. So preparing it will be scary. Anyway, I have to return the book to Varag, but I just thought you both might like to hear the poem."

Now Dauntay, who had taken the book from Tanita, held it out to Pamela. "It says 'freed' though. At the end he does get free after all."

8. ARRIVALS

When Pamela had first asked Yun Hee and Jesse to find a way for the children from the art workshop to take part in the event at the UN, Yun Hee had balked. "Of course I love them all, but are you kidding me? How can they perform at the United Nations? These kids are the ones their teachers call 'holy terrors'. I have been to events at the UN where there are children's choirs performing. Those kids are practically professionals. Everything goes perfectly, like clockwork. You *know* that's not going to happen with the kids we know."

"Well..." Pamela hesitated, twisting her hair. "I do know what you mean. The children who usually perform at the UN probably haven't the foggiest notion what it's like to see their own parents looked down on."

"Exactly," Yun Hee agreed. "With the children we know, even their parents are talked down to every day. There's always something that a teacher or a social worker expects from them, and they just can't manage."

"But don't you think the children deserve a chance to prove us wrong? People at the UN talk so often about children in poverty, but how often do those children get a chance to speak out for themselves?"

"Maybe it's worth a shot," Jesse said. "I'd just love to see Lissa up on stage. Can you imagine what her teacher would think of that?"

"You'd love it *if* it went well," said Yun Hee. "But what if the children embarrass themselves? I'd never forgive myself for putting them through that."

"Then we'll have to make sure they won't," said Jesse.

On the last Sunday in September, Yun Hee had a date with Travis. Like her, he sometimes worked on weekends. As a reporter for the New York Daily News, his schedule was never 9 to 5. It was because they often had trouble scheduling time to get together that she had started occasionally inviting him to help her run the children's activities. The kids sometimes poked fun at his West Virginia drawl, but his laid-back outlook on life ended up endearing him to them as much as to Yun Hee.

Now that they both had time off on the same day, they were eager to spend it roaming the many acres of the Brooklyn Botanic Garden. The sky was overcast and its opaque pallor, discouraging; but both of them loved the outdoors in any weather. When they arrived at the garden, the intermittent drizzle gave a particular sheen to the greenery. Yun Hee wanted to make a beeline for the Japanese Hill-and-Pond Garden, which gave her the feeling of being magically transported to a different century. But Travis was more partial to the composting exhibit. It amused him to watch New York hipsters struggle to learn skills that were a birthright for everyone in his hometown. Now he made no effort to suppress a smile as he watched one of them awkwardly and over-energetically poking a pitchfork into a smoking heap of dirt and straw.

"He's turnin' that compost into a slimy mess," Travis gloated.

Less enthralled with the spectacle, Yun Hee let her thoughts drift to the fast-approaching performance at the UN. She knew that by now Jesse and Pamela felt confident the children would be able to pull it off. But Yun Hee just couldn't stop worrying. She remembered, growing up, how terrified she had been of embarrassing her mother. She saw how hard her mother worked, raising a child alone in an adopted country where she never completely mastered the language. From a young age, Yun Hee helped keep track of her mother's bills and correspondence. As Yun Hee began to excel in school, however, her mother told her more and more often, "Just because you go to school, you don't know better than me." Gradually, Yun Hee stopped conversing with her mother, no longer expressing her thoughts and ideas. All the while, she remained her mother's spokesperson, the one who had to speak up whenever they left home together.

As an adult, when Yun Hee had gotten to know the children in the art workshop, she was struck by how different their childhoods were from her own. None of them were used to expressing their own thoughts in words. Nor had anyone ever relied on them for what they learned in school, as her mother had relied on her.

"Travis," she said, as they began to walk toward the orchid collection, "how am I going to make sure the children can perform well at the UN? You know how they are — so full of trouble."

"Well, sure they are! What kids don't act up?"

Yun Hee frowned. "I wasn't like them at all. I saw how hard my mom worked. She was always at the restaurant scrubbing pots. I was always careful not to make trouble in school so that no teacher would ever have to ask my mother to come to a meeting about me. I was her translator, so how would it look if I had to translate the teacher telling her that I misbehaved?"

"Okay, you're different," Travis conceded. "But it's natural for kids to be rambunctious. You don't want to know how many teachers were put out that I paid them no mind."

"Maybe it's lucky no one asked *you* to go onstage at the United Nations." They both laughed, but Yun Hee continued, "Look at Allan — he's always up to something. I don't know how to stop him. I'm not even sure his grandmother knows how either. And Tyrone! He has so much energy. To be honest, sometimes he scares me. I know he'd never hurt anyone, but once I took them to visit the Metropolitan Museum and he was so loud. He was swinging his arms everywhere. I was just terrified that he'd smash a statue or something."

Travis laughed again, "Oh, come off it! Museums have glass cases and iron railings all over the place. He couldn't have done a lick of harm. But, hey, if he had, I could have given you a banner headline: 'Yun Hee's Gang of Vandals Storms New York's Citadel,' just to make it up to your mom for that long worry-free spell of your childhood. She probably thinks you're due to rile up on a rampage any time now. Hey, I should get that headline printed up anyway, as a present for her."

"Don't you dare!" Yun Hee laughed too. "But seriously, since you're such a trouble-making boy, give me some advice I can use with these kids. When I was their age, I could lean on my teachers. They taught me so much! But Tyrone and Cedric seem to really hate school."

Travis set his jaw. "Are you sure it's not school that hates them? Some kids just don't fit in at school. And some schools are just messed up."

Yun Hee considered this. "I did look at the city records for their schools. Tyrone's school has really high absentee rates. And the teachers are so young."

"That's got to be hard. Teachers just starting out like to get advice from older ones. That's just common sense."

"True. And you won't believe this. One of the statistics about Tyrone's school shocked me even more. Most schools in the city punish about 1 or 2 percent of their students with a suspension. That's the average, for elementary schools and high schools too. But in Tyrone's elementary school, do you know how many kids get suspended?"

"I don't know... 10 percent?"

"It's more than 32 percent — one third of all the kids there. That makes no sense. They're still so young. How do children so young manage to get in such bad trouble? And why do teachers think that making them stay home from school is a punishment that will teach them something?"

"Maybe they reckon that any kid they suspend is going to get a whipping at home."

"Even if they do, that's not how children learn to behave."

As they reached the Japanese pond, Travis put his arm around Yun Hee's shoulders. They could smell the orchids. The smooth surface of the water was being dappled with raindrops that, in Yun Hee's eyes, blurred the boundary between heaven and earth. "Listen," Travis said, "I know you're worried. But deep down, you know they're good kids. When we needed to settle the tomfoolery of the youngest ones the other night, Tyrone is the one who stepped up. He knows his sisters listen to him more than to us. He corralled Shaniqua and Lissa like some kind of lion tamer."

Yun Hee smiled. Travis had a good point about Tyrone. He did help out, and often flashed a dazzling smile just when she least expected it. But he and most of the children also got angry often. They were quick to show it, lashing out at one another, at their families, at her and anyone else who happened to be around. Sometimes, Yun Hee heard other children calling them names, telling them they smelled bad, snatching away a knitted hat or a bag of potato chips, or insulting their clothes and their families. She understood the children's shame. But their rage always stymied her.

Now, gazing into the pond, she listened to the wind rustling the leaves. Once, she remembered, a boy taunted Tyrone: "Your mom had to borrow milk from us yesterday." That had been enough to make Tyrone go berserk, starting a fight that quickly led to mayhem as others joined in. A tired older man had leaned out of an upstairs window to shout at Yun Hee, "You're always playing with those kids; can't you control them?" His words humiliated her, but she had no magic wand — except to try involving the kids in a project. Whether it was a day for painting, or for working with wood or yarn or other materials, any manual activity seemed to calm the children's emotions. Once they were really absorbed, nothing else mattered — they became just like any other children who loved to paint and create things.

"Come on," Travis called, already striding toward the Japanese tree peonies. He must be on the way toward the local flora exhibit, where he enjoyed seeing plants in the exact setting that nature intended for them. Yun Hee drew a deep breath of the cypress aroma in the air and sprinted to catch up.

Glancing at her as she fell into step at his side, Travis blurted, "Hey, can I ask you a favour?"

Yun Hee was surprised. Travis never seemed to ask anything much of her. She often wondered if this was because of his habitual self-sufficiency or if he was trying to avoid complications in their relationship. "Sure, go ahead."

"Well, it's about my sister Dawn. She's the oldest." Yun Hee knew that Travis came from a big family, but in the ten months they had been seeing each other, she had not met any of his relatives. "Dawn is actually ten years older than me. She kind of brought up the rest of us, especially whenever our mom was feeling poorly."

"That must have been a lot of work."

"You bet — I wasn't the only troublemaker in the family."

"Poor Dawn!"

"Well, she's always been mighty good with kids. She has four of her own now, and she teaches Sunday School at church."

"Did you go to Sunday School when you were growing up?"

"Oh, sometimes I snuck off. But yeah, most of the time. Anyway, the thing I want to ask you is 'cause Dawn's coming to New York soon. She'll be here for a week. I'll spend all the time I can with her — but I haven't got any vacation days left so I'll have to work too. I'm just wondering if you could spend time with her, maybe show her around a little bit?"

"Um, sure." As soon as Yun Hee agreed, she felt uncertain. They might not have anything in common. It felt awkward already. "She's coming alone? She doesn't want to bring any of her family?"

"This visit's not about kin. I mean, she'll see me, of course. But the reason she's coming is for her birthday. She's turning 40. And a bunch of her friends at work decided that she ought to see New York City for once. So it's their present to her. They're paying for her to come."

"That's so sweet of them!"

"They're paying for a hotel too. They don't want her anywhere near some fleabag futon at my place."

"A very wise move," Yun Hee said. "What kind of work do they do?"

"Oh, they work at Walmart. Dawn manages inventory there."

Yun Hee tried to keep from frowning. She had never shopped in a Walmart, and she couldn't imagine what it might be like overseeing inventory for such a big company. Yun Hee found it hard enough to keep the supplies organized for her chaotic little workshops. What would she find to talk to Dawn about?

But as a mother and a Sunday School teacher, perhaps Dawn would have advice about handling children. Sometimes Yun Hee read books to the children. She had seen how a girl who was embarrassed at being asked to read aloud, who was always told she was doing things wrong in school, would dare to look over her shoulder at the page if she was the one reading. When she first met the children and saw that one of them had reached the age of 11 without having learned to read, Yun Hee thought the girl was just not very smart. The following week, however, the same girl could recite the entire book Yun Hee had read her. She had been smart enough to memorize it after hearing it just twice. Yun Hee was determined to give her and all the children every possible chance to use their minds and imagination. There were days when she felt that maybe she could learn to see the world through their eyes.

Her day in the park with Travis was a peaceful one, even when she realized that her sneakers were no longer as waterproof as they had once been.

But long after they said good-bye that night, Yun Hee's thoughts remained anxious. Tossing and turning in bed, she thought back to the museum outing she had mentioned to Travis. Despite all the walking, the children still had energy to burn at the end of the day. So when they left the museum, she had taken them to a well-groomed public playground nearby. She still felt ashamed remembering how mothers there had pulled their own children away, as though the children in Yun Hee's group were spreading the plague. Even Tyrone and Lissa's 4-year-old sister, Shaniqua, seemed to panic the mothers in that neighbourhood. What on earth did they think their children had to fear from sweet little Shaniqua? And if children were looked at as though they were monsters, weren't they even more likely to act out the expectations put on them? Sometimes even the children's own teachers could humiliate them. Yun Hee remembered that when one of the children tried to hide the fact that she was living in a shelter, it was the teacher who announced it in front of the class — and who told her she smelled bad. It was heartbreaking to see so many children growing up in shame and never getting a chance to shine.

By now, Yun Hee decided that her sheets felt too rumpled for her to fall asleep. She got out of bed to tuck everything in tightly. For good measure, she gave her bed a spritz of chamomile before lying down to try again.

Despite the restful scent, her thoughts continued to churn. Tyrone was worrying Yun Hee as he grew bigger. Already 10 years old! Just last week, Yun Hee had been shocked to find him in the middle of a group of clamouring boys, banging his own head against the wall. When her arrival had made them scatter, Tyrone had been furious, "You ruined it. We was head-butting. You bang your head and the other guys bet that you can't keep doing it, and then you win their money. I wasn't stopping yet; they should have paid me." His anger frightened her. Yun Hee could not imagine Tyrone behaving properly on a stage at the United Nations.

Jesse

For a few weeks now, Jesse and Yun Hee had been talking to the children about the United Nations. He had written a skit using most of what the children had said in these conversations. This Saturday, they would practice the skit all together for the first time. Since Johnny's family had been evicted from the neighbourhood where the art workshop took place, Jesse and Yun Hee got up early to make the long subway trip to the temporary shelter where Carmen was staying for the moment with Johnny, age 9, and his two younger brothers. The shelter didn't accept adult men or boys over the age of 10, so after picking up Johnny, they continued on to another shelter where his brother Montrell, age 12, was fending for himself. The boys' father, Mateo, whose immigration status was too uncertain for him to trust the shelter system, was moving around, spending some nights on a friend's floor and others on subway trains.

With the brothers in tow, Yun Hee and Jesse then picked up the other children for the rehearsal. Jesse had arranged to use the activity room of a public library. At first he had suggested using the library closest to where most of the children lived, but Tyrone and Lissa's mother, Darleen, had put a stop to that. "No way! That library is right in the middle of the housing projects where there was another shooting just last month. I do not want my kids going there." So they made a sweaty trek to another library.

When they got there, Yun Hee was disappointed. The bookshelves didn't offer much selection at all, and there were none of the decorations that could turn a library into a magical place for children. But Lissa began jumping up and down with excitement. She and the others who were making their first-ever trip to a public library were issued their own borrower's cards. Lissa's joy, when she was invited to sign her name on the library card, made Yun Hee glad after all that they had come. Kneeling down next to Lissa, Yun Hee pointed out the design on the card. "Look here, you see these signatures? All five are the autographs of famous authors from Brooklyn. They grew up here just like you, and they wrote books that lots of people wanted to read."

"Like what?" Lissa asked.

"Well, most were books for grown-ups, but see right here? The very first autograph is by Maurice Sendak. You've read his book *Where the Wild Things Are*."

"The Wild Things are cool," said Ashanti, Lissa's 8-year-old sister. "He's really from Brooklyn?"

"Yes he is. And you know where he got the idea for the Wild Things?" All the children were listening to her now. "From his relatives. In an interview once, Maurice Sendak said that when he was a kid, his parents always had more and more relatives coming to stay. They were new to the country and they couldn't speak the language yet. They were all pretty crowded together in his apartment, so he imagined them as Wild Things."

"Cool," said Johnny. "I bet his mom didn't like him calling their whole family Wild Things."

"Probably not." Yun Hee laughed.

In addition to Johnny and Montrell Ramirez, and Lissa, Ashanti, and Tyrone Walker, they had also brought along Tanita's brother Cedric, Ernestine Jones's grandson Allan, and Allan's cousins Willy and Sheray. They began with Jesse reading the skit to them and explaining what they would do, while Yun Hee passed out a snack. She started with Lissa and Cedric because they were the youngest children in the group. But when Allan saw that they had been served peanut butter sandwiches first, he started shouting, "Where's mine? You're gonna run out." It took all of Jesse's diplomatic wrangling to calm Allan down long enough for Yun Hee to serve all the children. Yun Hee had heard that Allan's teacher wanted him on Ritalin, and at times like this she could understand the teacher. Maybe Allan was afraid she hadn't brought enough food, but how could they ever get the whole group prepared with him acting out this way?

Once everyone was eating, Jesse seized the moment of calm to find out what the children understood about the event where they would perform. "Hey, I'm confused," he called out, "Why are we going all the way to the United Nations?"

"To help the poor," Johnny called back.

"Naw," disagreed Montrell. "People at the UN are rich. Maybe seeing me in this skit will help *them.*"

Then Sheray spoke up more quietly, "Not just you."

"That's right," Jesse said. "They'll see all of you up on stage, together." Looking at Sheray, he asked, "Why do you think we're going to the UN?"

Sheray thought the question over. "Is it like when people go to a soldiers' cemetery? They have to thank the unknown soldiers."

"Yes, sort of. There are people who died from poverty and we should remember them."

Hearing their words, Yun Hee began to feel hope that maybe bringing this most unlikely group of children to perform at the UN was exactly the right thing to do.

Eventually, they made it through the entire rehearsal, but suddenly Tyrone and Montrell were wrestling each other, thrashing left and right, and causing Sheray to cower against Yun Hee. When Jesse pulled them apart, Tyrone said, "This is just play-fighting, it's not for real."

"I know about play-fighting," Jesse answered, "but sometimes you can hurt each other for real, even when you don't mean to."

"I guess," Tyrone said. "Last month, we were play-fighting and I accidentally dropped the other guy for real, so he started chasing after me with a brick, and I had to run fast."

During the long subway trip to bring the Ramirez boys back home that evening, Jesse asked Johnny how their family was doing in the shelter.

"Our dad can't come visit. No one can, not even for my birthday."

"That's tough. Do you have enough space there?"

"Not really," Johnny answered. "It's one room for all of us, so my little brothers are always messing up my school stuff. Besides, there's always staff coming in the room. They don't even knock."

"Man, that's crappy, not having any kind of privacy. What about you, Montrell? Is it hard being so far from the rest of your family?"

Montrell glared. Then he said, "I feel like I'm locked down. You don't have nowhere to call your own." Looking at the obscenities scratched onto the train window, he added, "You're not free. It's like being behind bars."

Yun Hee

The next day was one of the Sundays that Travis had to work. He and Yun Hee had arranged to meet early in the day, so that before leaving he could introduce Yun Hee to his sister Dawn. They met in a bagel shop beside her Manhattan hotel. As Yun Hee made her way to their booth, she was surprised to notice how much alike the two looked. A family resemblance made sense; but they had more in common than their gently rounded chins and sandy hair. Somehow they both struck Yun Hee as looking like people from out of town. That didn't make sense. Travis had been living in New York for years now; and New Yorkers were so diverse that who could say who "looked" local or not? Wondering whether her impression had more to do with the open expression on Dawn's face or the no-nonsense cut of her short, greying hair, Yun Hee slid into the booth next to Travis.

After making introductions, Travis went to the counter to buy more bagels and a chai tea latte for Yun Hee, leaving the women to get acquainted.

"So," Yun Hee asked, "what do you think of the city so far?"

"It's a sight to see, all right. We took the ferry boat yesterday, over to Staten Island and back."

"Oh, that's a nice boat ride! And it's a lot cheaper than the tourist boats."

"It surely is. I liked seeing the ocean. In a city like this you all live so cooped up, with so many people in one place. It's right nice to be able to get out onto the water like that."

Travis slid back into the booth, pushing a steaming cardboard cup toward Yun Hee. "We took the ferry so Dawn could at least look at the Statue of Liberty."

"Yes, I saw it."

Travis turned to Yun Hee. "I wanted to take Dawn to Liberty Island, but they still haven't reopened the Statue. There ain't much point if you can't climb up to see out."

"Oh, that's true," Yun Hee said. "I don't think they've let anyone up top since 9/11."

"I'm not sure I'd have liked that anyway," Dawn said. "It's mighty high, and it looks claustrophobic to me. There can't be a smidgen of room to breathe in there."

Finishing off a bagel loaded with the lox that he had acquired a taste for since moving to New York, Travis looked at his watch. "Sorry, ladies. I've got to go earn my keep. See you tonight!"

Jesse

That Sunday, Jesse was welcoming a guest of his own. Ahmed's flight was arriving at JFK Airport in Queens. Getting his visa had required no small miracle. In addition to proving he was employed, Ahmed had also been required to show the American Embassy in Dar-es-Salaam three months' worth of bank statements establishing that he had enough income and savings to be able to afford to be a tourist in the United States.

"No wonder the people speaking about poverty at the UN are never really the ones in the toughest situations," Pamela had fumed. "If the US won't give any of them visas, how are they supposed to speak for themselves?" Ahmed, like Pamela, Jesse, and Yun Hee, was part of the All Together in Dignity full-time volunteer corps, and the small monthly stipends they received did not give any of them large bank balances.

Ahmed's basic level of schooling and lack of wealth made him likely to be refused even a short-term visa. When Jesse and Pamela had asked for advice at the US embassy, the diplomat they met had been of no help at all. "Why on earth should this young man make such an expensive trip? Surely you can find training programmes for him closer to his home."

"We've already received donations for the travel costs, but the point isn't to train him. He's the one who has things to teach other people," Jesse answered.

"That doesn't make sense. He doesn't even have a diploma. What on earth is he qualified to teach?"

Annoyed, Pamela launched into a long explanation: "Whenever the UN discusses poverty eradication, the dialogue is based on the assumption that wealthy countries like ours have all the solutions and that people in developing countries should do as they're told. But it's not true that we have all the solutions."

The diplomat raised his eyebrows dubiously. Undaunted, Pamela forged on, "If we did, you wouldn't have people sleeping in the streets and going to bed hungry in the richest countries on the planet. And the unfairness of ignoring the knowledge of people who themselves have lived in extreme poverty means that many countries are going to a lot of trouble just to replicate mistakes we've made here."

Unconvinced and impatient, the diplomat shooed them away. Pamela, kicking herself for not having been more tactful with the US diplomats, had then run herself ragged tracking down a high-level French minister who had supported All Together in Dignity in the past. He happened to be on a fact-finding mission in Haiti at the time, but once found, the minister agreed to write a strong letter of support to the US consular officer in Tanzania. The letter explained that he had often seen All Together in Dignity organize international events, and that none of its members had ever attempted to overstay a short-term visa. One of the most important aspects of their participation in an international event was returning home afterwards to share news of it with people who had not been able to attend. Thanks to this minister's letter, Ahmed had finally been granted a ten-day visa.

When Ahmed arrived in New York and made it through customs, Jesse was waiting for him with a denim jacket. "You might want to put this on. The weather is still warm for October, but it's a lot cooler than you're used to."

Ahmed's bag was not heavy, so they took a shuttle bus to the A-train subway line. The bus ride and the waits on several outdoor platforms as they transferred gave Ahmed a chance to begin looking around. Sunlight glinted off a water tower looming toward the sky. A car dealership was wreathed in colourful plastic pennants, each triangle aimed downward to steer the interest of potential customers. Farther on, spirals of barbed wire atop a chain-link fence protected a vast junkyard where wrecked cars were stacked in hunks of metal. A separate yard contained teetering piles of rubber tires amid rubble and weeds. Bright purple and orange graffiti on the brick wall around the tires seemed to be composed of bubble letters, but Ahmed couldn't make much sense of it. About a dozen yellow school buses were parked in a lot. A lumber yard was full of stacked pallets painted red or blue.

None of the buildings — commercial or residential — were more than three or four floors high. On the fire escape of one building, Ahmed could see a young couple in conversation, the man leaning against a window ledge and the woman sitting on the steps.

"I thought the buildings in your country were supposed to be the tallest," Ahmed said, laughing. "Even we have buildings taller than this."

It was true, Jesse realized. Most buildings in this part of the city were short ones. "That's because we're not in Manhattan. When we go there, you'll see skyscrapers alright."

Ahmed read aloud some of the billboards and signs: "'Believe in Something Bigger: Lottery Jackpot,' 'Happy Face Daycare,' 'Gotta leak? Get relief at the corner.' 'Alcohol: Cheaper than Therapy.'" Turning to Jesse, he reflected, "That one is sad. Alcohol can drive people to behave so badly. What does that one mean? 'Greater Zion Deliverance Tabernacle.'"

"It's a church."

"Really? But don't your churches have steeples?" The tabernacle was a long low-slung brick building.

"A lot of them do, especially in white middle-class neighbourhoods. But real estate in New York is expensive, and pastors want to be in the heart of every community. So in poor areas, a lot of churches just move into any kind of building."

"You mean a building that was already there before the church came?"

"Right. That one might have been a school or a post office or something before. Lots of storefront churches are much smaller, though. Look, that's probably a church too." Jesse pointed to a small building fenced in by a red metal grate. A small sign on its wall featured a cross and writing in the Korean alphabet. Beneath it, Ahmed could make out a translation: "Evangelical Crusade of Christ's Chosen Believers." Dozens of telephone and power wires stretched from corner to corner. Most were taut, but here and there, they sagged under the weight of running shoes, hanging in pairs. Perplexed, Ahmed asked, "Why are shoes up there?"

Jesse gave a wry smile. "Sometimes, kids toss their own shoes up there, just for fun when they are done wearing them or to celebrate the last day of school. I guess that's a pretty wasteful tradition here."

As their subway plunged below ground, the street slid out of sight. The continual screeching of the metal wheels beneath them echoed against the tunnel walls.

Ahmed said, "For us, going underground means working in a mine. Either that, or being buried. But here, people do this every day?"

"Twice or even three or four times a day," Jesse answered. "When I'm visiting the kids we know, I can end up taking a bunch of subway trips all in one day. There's a family we know that has been split up because they lost their home, so now they're in three different places. You can't see all of them without taking four different subway lines."

"Why did they separate? Can their relatives not take them in?"

"I don't think they have relatives here in New York. They're from the Dominican Republic. But they did try at first living with neighbours who took them in. That's hard though, because not only does it make a home really crowded, but sometimes the people who offer to take others in can lose their own homes. They're not supposed to have so many people there. It's against the law."

"A law against taking someone in? That's hard."

"Well, overcrowding is considered a fire risk."

"Are there many fires here?"

"In poor neighbourhoods, yes, there can be a lot. All it takes is a lit candle when the electricity's been turned off, or a faulty space heater in winter, and a whole building with lots of different apartments can go up in flames."

"But why is the family you spoke of in three different places?"

"There's an emergency shelter that had room for the mother and three of her sons. But the fourth son is over the age of 10. The shelter she's in doesn't allow any men or teenage boys. Since there are teenage girls there, I guess they just don't want to have to worry that anyone is hooking up. So the oldest son is in another shelter for men and boys. His father could stay there too, except that he doesn't have legal immigration papers."

"So where does the father sleep?"

"Sometimes, right here on one of these trains."

"At night?"

"Yes, the trains run 24 hours a day, and they're heated in the winter, so it's not as dangerous as sleeping outside in the cold. You could freeze to death in the cold here. The father also has a friend who lets him stay over sometimes, but he's pretty careful not to wear out his welcome. The friend has a big family and not much room. But that's where the father can go to shower."

"That sounds so hard. It is not what I was expecting of a place like New York," Ahmed said, shaking his head. "When young people leave home in Tanzania, they might have a hard time and need to sleep under a market stall or on the beach. But it's not because a law said that a friend couldn't take them in or that a father couldn't be with his family. And even if it is not easy to sleep under a market stall, their lives are not in danger from the weather. The family you are speaking about must be very courageous."

That night, Jesse met Dauntay and together they took Ahmed to Times Square. "Now *this* is what I thought New York would look like," Ahmed exclaimed. "I want to look everywhere at once." Craning his neck, he scanned the skyscrapers towering overhead. On the billboard nearest to them, a white man with chiseled features wore nothing but jockey shorts and flexed his rippling muscles. In an adjacent ad, a blonde woman with deeply tanned skin lifted a beer stein with one hand, while the other drew her skimpy scarlet dress still further up her thigh. A third billboard, with the caption, "Discover your inner Smirnoff," depicted a mouse outfitted like an art thief. The intrepid mouse was suspended by a cable above a mouse trap. Ahmed gave this one a quizzical look.

"Is it planning to steal the cheese?"

Jesse laughed. "I guess that's the idea. But I don't know how that's supposed to make us want to drink vodka."

Just then a particularly long, white limousine whooshed past them. "What was that?" Ahmed wanted to know.

"It's called a stretch limo. It's a very expensive car with a private driver. They tint the windows so you can't see inside, and it's like a little hotel room, with a television and a refrigerator full of drinks."

"Who is riding inside? Is it for the president?"

"Not usually, no." Jesse answered. "We Americans prefer our politicians to seem like the middle class. Stretch limos are more for celebrities, famous actors, or sports players. And teenagers too. There's a tradition where teenagers graduating high school all chip in money together to rent a limo for one night and have a party in it."

"I'd like to see that. Will you do that when you graduate, Dauntay?"

"Naw, I'm looking for a job."

Among the passengers getting out of a bus, Yun Hee and Dawn emerged. Jessie and Yun Hee made the necessary introductions. They had decided to welcome both of their guests by meeting up for a walk around the midtown area together.

Ahmed was still riveted by all the neon billboards, turning in every direction as images and slogans changed constantly. "So much light! It is bright like day."

"I guess New Yorkers just don't think much of the stars," Dawn commented dryly. "If you want to see real be-still-and-know-God scenery, you'd have to visit our neck of the woods."

His wonder unchecked, Ahmed asked, "How long is this light show?"

"It never stops," Yun Hee answered. "Billboards are like the subway, round the clock."

Ahmed gave a low whistle, trying to imagine how much money so much electricity must cost. "But there must be blackouts."

Jesse remembered how frequent the blackouts and brownouts were in Tanzania, often scheduled to take place at certain times of day to conserve electricity — at least in the lower-income districts. "A year ago, I would have said that blackouts don't really happen here anymore. But I would have been wrong because we actually had a huge blackout just this past summer."

"Yep," said Dauntay. "It was a hot day, 90 degrees. My sister Makayla had snuck into the movies, thinking she could cool down, but instead she got stuck in the pitch black."

"No light during the day?" Ahmed asked, puzzled because most buildings in Tanzania had windows and courtyards.

"Movie theatres have no windows, and neither do a lot of big stores or offices."

"And this happened in the entire city of New York?"

"Actually, it was a whole lot bigger than that," Yun Hee remembered. "It was in eight different states, and in part of Canada."

Not sure how much geography Ahmed had learned, Jesse added, "You could have driven about sixteen hundred miles without finding electricity. That's like going from Dar-es-Salaam out of Tanzania, all the way through Kenya, and halfway into Somalia."

Ahmed gave another impressed whistle.

"When it happened," Dauntay remembered, "there were so many helicopters circling over and over the city. They thought it might be another 9/11."

"You were scared it was terrorism?"

"Some people were," Jesse said, "but it was just a big technical failure — and they said something about overgrown trees interfering with the power lines."

"For heaven's sake," Dawn said. "It's power lines that interfere with the trees, not the other way around."

Jesse laughed. "I stand corrected. But at least on that day the trees overpowered the electricity grid."

"Did it last all day?"

"In some places it was about seven hours, and in a lot of places it lasted sixteen hours. But depending on where you live, some buildings stayed messed up for days. I have a friend here who lives on the twentieth floor of a building. Not only did he have to walk up all twenty flights of stairs for a few days, but the whole water system in the building depends on electricity, so he had to carry bottled water up all those stairs, for drinking, washing, and even flushing the toilet."

"That's crazy," said Ahmed. "I think we are right in Tanzania to live closer to the ground."

Dawn nodded, adding, "It's New Yorkers who are crazy. In West Virginia, we know better."

"Your country is very different?" Ahmed asked.

"Well, it's the same country — but a sight more neighborly. People in West Virginia are real friendly. It's not like here where everyone just looks right through you and rushes on past."

Jesse agreed. "It's true that New York is always in a hurry. When I was in Ahmed's country, I really appreciated that people always take time to greet each other and ask for news of everyone's family. But sometimes New Yorkers can be neighbourly too. Oh — we should cross the street here." As they continued talking, Jesse was shepherding their group east toward Rockefeller Plaza.

Dawn paused to look over a sidewalk display of sketches of Manhattan landmarks, including several of the World Trade Center sporting exhortations to "Never Forget." The sketches were covered by a sheet of plastic on a folding table near the curb. The vendor, an elderly Asian man in a baseball cap, sat hunched over on a folding stool.

Hastening her pace, Dawn caught up with the rest of the group. Jesse was still talking about New York. "I know the city has a bad reputation, but the blackout showed how much it has changed."

"That's true," Yun Hee agreed. "Years ago, there was another huge blackout in New York, back in the 1970s. A lot of people took advantage of the blackout to loot stores and burn them down. It took decades for businesses to return to some of the devastated neighbourhoods. But nothing like that happened this summer at all."

"Why not?" Ahmed wanted to know.

Still walking, they fell silent for a few minutes, thinking about it. Then Dauntay suggested, "Maybe 'cause of 9/11? At first, we did think maybe Al Qaeda was coming back to bomb us again. You don't go knock over a liquor store when you think you need to fight a war."

"I think you're right," Jesse said. "People were looking out for each other, helping each other to walk down huge black stairwells or out of subway tunnels."

"The subways stopped running too?" Ahmed asked.

"Yes," said Yun Hee, "and some of the trains stopped under the rivers where it's really far between stops. A friend of mine was stuck under the East River in the dark with her three little kids. But they didn't even wait for the rescue workers. Everyone on the train just helped one another to walk out, and a stranger gave her kids some water."

"Man, it was hot that day. We were all parched." Jesse remembered. "Even when the temperature in New York isn't as high as in Dar-es-Salaam, I think it feels worse here because of the pollution. And lots of us were walking over the Williamsburg Bridge to get home to Brooklyn, just like people did on 9/11."

They had walked to Fifth Avenue and now reached the east end of Rockefeller Plaza. Together, they stopped to gaze westward at the fountains bordered by shrubs. The blossoms alternated between golden yellow and burnt orange. At the far end of the plaza, the illuminated facades of the buildings rose far into the sky. Still remembering the blackout, Jesse continued, "When everyone was walking home, I felt bad for the girls in high heels. But when we got over the bridge, there was a bar that had set up an outdoor table to give out free ice water to everyone. A lot of people were just looking out for each other. Most Americans think New Yorkers are mean, but on days like that, you get to see that it's not really true."

Ahmed grinned, "So I came to a good place. You agree, Dauntay?"

Dauntay was frowning. "I don't know about that." Scooping a pebble from the flower bed nearest him, he tried to make it skip down the pool toward the mouth of a sculpted fish carrying a mermaid on its back. The pebble dropped to the bottom without a single skip.

"What's wrong?" Jesse asked.

"Last week my friend Caleb got sentenced to three years in prison. But he's not a bad guy. He didn't really hurt anyone."

Dawn's eyebrows shot upwards dubiously.

"Wasn't it a police officer he wounded?" Jesse asked.

"Yeah, but the cop is okay now, and Caleb didn't even know he was a cop. He thought he was protecting himself. But when he got to court, the lawyer didn't say none of that." Dauntay tried to skip another stone in the pool, again without success. "When the lawyer talked to Caleb's mom, he was rude. And he didn't make any sense. She has no idea what that lawyer was talking about."

"That's not right," Jesse said. "I don't think Caleb really had violence in his heart."

"Nonsense," said Dawn sternly. "If he was fool enough to shoot a police officer, he belongs behind bars."

"I've met Caleb," Jesse explained. "I think that was a day when he just got scared and did something very stupid. When you grow up faced with violence all the time, it's too easy for one thing to lead to another. I'm not saying he's innocent. But maybe his sentence should have been shorter. The lawyer should have taken the time to get to know Caleb and his family. It could have made a difference if he had said the right thing to the judge."

"Prison is a terrible thing," Ahmed said gravely. "A lot of people get sick in our prisons from malaria or tuberculosis."

"There's TB in prisons here too, but the United States got rid of malaria back in the 1940s," Jesse said.

"Malaria, here?"

"In the south, yes. People were still dying of it in the 1920s and 30s. I heard once that it was because of diseases like malaria that the south had slaves when the north didn't. Farmers in the north worked hard, but they could manage on their own.

In the south, though, so many people were getting sick that the rich decided they needed more and more slaves for their plantations to work. It was an evil system."

"Prisons in Tanzania can be evil too. I know people are not treated like human beings in prison. All they can do to survive is to hold onto their faith. It's so crowded, the prisoners often don't even have room to sleep," said Ahmed.

"Conditions in prisons here are probably not as crowded," Jesse said, "but the US puts a higher proportion of our citizens in jail than any other country. It's even higher than Russia or South Africa, and much higher than Nigeria or Kenya."

"And we're supposed to be the 'Land of the Free'," Dauntay said.

"We're all born free," Dawn said. "But prisons are built to protect innocent people from being hurt." She picked up a small stone and skipped it neatly down the pool. "Next time, try a more underhanded throw."

Blandine and Varag

The next day, Mira's nephew Alejo Prieto found his way to a taxi outside the airport. Blandine's doorman let him into the apartment, so Blandine did not meet him until she got home from work. The 17-year-old was sprawled out on the living room couch, an iPod in his ears making him oblivious to her arrival. From fragments of music escaping his earbuds, Blandine thought she recognized Beyoncé's "Crazy in Love." She crossed the room into Alejo's line of sight, prompting him to get languorously to his feet to greet her.

"Hey, thanks for letting me crash here," he said.

The boy was as tall and lanky as Varag, but blond and blue-eyed. His hair was styled in the latest fashion, longer hair in the middle sprouting up from the short sides. Did they call that a "faux hawk"? Although Blandine had seen the look advertised in her hair salon, it made her think of baby hedgehogs. On the floor, she saw a backpack splayed open, offering a view of the boy's underwear and socks.

"You can put your things in the guest room, just through there." He obliged, disappearing behind a closed door, which suited Blandine.

When Varag got home, Blandine was setting the table. She knocked on Alejo's door, summoning him to a dinner of swordfish, Brussels sprouts, and roasted potatoes. Blandine did not often serve potatoes, but tonight added them to the menu acknowledging to herself that she shouldn't expect a growing boy to subsist on her low-carb diet.

As they ate, Varag tried to grill Alejo, asking about his upcoming college interviews, scheduled at Columbia, NYU, and Rutgers. "I'm sure they'll ask you about current events. Tell me what you thought of David Brooks's New York Times column the other day."

Seeing Alejo's blank stare, Blandine wondered why her husband assumed that everyone spent as much time as he did dissecting the most obscure news items. She filled him in: "Brooks wrote about what he calls 'presidency wars.' He regrets that Americans stopped arguing about public policies and moral values. Instead, Brooks says, all they do is keep re-hashing the fight over who should have won the election in Florida."

"You mean people keep saying that 'Bush stole the election from Gore,' instead of talking about his foreign policy?"

"Exactly," answered Varag. "Each side feels real hatred of the other, and people have stopped trying to understand their opponents' point of view. Brooks argues that it would be more constructive to criticize policies than to vilify one president or the other. What do you think?"

"I don't know. I haven't really thought about it. …" Alejo reached past the Brussels sprouts to help himself to more potatoes. "I did think it was crazy, though, when everyone got so angry at the Dixie Chicks."

Now it was Varag's turn to frown in puzzlement. "What are Dixie Chicks?"

"You know, that country music trio from Texas? Right before Bush invaded Iraq, they were playing a concert in London. On stage, they told the audience that they were ashamed of Bush, and ashamed that he's from Texas too. So they got death threats and a lot of Americans started boycotting their music. Pretty stupid."

"What was stupid?" Blandine asked. "The death threats or their remarks?"

"Well... both, I guess." Alejo gulped down a mouthful of wine. "They're just these little blonde singers. Making death threats against them doesn't seem very tough. It's like threatening baby kittens. But what they said was kind of stupid too. They weren't even in the country. They just started dissing their own president while they were traveling. That's going behind someone's back. But anyway, I don't like country music."

Blandine rolled her eyes at the non-sequitur and headed to the kitchen to bring out a fruit salad.

"Let me get this straight," Varag growled, making no attempt to hide his exasperation. "Your only objection to the death threats is that they were made to women who are likely to lose a fist fight?"

"Oh, I don't know about that...." Alejo began trying to imagine the fist fight. "They're tiny, but they might be pretty scrappy when it comes down to it. I could see them winning in an all-out cat fight. You know, by scratching and hair-pulling. Oh — biting too. I bet they would bite."

"But don't you realize —"

"And heels! I don't think they wear stilettos, but they've got these boots with bad-ass heels that could do a real number on you."

That night as Varag and Blandine were getting ready for bed, Varag was still fuming: "How does that boy's mind even work? I don't think he's capable of following a line of reasoning for two sentences in a row."

"Well, he's young." Blandine felt no warmth toward Alejo, but worried that if Varag's belligerence went unchecked, their guest's visit would feel unbearably long.

"Ridiculous!" Varag sputtered. "Lots of teenagers his age compete on debate teams. Remember the Model United Nations students? They weren't yammering on about cat fights."

"True. But neither were they drinking wine while being interrogated by a rabidly political economist like you. You do get so passionate, darling. Perhaps you intimidated him into idiocy. Besides, it isn't as though he plans to major in international relations. His dream is to work in Silicon Valley for an internet start-up."

"Well, thank God he's not going into politics. But he's almost old enough to vote. What is the world coming to when a boy like that, with every advantage in life, is so stubbornly foolish about world issues?"

Tanita

The next day at work, Tanita found time dragging by slowly. "Good morning, ma'am, if I could have a few minutes of your time —." Click.

So many people hung up on her before even realizing that she wasn't selling anything, only asking survey questions. Tanita often wanted to vary her introduction depending on the voice that picked up the phone. Even the single word "Hello?" could give you clues about a person's age and gender, and whether English was their native language or not. But the scripts were detailed and Tanita was expected to follow them to the letter. And so many people screened their calls nowadays that it was harder and harder to get anyone to answer a stranger's call. Tanita often worked until late into the evening, trying to catch people during dinner and out on the west coast where everything happened three hours later than in New York. But today she had scheduled a shorter shift so she could work with Ahmed on the message for the United Nations.

Finally — time to clock out. She hurried downtown, trying to clear her mind, where she felt her thoughts muddled by the phone calls she'd been making. At the All Together in Dignity centre, it was Yun Hee who answered the door. "Come on in! I'm in the middle of writing a report, but you'll find Ahmed downstairs."

He sat at a folding table facing glass doors that looked out on a small courtyard. The concrete walls displayed a mural in lively colours showing adults reading books to children under a tree. As

Tanita sat down beside him, Ahmed said, "I am glad we are supposed to write together. Alone, I would have no idea where to start."

"Then we're in trouble because I have no idea either." They both laughed. "What I do know a little about is the kind of people we'll be speaking to. One of the ladies from the United Nations came here to a meeting, and then we went to the UN to meet with a man there."

"What were they like?"

"The lady seemed to me really full of herself. She's ready to tell us everything there is to know about poverty and what governments should do about it. I wouldn't know what to say to her."

"I see... There are people like that in Tanzania too. But what about the man?"

"I'm not sure. He also knows a lot. But he doesn't act like he thinks he knows *everything*. When we met, he sounded pretty curious about our work and about what we have to say. And Pamela told me that she knows he gets discouraged when the UN's approach to fighting poverty doesn't work."

"Jesse also told me there might also be some university people present."

"I guess he means Professor Helen. She's really nice. She knows a lot herself, but somehow she's on our side. She jumps right in when we need her help."

"I look forward to meeting her. But the first lady, the one you say is hard to talk to.... I remember when Jesse was in Tanzania, I went with him to meet someone from the UN Development Programme there. This man was Tanzanian like me, but from a high, educated background. Never did he speak to people who go barefoot and live in the streets. He was preparing for the World Day for Overcoming Poverty like us, but he did not think that people living in poverty should be invited."

"You're kidding! Then who would he invite?"

"Only people from important embassies and ministries. His idea was that the World Day must be a time to tell all of them how much the UNDP accomplishes, so they would continue funding his work."

"And he didn't think people living in poverty should even be in the room for that?"

"He hated the idea. Then later he said, 'Maybe they should come so we can tell them what to do so they won't be poor anymore.'"

"He thinks people are still poor because they haven't come to a meeting where he could tell them what to do?"

"He did think so, yes. It was very hard to work with him. But one day we stopped by this man's office. He did not expect us. We went only to deliver the programmes we had prepared for the event. He invited us into his office, and he spoke differently than before."

Outside, they saw an empty plastic grocery bag waft slowly downwards, eventually catching on a small shrub beneath the mural.

Ahmed continued, "He had just come back from the north of the country where there was drought and famine. He was very sad. He had lost heart. And then he said, 'Maybe you are right that this World Day can give all of us courage. Maybe it will help me to hear the messages from poor people.' And when the day came, he really listened to what people said, and he took the time to speak with them afterwards. It was so much of a change."

"It sure was. Well, I guess we'll have to imagine talking to someone like him and see what we have to say together."

An hour later, as they were making notes together, Jesse came into the room with a large bottle of soda. As he poured it into three cups, he said, "Hey, I hope I'm not interrupting your flow. I was just out visiting Mateo Ramirez."

"How's he holding up?" asked Tanita.

"Like you'd expect. It's hard. But he promised to join us at the UN. I told him he won't need any kind of ID just to go through the metal detector."

"There's a metal detector?" Ahmed asked.

"Yes, access to the garden is restricted, so everyone is searched. Our names have to be on a list. But Mateo can just tell them his name without showing ID. Pamela says it will be fine because one of us will be right next to the guard to vouch for each person. Anyway, the reason I'm interrupting you is because, if you don't mind, I have something here I want to share with you." He pulled a folded piece of paper from his shirt pocket. "Tanita, you told me about that poem you read with Pamela, and that reminded me of a poem I really like. I was thinking it might help you with your writing. This was written by Karen Erdman. She calls it '(a poem about death)'." Jesse proceeded to read aloud:

> *I am twenty-three years old*
> *and no one I know is dying*
> *So I continue to grow*
> *a green bristling shoot*
> *through the cracks*
> *of a grey and white-columned city*
> *not pearly, delicate with dew*
> *but coarse, with fibres twining through*
> *the ways I know to survive.*
>
> *Death is not shiny and new*
> *to all my passersby on nighttime streets*
> *A man died cold on the street last night*
> *Six children hot in a tenement fire*
> *And thirty-seven other murders last month*
> *AIDS is another death for gaunt brown women*
> *tracks streaked down their arms*
> *for moonlit hookers who before might have been*
> *left stabbed in an alley*
>
> *But to me death is a novelty*
> *a bright nauseating toy*
> *Each death a brilliant pain*
> *sharp inside*
> *like the pin drawn from a grenade*
> *about to blow*

I am twenty-three years old
and no one I know is dying
but everyone I know
knows someone who is,
Friend, brother, nephew, son
tracked through knotted months or years
As friends stand watch on the road to dying
I stand watch over the grief of the living

I am twenty-three years old
and no one I know is dying

Unless you count
all of us.

The three of them were silent for a moment. Then Ahmed echoed, "'Stand watch over the grief of the living.' Sometimes, that is the only thing we can do."

"But it can't be," Tanita protested. "If we can't do nothing but grieve or stand watch, what's the point of a world day like this?" She looked at Ahmed. "Remember the man you were telling me about?"

"From the UNDP?"

"You said he changed. Maybe now he's doing more to help. So what changed him? What can we say to change the mind of the lady at the UN here in New York?"

"That's a big question." Ahmed thought for a moment. "People like that man go to high-level, good schools. They are raised to be not like the rest of us who may not go to school at all." A taxi horn blared in the street. "But they forget that they too could be in our place. They could fall ill or be in an accident. They could lose their job. They learned many, many things in their schools. But we learn things in life."

"Yes." Tanita was nodding her head.

Ahmed continued, "We can tell them what it feels like to have nothing certain, to worry all the time about how to feed your family."

Tanita added, "And to have people look down on you. To have them put you in a category and assume that you're not even good enough to raise your own brother."

"Your brother?" Jesse asked. "Did someone actually say that about you?"

"Well, yes. It was this stupid psychologist lady who had to evaluate Cedric for special ed. I don't want to put *that* in the speech. But I feel terrible. She thinks I'm too young to take care of him: I'm not strict enough, I have a bad temper — everything."

"I see you with Cedric all the time, and she's dead wrong. He's lucky to have you as a sister. But I hear what you're saying about how people assume things and stereotype you."

"Yeah, they think they know you when they don't. And it's like Ahmed was just saying too: they just don't know what it's like. I remember what they used to say to my mother: 'Just get a job if you don't want your kids living in a shelter,' or 'Where's their father? It's your fault for raising kids on your own.' I saw the way people looked at her when she had to beg for help." Tanita clenched her knuckles. "Sometimes pity — that was bad enough because we were supposed to be grateful for that pity — but sometimes people looked at her with hate. They couldn't move away from us fast enough. Just full-on hate."

Ahmed was looking at Tanita sorrowfully. "That must have been very hard for your family. But all that hatred.... I am wondering: where did you put it?"

"What do you mean?"

"I mean that —" Ahmed hesitated, worried his question might hurt her feelings. "You sound so angry: about people treating your mother badly, about the psychologist who insulted you. And anger can harden into hate."

"So you think the psychologist is right. I have a bad temper." Tanita was glowering.

"No. I speak not about your temper. I speak about your heart. When anger becomes hate, it weighs on the heart. I have felt hatred too. I think everyone must feel hatred sometimes. I felt it when my father died."

"You did?"

"He was ill, and therefore he died — but there are more medicines for rich people. If we had been rich, I know there are medicines he could have taken. And so I hated everyone with money, everyone who did not hire him, everyone who did not pay him money that can save lives."

"Well, you're right. He shouldn't have died, and it's not fair that medicine is so expensive."

Jesse broke in, "But you say you felt that hatred *before*. Why don't you feel it now?"

"I don't know.... But maybe because of my mother. That line in the poem you read, about keeping watch over grief. That is what she did. She saw my anger, she saw that it would harden to hatred, she saw it weigh on my heart. She feared that with hatred I would strike out and become violent, maybe even a criminal. She missed my father just as much as I did. But she was stronger to not hate anyone. She was strong to soften my hatred."

"How did she do that?" Tanita wanted to know.

"I think that maybe it was her faith. She believes that my father's life meant more than his death. She believed — even when hatred had me tied in knots — that I could do better, and find peace. She believes that it is important to honour all people, even those we can't see. My behaviour must always honour my father, even though he no longer walks beside me."

Blandine

For their second dinner together, Blandine offered Alejo a choice of take-out menus. She hoped that if she could fortify him with food he liked, he might be able to hold his own in arguing with Varag. To her surprise, he chose well, picking a Salvadoran restaurant that made delicious pupusa tortillas stuffed with meat and beans. But at the last minute, when the food had been delivered and Blandine had just put on Varag's favourite Miles Davis CD, Varag texted her that he needed to work late.

Removing the third place-setting, she steeled herself for an intimate meal with Alejo and invited him to join her at the table.

"How did your interviews go?" she asked.

Alejo had begun wolfing down a chicken tamale, but suddenly looked sheepish. "I think Rutgers was fine. But I don't know about the Columbia lady. She was just on my case for no reason. I don't think she liked me very much."

"What makes you say that?"

"We were just talking away, and I was telling her about the road trip I took last summer, but suddenly she started getting angry at me. Pretty stupid."

"Why would that make her angry? What happened on your road trip?"

"I don't know.... It wasn't even that great.... My friends and I took Route 66 out to California, you know, just chilling, kind of like Jack Kerouac?"

Blandine smiled. "I've never done that, but the vistas must be magnificent out west."

"I guess. But that gets old pretty fast. And the food really sucked, just beyond weak."

Blandine laughed. "I can imagine that it is. You ate at fast food places and diners?"

"Yeah. Really greasy stuff, and too much hot sauce. I mean, I like hot sauce, but not when it's just covering up what they don't know how to cook."

"So what else did you say during your interview?"

"Well, I mentioned Kerouac because colleges like that kind of stuff, you know, talking about books. Then she asked what I thought about Kerouac's 'relationship to drugs and alcohol.'" Alejo drew air quotes with his fingers. "His 'relationship.' What a stupid question! Who talks like that? So then I thought it would be better just to talk about something else. I mean, of course we got wasted on our road trip, but that's not what you're supposed to talk about in a college interview."

"No, that's true. It certainly wouldn't make a very good impression. So did you manage to change the subject?"

"Yeah, that's when I told her about our game with the cops. The roads out there are so straight. They just go on and on for miles. And the speed limit is ridiculously low. I mean *no* one drives the actual speed limit out there, really no one. So obviously we were speeding. But we could do it without breaking any laws at all, so it was okay."

"What do you mean you didn't break any laws? The speed limit is a law."

"Sure, but not for us. We were using my friend Dylan's car. And his father is an ambassador, so they have diplomatic license plates. In DC, no cop would ever even bother to pull us over. They know all about diplomatic immunity. But out west, they had no clue." Now Alejo was laughing.

"You mean that you would get pulled over for speeding, and then you would tell the police that they aren't allowed to give a ticket to a diplomatic family?"

"Yeah, that blew their minds. Those dudes would keep us sitting there in the hot sun while they were scratching their heads and radioing to other cops to ask about us. So that was the game. We used to bet with each other about how long it would take them to finally wise up to the fact that they had to let us go."

Blandine leaned her head onto her hands with a deep sigh as Alejo continued chuckling. Finally, he looked at her. "You're looking just like that Columbia lady did. You don't like me either. I don't know what your problem is." Abruptly, he pushed back his chair and strode out onto the terrace.

It would be so easy just to clear the table and leave him alone. But Blandine thought of Mira. At least for these few days, it had become Blandine's responsibility to stand in for his aunt. Mira would have been deeply troubled by the kind of person Alejo was becoming. So, carrying her wine glass for fortification, she joined Alejo on the terrace.

"Alejo. It's not true that I don't like you. But why don't I try to explain why your interview went badly. After all, you have another interview tomorrow, and you don't want the same thing to happen. Right?"

The boy took a long drag on his cigarette, gazing past her at the Queensboro Bridge lights glinting off the river. "Whatever...."

Ignoring his lack of interest, Blandine forged ahead. "You say you broke no laws. But that's not actually what diplomatic immunity means. Do you know why it exists?"

Alejo shook his head.

"Every country must have a way to communicate with every other country. That's how we try to avoid wars, by making sure that a head of state can look into the eyes of an ambassador to send important messages."

"Yeah, I know that."

"Good. I don't mean to talk down to you. But this is why diplomatic immunity is important. It exists to protect diplomats from the abuses of tyrants and dictators. Imagine that Dylan's father had been assigned to the embassy in Iraq under Saddam Hussein. What if Hussein hated Dylan's country and decided to harass his whole family, throwing them into jail on trumped up charges? If that could happen to a diplomat, then there would be no way to prevent war at all. That's why diplomatic immunity exists."

Alejo said nothing.

Blandine continued, "But here in New York, there are quite a lot of diplomats in a very crowded space. And diplomatic immunity is often used — some would say abused — just so that a person running late can get a free parking space."

Alejo laughed. "That's cool."

Blandine sighed again and took another drink of wine. In the streets below, a horn sounded impatiently. "Listen, Alejo. You want to understand why your interview went badly, right?"

"I guess."

"Well, here it is. When people — and I think particularly people your age — enjoy privileges that others can only dream of, they sometimes have a sense of entitlement. That means feeling that it's their birthright to have expensive things — the latest smartphone, or the money for tuition at an Ivy League university — and also to get away with things, without facing the same consequences that most people would have to face."

Alejo looked away, a sharp flick of his wrist aiming his cigarette ashes over the balcony railing.

Blandine flinched as a sudden breeze threatened to blow the ash toward her.

Buttoning her cardigan, she made herself count to ten in her mind so that she could be sure her voice would be calm when she continued. "This doesn't make you a bad person. Luckily, you and your friends didn't harm anyone. You were just trying to enjoy yourselves. But perhaps it would help if you tried to imagine things from other people's point of view."

Alejo laughed weakly. "Maybe cops need to do that too. I think we were actually helping them. For once, they got the experience of not having the law on their side."

A stronger gust of wind made Blandine shiver. "I'm going back inside now, but if you'd like dessert, I bought some pastries you might like."

9. A LANTERN

The day had finally come. It was October 17, the World Day for Overcoming Poverty. In the Bronx, Brenda Jones got a phone call from her mother. "Today is that event at the United Nations," Ernestine reminded her.

"Today? I don't think I can make it, Ma, I'm not feeling too well."

"Don't give me excuses. Don't you want to see Allan? He's going up on stage with the other children, he's been practicing real hard."

"I don't know..."

"Remember the commandments: honour thy father and thy mother. Now I'm not young anymore and if I'm going all that way into Manhattan, you can do it too, You come to 46th Street and First Avenue."

Helen

The night had been long for Helen Jansky. Although her body had waited until she was 60 for menopause to set in, her hot flashes were now severe. Two of them had woken her up in the night, leaving her drenched in sweat and feeling fragile and dizzy. She considered calling Pamela or Tanita to explain that she wouldn't be at the UN after all. But she had looked forward to this event. It made her angry to think that her own hormones might keep her away from it, so she made up her mind to go.

Pamela

For the second time in a few weeks, Pamela was preparing food with Ornella and Tanita's grandmother, Cheryl Brown. This time they had more help: Ornella had brought her husband's niece, Darleen; and Ernestine Jones too had insisted on coming early to help. As they prepared sandwiches to be served after the big event, Pamela frowned. "Now why is it that none of the men ever help us with the food?"

Ornella laughed. "Bite your tongue, child." She slathered a roll with mayonnaise. "I don't want Jesse in our kitchen; he'd only be stealing tastes of things."

"That's the truth," sighed Darleen. "It's the same with Dauntay and Tyrone. I have to keep them far away from the food if I want to make something nice without them digging in before it's even ready."

Varag

When Alejo emerged from the shower that morning, Varag handed him an invitation printed on heavy card-stock. "After your interview is over, come meet me in midtown."

"How come?" Alejo reached past Varag into the refrigerator to grab a cream tart from the previous night's dessert pastries.

"There's an event in the UN garden that I think you should see."

Alejo shrugged. "Sure, whatever," he said through a mouthful of oozing custard.

Ahmed

A few blocks away from the UN, Jesse told Ahmed, "I need to stop at the bank first. Don't worry, we have plenty of time." Seeing a line at the ATM, Jesse took Ahmed into the bank lobby and gestured toward an empty armchair. "Just have a seat. I won't be long."

Sinking into a thick leather cushion, Ahmed looked around. Among those already using ATMs was a natty elderly gentleman in a motorized wheelchair. While several ATMs had screens too high for him, the one he was using was at the appropriate height. When he had finished, the bank doors slid open automatically to make way for him. Watching him effortlessly navigate along his way, Ahmed thought of the grueling efforts it took at home for people with disabilities to get around. Even those who could afford a wheelchair needed such strong arms to be able to make their way over rough unpaved terrain.

A pair of young men, both wearing torn jeans and sweatshirts, had just finished meeting with a banker. As Ahmed marvelled at the casualness of their clothing for such a formal occasion, the men surprised him even more by holding hands with each other. Then one of them helped himself to a bright blue lollipop from a glass jar as the couple left the bank.

"All set." Jesse had finished with the ATM.

Ahmed was about to tell Jesse what he had seen when his attention was caught by a dainty Yorkshire terrier. Clad in a distinctive houndstooth sweater, the dog led its owner from the entry vestibule toward a counter inside the bank itself. As the dog sat below the counter gazing up, its owner — a well-dressed woman in her fifties — reached into another glass jar to take a dog bone for her pet.

Sprinting now to catch up with Jesse, Ahmed decided that it would take a very long time indeed for him to understand a startling country like the United States.

Tanita

Ahmed and Tanita had been up half the night practicing their speech, but Tanita was too keyed up to feel tired. In the morning, she met Helen outside the gates of the United Nations. Staring up at the long row of world flags, Tanita felt dazed that the big day was here at last. "So many countries in just one building," she sighed. "I just love seeing all the flags."

"There are certainly a lot of them," Helen said, rubbing the back of her own neck and wishing she felt more energetic. "I suppose this is where the world can come together. Or it can try, anyway." Turning from the flags to look at Tanita, Helen asked, "How are you feeling about today?"

Tanita sighed. "Honestly? I don't even know. I should be tired because we were up late. But instead I feel like there's electric shocks going through me."

Helen smiled wanly. "I didn't sleep well and I *am* tired. I could use some of your electric shocks. But I know how that can feel — and I know you too. I don't think it's stage fright, I think it's adrenaline. You know, the way athletes feel before a race?" As Helen spoke, she and Tanita joined the long line to go through security, behind a chattering group of students on a field trip. "All of us are so proud of you."

"Thank you, but you're not the one I'm scared of. I already know you. But these UN people — we have nothing in common. What if what I say doesn't make any sense to them?"

Helen thought for a moment. "Listen, Tanita. Years ago, I remember watching a comedian do a routine. He was poking fun at a rich televangelist's wife for donating make-up to poor women."

As the line inched forward, Helen admitted, "I laughed, right along with everyone in the audience. But the more I thought about it, the more I wished I hadn't laughed."

"How come?"

"The whole reason the joke was supposed to be funny was that many people can't imagine why a woman in poverty would worry about make-up when paying for groceries and rent might be more urgent concerns for her. Make-up sounds like a luxury. But doesn't everyone deserve some luxury in life?"

"I think make-up helps women get jobs," Tanita said.

"Yes, and why shouldn't any woman be able to look her best, whether to get a job, or just to feel in a good mood while caring for her family?"

"True. No one wants to look skanky."

"Exactly. But it took me time to realize that a joke I'd already laughed at wasn't actually funny. And it's possible that some of the people who hear you speak today might need that time too. They might listen, but not really get it — and you never know, they just might keep on thinking about it in the future."

By now, Tanita and Helen had both been cleared by security. There was an hour left to wait before the event began. "I promised Pamela I would help organize the chairs and the guest book in the garden," Helen told Tanita, "but you can wait indoors. There are always a few exhibits on display you that might want to see."

As they walked into the lobby, Tanita happened to glance to the right where a large panel of stained glass was almost hidden in a dim alcove. "What's that?" she asked, leading Helen toward the panel.

"It's by an artist named Chagall who grew up in Russia in the late 1800s. His father worked carrying barrels for a fishmonger, and Chagall said he often put fish in his artwork out of respect for how hard his father worked."

"Funny, I don't see fish in this one. But look, there's flowers and children... and is that an angel?"

"I think so. This is called 'Peace and Human Happiness.' I don't know why it was installed in such an out-of-the-way corner. There's hardly enough light behind it, but it's very beautiful." Glancing at her watch, Helen said, "I'd better set up that guest book. See you in a little while."

As Helen hurried back outside, Tanita remained before the stained-glass window, letting its deep blue colors wash over her. She was drawn to a couple, clutching a baby together while gazing into each other's eyes with a trusting kind of love. Hidden or not, Tanita decided that this was exactly the right kind of artwork for a day about ending poverty.

Yun Hee

Finally, Yun Hee had got permission for all the children involved in the skit to miss school for this event. Even armed with signed notes from every parent and a beautiful programme with the UN logo showing what the children's role would be, it had been an uphill battle for their school to agree. The office staff seemed annoyed that she kept bothering them.

The principal had said, "You know, we have some very good students here who could better afford to miss class. What do you want with the kids who will probably be left back again next year?"

Yun Hee knew that this whole underfunded school had been issued a failing grade by the Board of Education for two years in a row now and might be shut down entirely in a year. Still, she was hard pressed to feel empathy for a principal so quickly resigned to the prospect of these children's failure. It took every last ounce of her patience to remain polite while insisting that these were exactly the children that international diplomats needed to meet. And yet, even as she made her case, she had remained a little doubtful herself whether these particular children could keep their composure under pressure.

So when Yun Hee was picking up the children that morning, she couldn't believe her eyes when she saw Tyrone. Ready in a freshly ironed shirt and slacks, he stood with perfect posture, his head held high, grinning from ear to ear. Yun Hee had brought extra copies of all the children's lines for the skit, but Tyrone had his own copy already in his hand. "I been practicing," he told her proudly, strutting down the stairwell carefully to keep his clothes neat. Long before they even reached the sidewalk, Yun Hee began snapping photos of him. She couldn't wait to show them to the principal.

Then Yun Hee did a double-take. She had been glad to see that Shaniqua, Lissa, and Ashanti — Tyrone's three younger sisters — were dressed and ready as well. But why was 15-year-old Makayla with them? Although not much older than Montrell, she had dismissed their skit as "babyish" so Yun Hee had not written a letter requesting that she be allowed to miss school.

But when she asked Darleen Walker, their mother's response was simply, "Why can't she come too? I want her to see the show."

Yun Hee wanted to object, but the school day had already begun, and she wasn't comfortable criticizing a mother in front of her children for a parenting decision. So Makayla took the subway to Manhattan with them.

On arriving at the UN garden with the Walker family, Yun Hee saw Dawn. Once again, Travis was off working, so to avoid leaving Dawn at loose ends, he had urged her to meet up with Yun Hee. She tried to introduce the children: "Say hello to Mrs. Pruitt. She's a friend who's visiting New York this week." Lissa, however, was the only one to make the greeting. Makayla had already spotted Jesse and gone over to talk to him. The other children were scampering across the lawn, relieved at being outdoors after the long subway trip.

Seeing Yun Hee's embarrassment, Dawn shrugged it off. "Don't you fret. I know how skittish kids can be."

Admiring Yun Hee's flared dress with a cabbage-rose print, Dawn added, "You look cute as a button, all gussied up today."

"Thank you. And I like your jacket," Yun Hee said uncomfortably. The busy geometric pattern of greens and browns on Dawn's blazer did not actually appeal to her, but Dawn had clearly made an effort to look her best.

Yun Hee knew she needed to settle the children down to prepare them. But she felt bad leaving Dawn alone. Seeing Helen Jansky spread a tablecloth over a folding table, Yun Hee decided to introduce her to Dawn.

"Nice to meet you," Helen said briskly.

"I actually need to round up the kids," Yun Hee said. "Maybe Dawn could help you set things up?"

"Sure," Helen said. "Are you handy with masking tape? We want to stick some construction paper underneath the seat of every folding chair."

Blandine

As Blandine was finishing up a draft of a statement on development, a text message from Varag popped up on her telephone: "Meet me in the garden for Pamela's event?"

Since it was noon, Blandine decided she could reasonably slip out of the office for an hour. It felt strange to be going toward the UN garden. It had once been a lovely place for a lunchtime walk, but since 9/11 security measures had kept it closed almost continuously to the public, and even to most UN staff. Today, the metal barrier was ajar and a guard was checking people's names against a list.

In the security tent, Blandine's diplomatic ID card always allowed her to sweep by the long lines of tourists. However, today she hesitated to do so. Remembering her words to Alejo about diplomatic entitlement, Blandine decided for once to wait her turn. In front of her was a heavy-set Hispanic woman with four boys. "My name is Ramirez — Carmen Ramirez," the woman told the guard. "I must be on your list. I know Pamela wouldn't forget me, not today of all days."

"Please open your bag, ma'am."

Still talking, Carmen began unzipping a frayed and stained backpack. A paper clip had been threaded through the broken zipper pull, and it opened slowly, catching several times.

"Thank you. Yes, you are on the list. The young children are fine, but what's your older son's name?"

"This here's Montrell. All the kids had better be on that list too. They're a part of the show; they been practicing time and again —."

By now, the guard was satisfied and waved Carmen's family through, adding, "No running!" as Johnny and his brothers began racing each other down the stairs into the garden.

Following them, midway down the garden path Blandine saw a table set up with a display of programmes, a guest book, and a pile of shapes cut from construction paper. Were they meant to be teardrops? As she approached the table, a young black man leaned toward her, holding a programme in her face: "Here, take one." Blandine was startled. His baggy jeans and the way he wore his jacket made her think of the words "gangsta rap" without even being completely sure what that meant. He was so close to her that she could smell his sweat. Had they been anywhere else, Blandine knew that she would have turned to get away from him. But she could see Varag over by the folding chairs with Alejo in tow — how had he managed that? — and so she simply took the programme and signed the guest book.

As Blandine turned away from the table to head towards Varag and Alejo, she almost bumped into a young black woman wearing dangling earrings and a lacy beige sweater over tight jeans and boots.

"Hey, Ms. Dulavar!" said the woman whose short hair was freshly curled. "I didn't know you'd be here too."

Blandine's mind reeled. It took her a long moment to realize that this well-dressed, smiling person was Sharmaine, whom Blandine had only ever seen wearing frayed T-shirts and a worn scarf knotted over her hair. Although Blandine was never at a loss when meeting people at receptions, now she had to rack her brains for some kind of small talk. Had she ever spoken to Sharmaine about anything other than furniture polish and recycling newspapers? What would Varag say to her?

Suddenly, Blandine realized that Varag had never met Sharmaine because he was invariably at work when she came. As Varag strode over to join them, Blandine began imagining how inappropriate her introduction could be. She might say, "Darling, this is Sharmaine, who does such a good job waxing our hallway floor." Or perhaps, "Sharmaine, this is my husband, whose dirty socks you always find under the bed."

Instead, she remained silent as Varag put his arm around her. "Are you alright, Blandine? You look pale."

"Oh, she's just surprised to see me here," Sharmaine said calmly. "I'm her housekeeper."

"Really? Then I should thank you for your excellent work because I'm Blandine's messy husband. So, how did you get involved with All Together in Dignity?"

"My kids and nephew go to the art workshops they do in the street. They just love it so much that now they've even got my mother going to their meetings."

"Do you go too?"

"Naw, I don't have time for meetings. But I really want to see the kids perform today, and I just got fired from one of my regular jobs so I had time to come."

"Fired?" Blandine asked, startled out of her awkward silence. "But why?"

"The lady said she'd rather hire a man who can lift more furniture. I don't know what she's talking about. Who does she think has been vacuuming under her couch for three years now? Anyway, if you know someone looking for a cleaning lady, would you let me know?"

A boy ran up to them. "Can I have some gum, Aunt Sharmaine?"

"Not now, Allan. Look, Yun Hee's already getting the other kids ready for the show. You'd better get going." He ran off.

"Is that your son?" Varag asked.

"No, my nephew."

"Blandine has a nephew about the same age."

"Oh, we hardly ever see him," objected Blandine. "His family lives in Thailand."

"Thailand!" This caught Alejo's attention. "Oh man, I'd love to do the river tubing there. There's this amazing 'death slide' for tubers in Laos."

Wondering if he realized he was conflating two different countries, Blandine put her hand to her forehead. She hoped she would not get a migraine.

Ignoring Alejo, Sharmaine gently asked Blandine, "Why does your family live so far away?"

"My brother works for the UN Development Programme."

"You must miss seeing his kids grow up. I live with Allan, so I never have time to miss him."

"Do you have a big family?"

"I have two children: Little Willy, over there in the blue shirt. And Sheray is the one in all the stripes."

"What a pretty hairdo she has." Sheray's hair was in two puff ponytails atop her head, crowned by a bright red headband.

Hearing her mother point her out, Sheray raced up to them. Pointing proudly to the array of bright colors on her shirt, she shouted, "Check out the rainbow," and then ran back to Yun Hee as her mother laughed.

Brenda

A few feet away, Ernestine Jones greeted Sharmaine's sister, Brenda, with a warm hug. "You made it. It's so good to see you. Oh, and I have the papers." She began digging into her pocketbook for the custody papers Pamela had given her. "I know they're in here somewhere."

Brenda frowned. "Ma, you know, I'm in a programme. I'm getting clean. What if Allan comes to live with me again instead?"

Abandoning the search through her handbag, Ernestine drew a deep breath and looked her daughter in the eyes. "Of course, I'd love for you to live with Allan again. You're his mother. All I wanted was to be able to take care of him properly for as long as you needed me to."

Ernestine hesitated. As much as she longed for her daughter to be the one raising Allan, she was afraid. The demons of addiction were so powerful. What would things be like for Allan if Brenda couldn't hold out against them? Then she said, "I tell you what. Why don't you come to live with all of us instead?

Allan likes the neighbourhood, and I think he'd miss Sheray and Little Willy if he moved to the Bronx now."

"I don't know, Ma..." Brenda was twisting her hands. "Let me think about it for a while."

Helen

Dawn's straightforward efficiency had ensured that the tasks assigned to Helen were all completed in time. As guests arrived, they distributed programmes and invited each one to sign the guest book. During lulls between arrivals, Helen tried to make small talk, asking Dawn about her sightseeing around New York.

"My brother has really gone all out to show me a good time. We took that there cable car over the river," Dawn said, pointing a few blocks uptown.

"Oh, the one that goes to Roosevelt Island."

"Yes, and from the Spiderman movie. My husband will be green with envy. And we went to see a show too."

"Which one?"

"The Lion King. I just don't know how they thought up those costumes, but they sure knock your socks off. Seeing the show was my brother's birthday gift to me."

"I haven't seen it myself, but it certainly has wonderful reviews. A lot of visitors enjoy shopping in New York too. Have you shopped too?"

"Oh, of course. It was a group of my friends who paid for my trip, so naturally I need to find good souvenirs to bring back to all of them."

"Have you found things they would like?"

"There are some pretty souvenirs near my hotel — but they do cost an arm and a leg. So my brother took me down to Chinatown instead."

"Yes, it's much cheaper to shop there."

"Sure, but even there, some of the storekeepers are cheap as dirt. You have to look out not to pay the first price they ask. But Travis is good at jewing down the prices, so eventually I got gifts for everyone on my list."

Helen's full attention was on Dawn now. "Did you say he 'jewed' down the prices?"

"Sure, they let you bargain in Chinatown."

"You know, I'm Jewish." Queasily, Helen's thoughts flashed back to the bullies of her childhood calling her father a "dirty kike."

Dawn did a double take. "No. I didn't know that."

Helen felt nauseous. Rubbing the back of her neck again, she hoped she was not going to have a hot flash.

Dawn swallowed awkwardly. "I didn't mean to hurt your feelings. Where I come from, it's just an expression."

Helen snapped, "Many expressions have bigoted origins. That use of the word 'Jew' is derived from an ugly stereotype."

"Well, I already apologized. You don't need to fly off the handle like that and talk to me like I'm stupid." Tears welling in her eyes, Dawn turned away and crossed the lawn to take a seat.

Too late, Helen realized how harsh her words had been. Should she be the one to apologize to Dawn now? But there was no time. Pamela was coming over to take her place at the guest book, and cueing Helen to begin emceeing the event.

Wishing she had stayed in bed after all, Helen walked to the podium. As she called on everyone to take a seat, a small youth choir began singing,

> "Oh-oh freedom,
> oh-oh freedom...
> Before I'll be a slave,
> I'll be buried in my grave,
> and go home to my Lord, and be free."

Blandine

Varag steered Alejo by the elbow down a row of chairs, and Blandine followed them. As many voices in the crowd joined in with the choir, Blandine remembered once having listened to the same song at a coffeehouse gospel concert with Mira. "...Buried in my grave..." There was no grave site for Mira; her ashes had disappeared on the wind. Did she feel as much freedom in death as she had in life?

"Look," Varag whispered. "That's Tanita. You remember, we met her at the German reception?"

"She's hot," Alejo said, appreciatively sizing up Tanita who was wearing the same bottle-green dress as on the night of the reception, this time with oversized hoop earrings.

"She's been working very hard to prepare for this," Varag said, still in a whisper, but more sternly. "I met with her and Pamela when she was preparing, but I don't know if that was much help."

Tanita and Ahmed

Hearing Helen introduce her, Tanita felt the pit of her stomach plummeting. What was she doing here? She fixed her eyes on her grandmother in the front row.

Next to her, Ahmed drew his shoulders ramrod straight against his suit. Jesse had told him that some people at the UN wore dashikis, tunics, and other traditional African clothing, but being in New York made Ahmed want to blend into the crowd of western suits. He touched a hand to the knot in his tie to be sure it was properly in place.

As they stepped up to the podium together to begin, Tanita tried to forget the impressively dressed strangers in front of her and to think only of the people she was speaking for.

"Sometimes we feel that people look down on us." Tanita heard her own voice echo uncertainly in the microphone. Clearing her throat, she tried to speak more steadily, "If you look a certain way, people put you in a category. If you talk a certain way, people put you in a category. If you don't have a job, if you don't have a home, people put you in a category."

Now Ahmed spoke, his accent crisp and musical, "People should not forget that tomorrow they might not have good health, a job, or a home. Now they take it for granted, but tomorrow, they never know.

"We do know what it is like to live from day to day.

"We know what it is to have our dreams and aspirations halted, while we have to scrounge around just to get by.

"We know what it is to sleep in marketplaces, in subways, in parks, in unsafe shelters.

"We know what it is to feel useless, to feel that we're no fraction of anything positive, to be looked at as being lazy, to feel shame coming down on us.

"We know what it is to have others decide whether we are successful or not, to have others believe that we don't want to get out of poverty."

Tanita continued, "We know what it's like to have others assume that we're scheming and scamming and that we just can't be trusted.

"We know what it's like to be unable to walk down the block without having the evil of crack cocaine pushed at us.

"We know what it's like to have others make us feel like we've died, to feel invisible and voiceless. 'Take a bath,' they say — but they don't offer the use of their bathroom. 'Get a job,' they say — but no one wants to hire someone who's tired, someone who's hungry, someone who's afflicted.

"I would like to better myself, to have more strength, to be closer to God. But people in this world have so much hatred. Go ask the homeless in the streets about hatred. Look at the panhandlers. They see hatred in people's eyes all day long. Go to the streets where anything goes down in broad daylight, the streets where drug dealers and pimps have free rein to wreck people's lives, right in front of the kids, and you can learn about hatred."

"Then," said Ahmed, "look at what people do to find peace of mind. Look how hard people work for survival, finding shelter, carrying whatever they own in the world, crossing a city on foot to find a job or a meal. Faith is something we try to hold onto, even if it doesn't put food on the table. Without faith, we have only despair, envy, and desperate acts. Without faith, we have only blame. And as much as I sometimes do want to blame everyone for the evils of poverty, blame does not heal any of us. We can blame one another, and we can blame ourselves year after year, until the sky turns silver — but blame won't ever protect our children."

"We need to have faith — faith in God or at least faith in one another." Tanita took a deep breath. "But even when we manage to hold on to faith, and even after all the efforts people make to survive, we don't find places where we can express ourselves, where we can participate and make choices. Instead, we're just shuttled back and forth from shelter to job center, depending when each service is open. We have to be quick and say nothing, as though all the misery in the world is our fault and nothing will ever change.

"Sometimes people who are stronger try to demand respect by refusing to take shabby clothing, refusing to have their dignity trampled on. But when they do, they are told that beggars can't be choosers, that they should be grateful even for hand-outs of clothing that is old and stained and torn. They should be grateful for the chance to stay in a shelter filled with violence, a shelter that could turn their own children against them.

"Faith is something we try to hold onto.

"But for us to have peace of mind, we need a home with food on the table, we need to be treated like others.

"For us to have peace of mind, our children need teachers who believe in them. They need the opportunity to know the joys of painting, of dancing, of learning, of finding their hidden talents so they will know what they might be able to make of themselves one day.

"And we need that peace of mind and that faith in one another to be able to draw strength from times of tribulation and struggle."

Tanita looked at Ahmed. The scariest part was coming up. He retrieved a small bongo drum from the side of the stage. Sinking onto a stool, he wedged the drum between his knees and began to beat out a slow rhythm with one hand. In the other hand, he clutched his copy of the words they had written. Now they spoke in shorter turns, rapping out the end of their message. Tanita began:

There are people you shun,
the banks in collusion —
Where's the solution?

    The world's in a bind,
    the rich are wined and dined,

and getting their shoes shined.
But the poor can never find
the slightest peace of mind.

When will injustice end?
So many people want to lend
a hand; they want to mend
what's wrong; they want to send
a song to say:

> 'Hey, no need to be hateful
> and it's not about acting grateful
> for being told what to do.
> Instead, let's try something new.'

If we get to know one another,
reach out as sisters and brothers,
that's a way to change the future.

> It's a tall order — you sure?

We won't end poverty overnight,
but this cause is worth a fight.
No matter how empty my purse,
someone else is doing worse.
It's about the whole community,
reach around the world, every city.

> Unless we include everyone
> Our work will never be done.

Today, we honour unmarked graves.
Today, we make a vow to save:
all the people the world forgot,
whose potential must not rot,
girls and women whose steps leave no trace,
a kid treated like a 'social case,'

a dad afraid to show his face
cause he found no work no place.

All people on this earth
deserve a sense of worth.
We can do so much more
together — let's open the door.

People applauded as Ahmed and Tanita stepped down from the podium, both of them letting out a sigh of relief that they had said what they wanted to say. Helen invited everyone to observe a moment of silence.

Blandine

When the silence ended with the choir singing "We Who Believe in Freedom Cannot Rest," Blandine was startled to hear Jean-Christian's abrupt voice. Seated just behind her, he was leaning forward to talk to her in a voice just barely lowered beneath the melody.

"Aren't they done yet?" Jean-Christian fumed, looking at his watch. "I can't see why the ambassador insisted I attend this time-wasting event. The homeless are just too lazy to work. They refuse to become part of society."

Uncomfortable, Blandine wondered where Sharmaine was sitting and who had heard Jean-Christian. Not sure how to respond, she simply frowned and shushed him. Now children were swarming onto the podium and she had no intention of looking like a rude spectator.

Montrell stood on the podium holding a lantern. The flame inside it, made out of coloured cardboard, was very small. "This is the lantern of hope. It's my job to keep the lantern lit, but the wind is so strong that I'm afraid the flame will go out."

The younger children, their shoulders covered by capes of pale grey with dark grey clouds of felt stitched onto them, began circling Montrell and giving reasons why it was hard to keep their hopes up.

"When people who don't live near us come into our neighbourhood, they see the bad things."

"Then they look at us in a certain way."

"What's hard is not just being poor, it's also when people look at us and don't smile."

"It's not fair when people call names and start fights."

"It's not fair when your family has no place to go."

"It's not fair when you don't get a chance."

"It's not fair when you have no friends."

As they circled, Montrell knelt lower and lower, sinking to his knees. Hesitant, Allan looked anxiously off stage at Yun Hee, who smiled and prompted him by miming his next move.

Leaving the circle, Allan now pushed the sides of his cape back over his shoulders, showing the outline of a yellow candle on his shirt. "The most true face is the face of a grown-up who is smiling," he called out. One by one, the others too, turned back their capes showing candles.

"I believe in peace."

"I believe in friendship."

Cedric frowned as the felt candle almost came unstuck from his shirt, but he remembered his line, "I believe in freedom." Relieved he hadn't forgotten it, he decided to add, "I believe in trains too!"

Some of the audience laughed at that, but Lissa ignored them, stepping up to the microphone for her turn: "I believe I can learn in school."

"I believe all children should have the same chances."

"I dream of being a shooting star like all the stars."

"I dream of being a beautiful colour like all the colours."

"I dream of being a bird, a messenger of joy."

Behind them, Montrell drew himself up to his full height as they spoke, lifting high above his head the lantern, now lit with a large cardboard flame. "The lantern of hope is burning strong. Together, we can be the friends of all the children in the world."

Yun Hee joined the children on stage with her guitar and together they sang:

"All of us need love to grow

and learn the things we need to know
A chance to say what's true.
Kids all need equality, so treat us all respectfully
And we'll respect you too.

Every child should have a chance to draw
And write down all her most important thoughts.
Every child should have a chance to play guitar
A chance to look outside and see the stars.
Children should feel good about themselves,
Not wish that they were someone else,
not someone else.
Every child should have a chance to play each day
A chance to pray, in their own way..."

When the song was over, Helen came to the microphone again and invited all the guests to look under the seats of their folding chairs where more candle flames made of yellow construction paper were scotch-taped. "Before you leave, we'd like you to write your own messages of hope on these flames. Then please share them with us by adding them to the lantern of hope."

Brenda

Allan had already run up to hug Brenda, who was standing in the back, smoking a cigarette. "Mom! Did you see me, Mom? I didn't mess up. Did you see me?"

"You looked so big up there." She grinned down at him, and added with a catch in her voice, "You're growing up so fast."

Blandine

As people milled about, Blandine went to add her paper flame to the lantern. Varag appeared at her shoulder. "What did you write?"

Turning the paper over, she showed him her neat script: "From the poetry and magic of children comes hope."

10. BELONGING

With the stress and formality of the event behind them, the members of All Together in Dignity headed across the street to a room where Jesse and a few college students had set up refreshments. Blandine had rushed back to work, like most of the UN and embassy staff. Varag, however, had agreed to join Pamela and the others. When Alejo heard there would be snacks, he was glad to tag along. Yun Hee urged Dawn to join them as well.

Seeing Dawn join the group, Helen Jansky told Pamela, "I'm sorry, but I need to get going now."

Pamela frowned. "But why?" Noticing the tired and unhappy look on Helen's face, she added, "It was so lovely of you to be our compere today."

Puzzled, Helen asked, "Your what?"

"Oh, I forgot. Here, you say master of ceremonies. It was terribly helpful of you to do it. I know that our members are comfortable with you, and the UN officials are as well. You've worked hard, so now you could do with us pampering you for a bit."

"But there's one person I've made very <u>un</u>comfortable," Helen confessed. "Yun Hee asked me to make her friend welcome, but I ended up embarrassing the poor woman. So I think I ought to let her alone."

"No wonder you look so sad. But if it were me who felt beastly, would you let me just slip away? I know you; you'll only feel worse if you don't patch things up. Please, do come." Taking Helen by the elbow, Pamela steered her firmly across the street.

As their group approached an uninspiring building on 44th Street, Ahmed read its name aloud, "The Church Center for the United Nations. Is this a church?"

"Not exactly," Pamela answered, "although there is a chapel in the building that's used for prayer services. But most of the building is offices and meeting rooms used by non-profit organizations like ours." Holding the door open for their whole group to enter the lobby, Pamela continued her explanation to Ahmed: "The meeting spaces are mostly used by non-governmental organization committees. They include groups of different religions, and also groups that are not at all religious."

As they rode an elevator upstairs, Ahmed asked, "What are the meetings about?"

"All sorts of topics: human rights, protecting the environment, economic justice, and so on. Some of the groups that rent permanent space here are Christian, and others are universities or secular NGOs."

By now they had entered a room where Darleen Walker and Jesse were trying to make sure that each child got a plastic cup of juice and a sandwich, and that nothing got spilled. Darleen, overhearing Pamela, jumped into the conversation. "I was raised to be a Christian. My mother was from the South, and it's just what you do. You get up and go to church on Sunday. But when the tithing at church goes to pay for a fancy new car for the preacher, I draw the line. It's hard enough to make ends meet. His car ain't what I'm working for."

Tanita's grandmother had settled with her styrofoam cup of sweet, milky coffee into a chair with some cushioning, more comfortable than the folding chairs had been on the UN lawn. She said, "What I don't hold with is every different church telling me they're better than the next one. It's like hearing commercials for Coke or Pepsi! A church ought to tell me what they do to stand by folk who are in trouble."

"It's God who stands by folk," declared Ernestine Jones.

"That may be," put in Tanita, "but it's people who can use religion to divide us all up into categories. There's rich and poor categories where you have the people who always sit up front in church because they can make big donations and get their names written on the pews, while others are always in the back."

"I hear you," Darleen responded.

Tanita continued. "And there's the categories of which religion you join or not. One of the ladies I work with is always trying to convert me, telling me that Cedric won't be saved unless I bring him to her church. She makes me crazy. You can't talk to her about anything else."

Pamela pulled a chair over to their circle and settled Helen into it. After taking a deep breath to smell the cup of milky tea handed to her, Helen spoke up, "People getting pressured to convert is something I worry about too. In a number of prisons, the government has started funding religious programmes geared to help prisoners fit into the community after they've served their time. That's an important goal — but the programmes are very much based on Jesus and the Christian gospel."

Varag frowned. "Do they require participation?"

Glaring at Helen, Dawn spoke up. "Of course not! They're doing the Lord's work — but even when you lead a horse to water, you can't force him to drink it."

"That's true," Helen admitted. "They don't require it. But I've heard a Muslim prisoner say he joined a Christian programme because he was afraid that if he didn't, he wouldn't be released on parole. How can people feel free to choose whether to convert when they are in prison and a programme like this seems like their only chance for early release?"

"That's a good question," Varag said. "So why doesn't the government fund similar programmes for prisoners who may not want to convert to Christianity?"

"I am a Muslim," said Ahmed, "but I don't think God wants us in different categories, whatever our religions. Practicing any religion is a way of being part of a community and reaching out to one another."

Ernestine Jones said, "Not everyone believes in God, but people who don't believe have to have a powerful, powerful mind. God is the only one who can help you start over again when you have a millstone around your neck. He's the only one with you when you get thrown in jail. God is the only one who can help you get off drugs."

"What about our children?" asked Luis Marquez. "If I didn't have my son Alonzo to think about, I could be a crackhead right now."

Ernestine looked at Allan. Holding a granola bar, he was licking it slowly to make it last. Thinking of Brenda, who had left the UN immediately after the event, Ernestine sighed and said, "With or without children, anyone can get hooked on drugs. A lot of people want to stop but can't."

"What's the big deal about drugs?" Alejo asked. "Everyone should be free to enjoy themselves."

Laughter rang out from Makayla, who turned a flirtatious face toward him. "That would sure make a day like this less boring."

Dawn turned her sternest Sunday school teacher look at Alejo. "At your age, it's time you learned to outsmart the devil. You should be praying to fall not into temptation."

Ernestine also turned toward Alejo. Speaking more gently than Dawn, she tried to explain. "When you're living in some raggedy, torn-out building, you might be trying to find a better life, but nobody wants to try to help you get out. You can get hurt. And when a person gets hurt bad enough, help can come too late, the hurt is already in you. Then you think that drinking or drugs will blank that hurt out." Ernestine paused, remembering all the times she had wished that her daughter could resist temptation. "It's easy to think that drugs will help. You figure when you get high, your problems will be gone — but once that high is gone, the problems are still there, the hurt is still in you."

"The good book says that's when you've given in to Satan," Dawn said.

Turning to her, Ernestine pleaded, "I don't want to hear anyone putting others down for using drugs or alcohol. Once a person goes down that road of addiction, it takes a mighty powerful mind to stop."

Listening to her mother, Sharmaine bent over her chair to give her a hug. Then Sharmaine turned to Ahmed. "I want to thank you for what you said today about people who are forgotten in unmarked graves. A neighbor of ours died like that last year, forgotten. When she died, her two younger children were put into foster care because there were no relatives who could take them in."

"That's right, Ernestine added. "Her oldest girl was 17 and raising her own baby. She was the one who should have tried to figure out something for a funeral."

"Why didn't her church help out?" Dawn wanted to know.

"I'm sure they would have," Sharmaine answered. "But the daughter was grieving and she wasn't used to that heavy responsibility."

"She was just blocking it out of her mind," Ernestine said. "So by the time she even thought to ask the hospital for her mother's body, a month had gone by. That meant it was too late. The body was unclaimed. It went to a medical school."

Carmen Ramirez shook her head with sorrow, "That poor lady. Her daughter must feel just awful. That's when a priest should have helped. You don't just wait for that poor girl to figure out what she has to do."

"Someone should have stepped in to help her," Darleen said.

"But that's the problem nowadays," Carmen said. "Our young people don't go to church the way we did growing up. The priests don't even know them. And how can we protect our kids without the church?"

"Churches just can't compete," said Darleen. "The streets are speaking to our kids loud and clear." Giving Makayla a stern look, she continued, "No matter how we raise them, violence is waiting at every corner. How do we expect religion to compete with that? But what helps my kids is the art workshop. It's right out there on the street where we live. They don't have to look for it. And I hear how Jesse and Yun Hee talk to our kids. They want them to be their own person and to believe in themselves. Maybe getting confidence can keep our kids away from gangs."

For the first time, Helen beamed, "We sure saw that confidence today. Every one of your children was amazing on stage. They added beauty to the world. Coming to the UN, we're trying to make a connection between two worlds that don't know each other, worlds that don't know how to talk to each other. And I think the children made that connection —" Breaking off, Helen looked again at Dawn. Were they also from two different worlds? Perhaps Dawn had never before met anyone Jewish.

And, come to think of it, Helen wasn't sure that she had ever before met anyone from West Virginia.

"Worlds that don't know how to talk to each other... That is so true," said Sharmaine. "One of the ladies I clean for was there. And she had absolutely no idea what to say to me — oh!" Awkwardly, Sharmaine turned to Varag. "I know she's your wife. But I didn't mean no disrespect. It just felt strange, that's all."

"It's alright," Varag said, glad that Alejo had already slipped outside for a cigarette. It was certainly better for Blandine's peace of mind that Alejo not realize how disarmed she must have felt.

"You mean Blandine Dulavoir?" Pamela asked Sharmaine. "I saw you two talking and I did wonder how you knew each other because you weren't with us the day she came to our meeting in September."

"Do you mean that same UN lady who came to meet us is your boss?" asked Darleen. "I thought she was a real phony."

Now Pamela looked uncomfortably at Varag. To her surprise, he looked amused.

"What did she say at the meeting?" Sharmaine wanted to know.

"I don't remember her saying a single word," Cheryl Brown said. "She's a real quiet lady."

Pamela explained to Varag, "The reason Darleen was upset is that Blandine left our meeting before it was really over. But to be frank, we had got pretty far off topic. Everyone was talking at once. I think she must have felt uncomfortable. After all, we all knew one another pretty well already, but she had never met any of us before."

Susana Montoya spoke up, "But she did come again today." She looked at Varag, "She brought you there too."

"Actually, I brought *her*," Varag murmured to Pamela.

Susana continued, "And there we were, all together. Rich or poor, we sat down just like it didn't matter. People from all over the world, and we were kind of — well, I guess we were comfortable together. I'm not saying it right. But I can't think of another time when I've felt like that."

"Amen," Ernestine Jones agreed heartily. "And look at you two!" She turned to Tanita and Ahmed. "Amazing! You said things I wish I knew how to say. And saying them right out there, in front of all those fancy folks. Just amazing."

"They sure was," Darleen chimed in. "We might all be different, here and in Africa, but today we were just the same. All just trying to make things better."

"Today was special," said Cheryl Brown.

"Could you tell us why you say that?" Pamela asked.

Mrs. Brown took a moment to think, looking at Ernestine Jones. "I think people often feel empty inside. We might not even know why." Twisting her hands in her lap, she continued, "We have to fill that emptiness."

"How?" Varag asked.

"Well, it could be by singing your heart out like that choir today. Or it could be just by scrubbing dishes to get them sparkling clean. I think when we come together like this, it helps to fill whatever feels empty."

"I'm so glad we're here today," Susana said. "I think you're all beautiful people."

"We sure are! Check out the rainbow," called Sheray as the grown-ups burst into laughter.

Coming back from the restroom, Yun Hee realized that Makayla was no longer with the group. Feeling responsible for her, Yun Hee went downstairs to the sidewalk where she found Makayla and Alejo smoking cigarettes. His eyes hidden behind sunglasses, Alejo looked effortlessly nonchalant.

"Makayla, what are you doing? You're not even old enough to be smoking." Yun Hee wrinkled her nose at the smell.

Makayla blew a smoke ring and glared at Yun Hee, "I don't want to sit around inside anymore. This whole thing is just whack."

Blinking away the smoke, Yun Hee said, "Come on. Your teacher won't like that you skipped school. You should at least pay attention so you can learn something."

"You're not my mom. Why do you always have to be such a bitch?"

Feeling as though she had been slapped, Yun Hee turned away, only to see Dawn on the sidewalk behind her.

"I got a call from Travis. He's just filed his story, so we're going to meet for coffee."

As Dawn left, Yun Hee ducked back into the building wishing that she were anywhere else in the world.

Blandine and Varag

For Alejo's last night in New York, Varag and Blandine invited Octavia to join them for dinner. Sinking back into a distressed-leather armchair, Varag cradled a glass of refreshingly bitter aperitif in his hand. For Octavia, Alejo, and herself, Blandine prepared kir cocktails, pouring out splashes of sweet blackcurrant liqueur to which she added white wine.

Because it was a school night, Octavia explained, she had left the children with a babysitter but she brought their greetings to Alejo. "They are sorry to miss their cousin's visit, but the school year is too busy. We'll spend time with you at Thanksgiving."

Alejo frowned, "I don't know about that. I think my mom is canceling the whole holiday this year." Returning from the kitchen, Blandine passed around hors d'oeuvres of cheese-flavoured puff pastry gougères, fresh from the oven.

Octavia was startled, "What are you talking about? She always hosts it so beautifully."

"I don't think she's up to it this year. You know they're breaking up?"

"What? Your parents are getting a divorce? Why didn't Sasha tell me? What's going on?"

"It's dad. He's with someone else now and she's pregnant."

"Oh my God! That bastard!" Octavia shook her head. "I'm so sorry, Alejo, I should not speak like this to you about your own father. But, still."

Raising his eyebrows, Varag shot a quizzical look at Blandine, who returned it with a faint shrug of her shoulders.

"How awful for Sasha. What will she do now?" Octavia asked.

"I don't know. She says she wants to move back to Argentina."

Slowly Octavia nodded her head. "That makes sense. She wants to be with her family at a time like this. And Washington has never felt like her home. Why has she been playing the gracious society hostess all these years if not to help Ramiro in his career? Oh, what a selfish man!"

Alejo glared at Octavia. "Washington is *my* home. What am I supposed to do now?"

Octavia fell silent.

Blandine asked, "You mean that your mother would move now, in the middle of the school year?" Alejo nodded. "Would you want to live with your father?"

"Maybe...." Alejo hesitated, tossing back the rest of his cocktail and holding his glass out for a refill. "But he's moving in with his girlfriend. Her baby is due in February. I think it would be weird."

"So, maybe you will go with your mother," Octavia suggested, recovering her buoyant confidence. "You have enjoyed Argentina on vacation. You will see, it must be a lovely place to live."

Alejo frowned. "I don't know anyone there who's my age. And I have no idea if their school system even works the same way. It's not my country. I just want to graduate and go to college."

"Maybe there's a friend in Washington you could move in with?" This suggestion came from Varag, who saw no problem with a 17-year-old no longer being under his parents' authority. Blandine was more dubious, but Alejo was shaking his head anyway.

"The problem is that I'm not an American citizen. If I'm not with my parents anymore, I'm not even sure what kind of visa I might be able to qualify for." Glumly, he pulled out his cigarettes.

Blandine bit her tongue, reluctant to make the boy feel even worse. But she couldn't help looking at the cigarettes with an audible sigh.

To his credit, Alejo noticed her reaction and excused himself to smoke outside on the terrace.

11. FALLOUT

Despite Pamela's advice, Helen had not managed to speak privately with Dawn. She had planned to wait until the crowd thinned out, but was so absorbed in the debate that she had not even noticed when Dawn left. On top of that, she seemed to remember that Dawn was scheduled to take a bus home the next morning.

After trying for many hours to fall asleep, Helen decided that perhaps she could apologize to Dawn by letter. Throwing a crocheted shawl over her shoulders, she dragged herself to the kitchen to make some chamomile tea. After warming her hands against the earthen mug, she hunched over a yellow legal pad. The paper was ugly, but perhaps the letter would require a second draft. She could copy it onto a card once she figured out what to say.

> *Dear Dawn,*
> *I'd like to apologize for my tone of voice ~~earlier today~~ yesterday. While I cannot remain silent when I hear such bigoted terms,*

No. That was no good. It was probably the rigid judgment of the word "bigotry" that had pushed Dawn to tears in the first place.

> *biased*
> *silent when I hear such ~~bigoted~~ ^ terms*

Was that less harsh? Maybe it was no longer necessary to characterize Dawn's words at all? A pencil would make erasing easier, but Helen wasn't even sure she had one at hand. The permanence of ball-point pens usually suited her sureness with words, but now it meant scratching out:

> *~~While I cannot remain silent when I hear such bigoted terms~~*
> *While menopause has been depriving me of rest lately,*

But was that really an apology? Helen began to have the impression that she was not actually trying to soothe Dawn's feelings, but to justify herself. And why was she apologizing only for her *tone* and not her *words*? Dawn seemed to be a kind-hearted woman who had simply repeated a term used by people around her without thinking about it. Helen regretted more and more having made her feel so bad. Crumpling the entire page, she started fresh:

> *Dear Dawn,*
> *I want to apologize for my harsh words yesterday.*

Helen paused to remember Dawn's exact words before hurrying away.

> *You told me not to talk to you in a way that made you feel stupid. I have been thinking a great deal about that. I realize that's the meanest possible way to speak to anyone. I certainly never <u>intend</u> to make anyone feel stupid.*

Taking a sip of tea, Helen thought for a moment.

> *I wonder if it's a trap of my profession that I have fallen into? I teach young people. Of course, I hope that I don't make any of them feel stupid either. But year after year, a new crop of students arrives. They seem less and less aware of current events. And of course they enter my classroom because I am paid to know more than they do — about the subject I teach. But perhaps I forget that there are many things that they, and you, may know more about than I do.*

> *If I'm honest with myself, I certainly know as little about West Virginia as you have had opportunity to learn about Judaism.*

Hitting her stride, Helen now scrawled without pausing.

There's also a difference between academic knowledge and intelligence. I have met young children who had yet to start school, but who were already possessed of keen emotional intelligence, knowing just when their mother is feeling blue and how to cheer her up. And perhaps I have been turning into their opposite: a tenured university professor who is losing emotional intelligence.

This letter is starting to ramble — that's yet another occupational hazard of being accustomed to a captive audience and the responsibility of filling each class with my own ideas. Suffice it to say that I am grateful to you for having taught me a lesson.

Best regards,
Helen

The mug of tea had gone cold, but it no longer mattered. As she copied the letter over onto proper stationery, Helen began to feel reassured that now she would be able to get some sleep.

Yun Hee

The next morning was Saturday. Yun Hee had slept badly and wished she could stay under the covers all weekend long. But she always woke up around sunrise. Unable to fall back asleep and tired of watching dust motes sift in through the window screen, she leaned over the side of her bed to rummage through her CDs. She chose The Sundays. The strumming of "Here's Where the Story Ends" felt about right:

"People I see, weary of me.... It's that little souvenir of a terrible year, which makes my eyes feel sore...."

By the time the aroma of Pamela's coffee reached her room, Yun Hee decided that holding a hot mug might be worth dragging herself out of bed for.

Pamela had decided to decorate the room. Ahmed had offered them both a beautiful postcard of Mount Kilimanjaro, which she was thumb-tacking onto the cheap drywall of their living room alongside some photos of East Africa she had just cut out of a National Geographic magazine. "Just look at this!" she declared. "Wouldn't it be splendid to be able to go there some day?"

Yun Hee frowned. "I guess. Anywhere but here."

"What's eating you? The kids were amazing yesterday. You and Jesse really pulled it off."

Yun Hee took a swallow of coffee before responding. "It's true, they were amazing. But Jesse's the one who believed in them. I honestly didn't think they would manage it. And I'm just so mad at Makayla. She wasn't even supposed to come."

"Is that so? I hope her absence doesn't look too bad on her school record. Maybe if you explain to her teacher, it won't be so bad."

"Maybe I don't want to. It's not like she spent the day learning about the UN. She was just smoking, and flirting with grown men, and calling me a bitch."

"Oh, Yun Hee, I'm so sorry." Pamela remembered the way Makayla's normally abrasive attitude often seemed even more cutting toward Yun Hee than toward her own mother. "No wonder you're upset. But you mustn't take things like that to heart. She's a teenager. Weren't all of us hormonal brats at her age?"

"How can I not take it to heart? I really care about her whole family. I can't just pretend I don't even notice when she gives me those looks. It's like there are daggers coming out of her eyes. And sometimes the stuff I do just feels useless. Maybe I should get a different job."

"Like what?"

Yun Hee gazed at the National Geographic images. "I could be a travel agent. My uncle has his own agency now. That would be less chaotic than dealing with Makayla. I like the idea of helping people find a bargain and enjoy their vacation."

"Sure, but what about when you end up with a customer like Makayla? Even when people are rude to you because some baby was crying on their flight, you'd have to sit there and smile."

"That's pretty much what I do now."

"Why? You don't have to. Isn't the whole point of doing activities outdoors that when tempers are running high you can just walk away from each other and wait to calm down?"

"Not exactly. We do want the kids and parents to have that freedom they wouldn't have in a centre. But Jesse and I don't walk away from the kids. I want them to know that I believe in them."

Pamela smiled. "I thought you just said you *didn't* believe in them."

"Well, making it through that skit was a challenge. But I guess most of the time I do."

"Even Makayla?"

Yun Hee sighed. "The thing about Makayla is that she's always so sure of herself. Being with her makes me feel 15 again — and when I was 15, I wasn't popular or cool. She is. So next to her, I feel like such a nerd. But that doesn't mean I don't believe in her." Yun Hee found herself beginning to smile. "She's so brash. I can definitely picture her making something out of her life."

"Let's hope so."

Beginning to feel a little better, Yun Hee said, "There were a lot of ambassadors at the event yesterday. Do you think any of them were inspired to change their policies?"

Now Pamela was the one frowning. "I don't know about that. Ambassadors represent their heads of state. They can't just change things on a whim."

"I overheard someone from the US embassy saying he appreciated what Ahmed and Tanita said. But I guess the US needs to elect a different president to actually do something about poverty."

"No," Pamela said firmly. "I disagree. No matter who's been in power, the people in the deepest poverty have always been cheated, even by communists in Europe who talk so much about poverty. No matter what their stance is on other issues, no political party yet has considered people in poverty as intelligent partners to think about policy with. That's what needs to change, in every political party."

As Yun Hee, no longer listening, began flipping through the local newspaper, Pamela's mind was still on the events at the UN. "Did you see that Mrs. Jones's daughter came to the UN?"

"Of course, she had to see Sheray and Willie on stage."

"No, not Sharmaine. Her other daughter, who lives up in the Bronx. Brenda."

"Oh! Is she the one you went to see without Mrs. Jones?"

Pamela's face fell. "Don't remind me. I know, I shouldn't have expected her to sign custody papers, with me a perfect stranger to her. She didn't sign them yesterday either. I don't think she's going to." Pamela went back to decorating the wall.

Suddenly, Yun Hee called out, "Hey, we're in the paper."

Spitting out a thumbtack between her lips, Pamela rushed to see the headline over Yun Hee's shoulder: "Tough Crowd Comes to UN."

"Hey, what do they mean 'tough'?" Pamela asked. "Everyone put their best foot forward."

"Well, look at this quote from Jesse: 'When I first started the art workshops on their block, it looked like there was a war going on.' That's why they wrote 'tough'," explained Yun Hee.

"But to make it the headline! It's insulting. And it doesn't take into account the rest of Jesse's quote: 'But there is a very strong sense of being from the same block. They are like a family and they rely on each other.' He's right, they do. That should have been the headline."

"Oh look, they quoted Mrs. Brown about the art workshops too: 'They are cultivating the kids' minds.' Well said, Mrs. Brown!"

Pamela, skimming further down the article, suddenly gasped. "They also quoted Luis Marquez. Listen to this: 'It's a good thing they do these activities with the kids, since most of these kids' moms are on drugs, so the kids really need the support.'"

"Oh no!" said Yun Hee. "Does he have any idea how bad this is going to make the parents and kids feel? And the word 'most' just isn't true."

"Even if it were true, there's still a person behind every addiction. Talking about 'mums on drugs' without any context just feeds prejudice. It makes the readers forget that a person on drugs is also a human being."

Pamela's rant hit its stride as she paced back and forth. "They're just playing into a dichotomy of guilt and innocence where people look at a parent on drugs as the 'guilty' party, without looking at all the ways society abandons some people until they can't imagine options other than drugs."

Sighing, Pamela sank onto a chair and began speaking more slowly, "I remember one of the mothers our team knew in London. Even before she managed to get off drugs, she was so careful never to come to our activities unless she was sober. I think it was her way of respecting herself and her children."

Abandoning the newspaper, Yun Hee, still in pyjamas, padded into the kitchen to make herself some toast.

Pamela continued, "There were so many sides to her. She was more than just 'a mum on drugs.' When she did come, she really wanted to contribute something. And when she did finally manage to go through rehab, she actually thanked *us* for it. She's the one who did all the work of getting clean; but she said that we were the only ones who kept knocking on her door and inviting her to events. That mattered to her."

Rummaging in the back of the refrigerator, Yun Hee extracted an almost empty jar of grape jelly. "She must have been so strong to turn her life around like that. Yesterday though, I was a little worried," Yun Hee admitted. "If any of the parents or teens had been high or drunk, we couldn't have let them come to the UN." Smelling the toast begin to burn, Yun Hee quickly unplugged the toaster, which had long stopped working correctly. "They would have made fools of themselves. But I think that's what everyone else felt too. Well, maybe not Makayla. I never know what she's thinking. But the kids had prepared so much and maybe that's why everyone had so much discipline."

"Yes, and that's why this article is such a shame. Luis doesn't live in the same neighbourhood. He barely even knows the other parents. How can he judge them so fast?"

Yun Hee thought this over while pouring herself another cup of coffee. "Well, I get the feeling Luis's life hasn't been easy either.

When you've already seen the worst in people, it's hard not to judge, especially people you don't know yet."

"True," said Pamela. "Maybe it was just bluster. And because he hasn't come to our meetings often, he's not used to taking a step back to think about things with people whose experience is different."

"If the reporter had asked him specifically about Darleen, or about Mrs. Jones's family, I bet he wouldn't have sounded critical at all. It's generalizing about a whole group that got him in trouble."

"That, and being quoted in a newspaper," said Pamela. "Who would have thought: for once, we get a little attention, but it's negative."

"Do you think we could ask them to print a correction?"

"I don't see how. The newspaper isn't asserting that anyone is on drugs."

Yun Hee protested, "But they wrote that Luis *said* they are."

"Well, if that's exactly what Luis said, the paper didn't do anything wrong."

"How about the headline?"

"I hate it because I think it plays to stereotypes — but it's not something anyone can disprove either."

"Frankly, Mrs. Brown and Mrs. Jones *are* tough, and proud of it."

Pamela nodded in agreement. "Sure, but it's kids like Dauntay or Montrell who don't deserve to be labelled with a word that makes you think they should be frisked on sight."

"That's true. Both of them have got so tall now. I see how people tense up when they walk by."

"Darleen took me to meet Dauntay's teacher once. I think it was the woman's first year teaching. I had the feeling she almost wanted to back out of the room to get away from Dauntay."

"That's so sad," Yun Hee sighed. "She ought to see how sweet he can be with his little sisters. At school, he expects to be yelled at. So of course he tries to look tough."

"Yes, and he could tell she felt intimidated by him even though he hadn't done anything. No one deserves this kind of stereotyping."

Yun Hee carried her plate of burnt toast over to a table that held the desktop computer they shared, a clunky second-hand one received as a donation. Waiting for it to boot up, she explained, "I'm making certificates for the kids who missed school."

"Didn't the teachers already give permission?"

"Yes, of course, but I want the teachers to know exactly what they accomplished and what they learned."

"That's brilliant, so the teachers know they didn't just swan off to have fun. But what about Makayla?"

Yun Hee made a sour face. "Maybe I could make one for her just in case — but I won't give it to her unless she apologizes."

Early that afternoon, Yun Hee went to Manhattan to stock up on high-quality paints and brushes at an art supply store. Travis, working nearby, had time to meet her on a bench in Union Square Park. He arrived with a greasy bag full of fries for them to share.

Squirting a thin stream of ketchup, he listened to Yun Hee's frustration with the newspaper article. He agreed with Pamela: there were no grounds to ask the newspaper to retract or correct anything. But he did empathize with Yun Hee's dismay. "It's true, for a person who's not interviewed often, it doesn't seem quite fair. Let's say I'm interviewing a woman who's on welfare. I might be aiming for her to tell me something personal, maybe even embarrassing. She knows it's for the newspaper, and I didn't force her to say it — but she doesn't know that it might be for the lead story on page one."

"So you should warn her. Reporters shouldn't take advantage of the fact that some people have no experience at all talking to the press."

"But it's our job to be aggressive. If we weren't, you'd never learn diddly squat about corruption, or what politicians do behind closed doors. So we learn to use certain techniques — and then I guess we're just in the habit of using them on everyone."

"That's not fair. You ought to have a code of ethics like doctors do. You could do a kind of triage when you're interviewing someone. You should use your most aggressive tactics for people who have professional press agents, but then be the most careful with people who've never in their whole lives been asked what they think about something."

"Oh. come off it! We've got a heap of ethics, but that's not the way they work. One of the ethics rules at my paper is that for every article I interview a range of people as racially diverse as possible."

"What if the issue is about something that doesn't affect every race equally? Like for an article about sickle-cell anaemia, it's African-Americans who get the illness, so you would talk just to them and to doctors, right?"

"Actually no. It doesn't make any difference what the content of the article is. The policy requires me to get racially diverse opinions." As Travis spoke, a dull percussion beat began thumping nearby. They heard 50 Cent begin rapping, "Go, go, go, Shorty, it's your birthday." Then the beat cut off.

Yun Hee ignored it. "Well, that's one kind of diversity, anyway. How about economic diversity? How about every time you report on Wall Street, you have to interview someone homeless for the same article?"

"Interesting. Of course that would also mean that when I write about soup kitchens, I'd have to feature millionaires' opinions."

"Go, go, go, Shorty, it's your birthday." They both continued to ignore the pounding beat, which returned for a few moments before cutting off again.

Yun Hee conceded, "Forget it. That's silly. But what about all the other kinds of diversity? Does every article include someone of every major religion? Do you make sure you interview people both with and without disabilities for every article too?"

"Hey, our policy is gummed up enough as it is. Writing one article would take forever and a day if we tried all that." Travis had just reached the bottom of the French-fries' container. Crushing the cardboard into the take-out bag, he tossed both lackadaisically toward a nearby wastebasket. Not noticing as it ricocheted off the brim, he again heard, "Go, go, go, Shorty, it's your birthday." This time, Travis looked around for the source of the rapping. Realizing that it was the ring tone of a cell phone on the otherwise vacant adjacent bench, Travis picked it up to answer.

"Oh my God!" a breathless young woman responded. "You took my cell phone. I have to get it back."

"Now just hold your horses," Travis requested calmly. "Your cell phone is out in public all by itself. I only answered it to stop that annoying ring tone. Maybe you forgot it here."

"Don't you dis my music. *Everyone* likes 'In Da Club.' Where you at?"

"Nope, not quite everyone. Your cell phone and I are in Union Square. Could this be where you two got separated?"

"Shit! I'm in Prospect Heights now. I can't get back to Manhattan until later tonight. Maybe you could bring it to me here?"

Travis burst out laughing. "That just beats all. I do like to help people out, but I have a job to get back to. But I tell you what. There's a book vendor on the southwest corner of the square. He's usually here till pretty late in the evening. You stop fussing and I'll ask him to keep it safe till you can come fetch it." Travis hung up and began walking toward the book vendor.

Following him, Yun Hee returned to their conversation. "What you're saying is that your paper prioritizes fighting racism over all other forms of prejudice and oppression. Isn't that kind of ranking just another form of divide-and-conquer?"

"Well, you have to start somewhere. In a country like ours, racism is a pretty good place to start, don't you think?"

"No. 'If I can't dance, I don't want to be a part of your revolution.'"

"O-kay," Travis said slowly, drawing out the syllables. "I reckon you just quoted Emma Goldman to me. But it beats the heck out of me what dancing has to do with this conversation."

"When Goldman said that, she wasn't just making a point about joy. She was saying that any revolution that doesn't free everyone is not truly liberating for anyone. If you commit to fighting racism while doing nothing about the prejudice against people in poverty, it's as though you're defending the right for some people of all races to make it to the top of the economic ladder — while they sneer back at the ones stuck at the bottom. None of us is free until we all are."

The amused look on Travis's face made Yun Hee realize that she'd gotten carried away.

They had reached the book vendor, a heavyset black man who looked to be in his 60s. The plastic crates he had piled four feet high were crammed with second-hand paperback books of every kind. The vendor, sitting on a metal folding chair, smiled at Travis. "Back for more already? I got some new books right here." There was a Caribbean lilt to his accent.

"Nope, not yet," said Travis. "I'm still working on that bodacious book of Edward Murrow's broadcasts. There's more than twenty years of them, so I won't need another book for at least another week or so."

"Go, go, go, Shorty, it's your birthday."

Travis held the throbbing phone toward the bookseller. "Some girl forgot her phone in the park. Maybe you'd be willing to hang on to it until she can come back to get it?"

"Why not? I ain't going no place." The jovial man smiled as he answered the call.

As Travis walked Yun Hee toward the subway, he noticed a figure on a terrace high above the square. A woman in a colorful leotard was performing a yoga tree pose. The terrace, probably a common space for all the building's residents, was landscaped with shrubbery sculpted into geometric shapes never intended by nature. Travis marvelled that anyone could attempt to reach meditative calm in the chaos and commotion of the city. However, as the woman moved into a series of lunges, Travis decided that perhaps her goal was simply exercise.

Yun Hee's thoughts went back to her sidewalk parting with Dawn. Cautiously, she asked, "What did your sister think of yesterday?"

Travis considered this. "She didn't actually say much of anything. She was kind of in a rush to pack so she could skedaddle back home this morning." Then Travis remembered: "Oh, I clean forgot, but she gave me a card to say good-bye to you." Slinging his backpack around as he spoke, he rummaged around and drew out a slightly dented envelope to hand to Yun Hee.

As she hesitated, he asked, "Aren't you going to read it?"

Feeling cornered, Yun Hee drew out a card. It showed a teddy bear holding up a dark pink daisy. The words "With Thanks" were printed in copperplate script.

Inside the card, Dawn's handwritten script was almost as neat as the printing.

> *Dear Yun Hee,*
>
> *I'm much obliged to you for spending time with me even when you were working so hard to prepare the children for their big day. You did a good job with them. I know how ornery teenagers can be. But maybe your work with the younger children will keep them from losing their dreams as they get older.*
>
> *Keep it up, and do come visit us one of these days.*
>
> *Your friend,*
> *Dawn*

As she closed the card, Travis said, "Dawn wants us to come along and go to her place for her Thanksgiving shindig. She really liked you."

Something inside Yun Hee unclenched. She answered, "It's kind of funny because I didn't think we had anything in common — but I like Dawn too."

Pamela

By Monday, not much time was left to prepare for the panel discussion on gender and the Millennium Development Goals. Pamela had prepared a convincing CV for Florence Grenier to show Varag and had arranged for Florence's transportation to New York. Florence's speech would be in French, but since that was an official UN language, simultaneous interpretation would not be a problem. Pamela was glad to have almost everything squared away. There was just one last challenge to tackle. It required a telephone call. Pamela so preferred emails, where there was always time to weigh her words. But telling herself not to be squeamish, Pamela dialled the number of the Belgian Embassy.

"Blandine? This is Pamela."

"Yes? What is it?"

"There's an event that your husband is coordinating next week. One of our organization's members will be coming here from Montreal to speak on the panel."

"Then perhaps you should call him instead." Blandine realized she sounded brusque, but she had hoped that the Friday event was the last one that would bring Pamela back to the UN for a while. Blandine just couldn't help wondering exactly how much her husband enjoyed Pamela's company.

"Yes, I have been talking to Varag about the event. But since my question now is social, I thought it more appropriate to ask you."

"Social?"

"You see, I plan to host a small dinner party for our guest from Montreal. Would you and Varag be able to come? It will be the evening after the panel discussion, a week from tonight."

Blandine racked her mind for an excuse. But she knew perfectly well that they did not have another engagement, and she had seen Pamela too often to be comfortable telling her a bald-faced lie. "I suppose we probably could."

"Oh, thank you; that's splendid."

Yun Hee

When she got to the Walker family's block that afternoon, Yun Hee saw Jesse already setting up the art workshop. Tanita was just turning the corner with Cedric in tow. As soon as he saw Jesse, Cedric yanked his hand free and sped up the block toward him.

On her way into the Walkers' apartment building to invite the children downstairs, Yun Hee noticed that the building was in even worse condition than it had been on Friday. A ground-floor apartment door had been boarded up, and some kind of fluid was leaking down the walls of the stairwell. It smelled of stale urine. She saw that someone had scotch-taped the ten commandments to the wall. "Thou shalt not bear false witness" made her think of the newspaper article. But Yun Hee didn't think Luis had actually borne false witness — no one could be prepared for the way Travis said journalists were trained to get the most sensational quotes. But what about the author of the article? Was it a form of bearing false witness to twist someone else's words into the most sensationalistic context?

Mounting the stairwell, she wondered whether Darleen had seen the article or not. The paper was sold in their local corner store, and both Lissa and Ashanti looked adorable in the photograph accompanying the article, so odds were that, even if they hadn't planned to buy the paper, a neighbour would have pointed it out over the weekend. Sure enough, when Yun Hee knocked, Darleen flung the door open in fury. "Look at this crap," she said, waving the newspaper at Yun Hee. "How dare he say we're all crackheads?"

"Pamela and I are angry too. It's not true and it's not fair. But you know, I don't think Luis meant to hurt anyone by saying that. Journalists have a way of distorting things. Sometimes I've said things that other people misunderstood or took out of context."

"That man is bugging out. He don't know what he's talking about. I hope he knows better than to ever come back to any of our meetings."

"I really don't think Luis had any harm in his heart when he said that. He just didn't know how it would look in the newspaper."

"Maybe, maybe not. But I hate this. Whoever wrote it sure don't live here. He don't know what things are like. He don't know how hard it is raising kids here. Just take last night, we got no sleep. It's 'cause of the upstairs neighbours. They only have the one key, so all night long one of them would show up downstairs and start hollering for the others to throw down the key. Plus they're still learning English. They only came here a while ago, from Haiti, you know? So I think that's why the mom doesn't know how to get rid of New York boys yet. They've got teenage girls in the family, and so boys are always hanging around them, just like they try to with Makayla when Dauntay isn't around. And last night, they got into some kind of big fight up there, mad crazy. I don't like having all that right upstairs from my own kids, it's not right. No one who don't live here has any idea what we put up with."

Having vented some of her anger, Darleen looked again at the newspaper in her hand. "Just look at this picture, though. Don't my girls look gorgeous? I'm gonna put this in a frame, right here on the wall. Only I'll cut the article off first."

Breathing a sigh of relief that Darleen's outburst was over, Yun Hee shepherded Ashanti, Lissa, and Shaniqua downstairs. Cedric had been joined by Sheray, Willie, and several other children from the block. Seeing that Tanita and Jesse had the activities in full swing, Yun Hee decided to knock on the Joneses' door to see why Allan had not come outside with his cousins.

Mrs. Ernestine Jones opened the door. "Come on in. You're looking for Allan?"

"Yes, he usually comes outside with his cousins."

"Sharmaine went to the corner store and he tagged along. They'll be back soon." Mrs. Jones turned toward the stove near the door where she began stirring a simmering pot of beans.

Yun Hee could smell onions beneath the beans. "How are you doing today?"

Mrs. Jones pursed her lips. "The school started his medication today."

"You mean the Ritalin?"

"That's right. They say he has 'attention deficit hyperactivity.'"

"In that case, maybe it will be good for him to take Ritalin. They think it will help him focus on schoolwork better, right?"

"I'm not rightly sure they know what to think. They say they'll be changing his dosage all around until they find the right one for him. They're experimenting on my grandson."

Yun Hee was surprised. "Why don't they know the right dosage for his age?"

"They say the side effects are different for every child. Look at this...." Mrs. Jones broke off her stirring to look through some papers on her kitchen counter. Pulling out a form mimeographed in blurry grey ink, she thrust it at Yun Hee. "See all those? Those are the side effects we should be watching out for."

Yun Hee scanned the long list: "Fast heartbeat, high blood pressure, chronic trouble sleeping, dry mouth, feel like throwing up, head pain, loss of appetite, nervous, over excitement, upper abdominal pain.... My gosh, I see why this is overwhelming."

"And that's only the top of the list. It starts with the most common side effects, but look down there at the other side effects. There are words I've never heard of."

"Like dyskinesia? I don't know what that means either. And it lists 'aggressive behaviour' as a possible side effect. That's crazy. They want children to behave in class but end up giving them something that could make them aggressive?"

"No rhyme or reason whatsoever."

"I'm so sorry. I know you didn't want him to take it in the first place."

Mrs. Jones sank into a metal folding chair. "Well, it's true, I still don't. But maybe it will help after all? Ever since Allan started school, his teachers have been asking me, 'What's wrong with that child?' Even Sharmaine doesn't understand why he never listens to us and is always losing his things."

Yun Hee thought about Allan's behaviour during the art workshops. "I know that he gets bored quickly when our workshop doesn't inspire him. But when it does, he can really focus on the activities he loves. He's a great kid. Maybe he just has too much imagination for his school."

Mrs. Jones smiled. "This is why it's always nice to talk to you. You don't look at Allan as if he's only a troublemaker."

"Of course he's not. But it must take a lot of energy from you to keep up with him, and to be taking care of Sharmaine's kids whenever she's at work."

"You can say that again. But it's not the energy that's the hardest part. It's the responsibility. Allan is Brenda's child, not mine. He will always be her child, and that's important to me. At the same time, I have to step up and carry the responsibility for him. So I make decisions for him every day that might not be what she would decide if she moved back home with us." Seeing Yun Hee glance discreetly at her watch, Mrs. Jones added, "I know, you ought to be getting back out there with the children. But it's real nice getting to talk to someone outside the family for a change. Make sure you stop by again soon."

"I will, I promise."

A few hours later, when the workshop was finished and the children had scattered, Yun Hee ducked into a corner store for three cold sodas. Sharing them with Jesse and Tanita, she looked around for a nice place they could sit. It was frustrating that there wasn't any place really relaxing. Even the few fast-food places in walking distance were just counters. You could pick up fried something-or-other to go, but there was no seating. But the weather was nice, so the three of them sat on a low cinder-block wall next to the subway station.

Smiling at the others, Yun Hee said, "I still can't believe the kids did so well on Friday. Tyrone looked so sharp, and did such an amazing job — all the kids did. I was just so impressed by them. Just wait until we show the photos to their teachers at school."

"Cedric impressed me too," said Tanita. "Even though he added the part about trains. But I wasn't sure he'd manage to say his line at all, and he did it, even though he was scared."

"Well, how about you and Ahmed?" Jesse said. "What you wrote was really powerful — especially when you started rapping. I know you made a lot of people think. I bet for a lot of them it was the first time they heard anything like it."

"That's true," Yun Hee agreed. "I overheard some of the UN staff commenting on what good speakers you were. Maybe they'll invite you back for some other event."

"Oh boy, I wouldn't want to do that," sighed Tanita. "Once was plenty. I was so stressed out. I haven't hardly slept all month."

"Well, just what *do* you want to do next? I know you've thought about going to college. What kind of job do you think you'd like to study for?"

Tanita was silent for a moment. A breeze against her cheek drew her eyes down the broad avenue where she could see the sky starting to blush with streaks of pinkish-orange as the sunlight waned. "Actually I think sometimes about becoming a lawyer. In one of those free legal advice clinics, you know?"

"Wow! What made you think of that?"

"It just seems like the law is always on the side of landlords who never want to repair anything, or bosses who harass you...."

"Or the caseworkers who pushed Mrs. Jones into putting Allan on Ritalin with the threat of foster care," Yun Hee added.

"Half the time I don't even think it is the law that's against people, but it's so hard for everyone to understand all the paperwork and legal jargon around us." Tanita paused to take a deep breath. "I really do think I'd like to be a lawyer. Even if it takes me a while to earn tuition."

"Hey, there are scholarships out there, you know," Jesse said. "I bet if we put our heads together, we can find someone who'd consider it an honour to put you through school. And maybe someday you'll end up a judge."

"I'll drink to that," Yun Hee said, raising her plastic bottle of soda to knock softly against theirs.

12. PERSISTING

On the following Monday, Pamela was back in a sterile UN conference room, this time with Florence Grenier for Varag's panel discussion on gender and the Millennium Development Goals. She would have liked to bring Tanita to cheer Florence on, but since Tanita had so recently taken a day off work for October 17, she couldn't afford to do it again.

Pamela found Jean-Christian Roche-Fontaine an insufferable speaker, brimming with haughtily contrived platitudes about economic growth being sure to trickle down, and about microcredit magically ending sexism. Although being asked to join the panel herself had intimidated her, hearing Roche-Fontaine made her glad that Florence was there to offer a rebuttal. Florence's speech described a completely different way to imagine building partnership with both women and men who live in extreme poverty, learning from their life experience and intelligence.

Mai Trong Pham's presentation was much more interesting than Jean-Christian's had been. Her organization supported young women in Southeast Asia trying to escape forced sex work. She spoke in a gentle manner brimming with courage and imagination. So when the panel discussion ended, Pamela invited Mai to join her and Florence for a cup of coffee. Florence did not get much practice speaking English, but was comfortable enough in the language for an informal chat.

"You were both very good speakers," Pamela said. Turning to Mai, she asked, "Have you spoken at the UN before?"

"Not in New York, but once in Geneva, and several times at UN conferences in Asia."

"Do you like public speaking? Or would you rather be working in the field?"

"You know, I think public speaking *is* a kind of fieldwork. Here, you have a whole audience of people who can really affect policy. Or you can speak to a group of businessmen, the ones who are usually driving the sex tourism industry, although that's a much tougher audience."

"So you're comfortable speaking at the UN?"

Mai smiled. "No, I wouldn't go that far. I do get frustrated with the hypocrisy of human rights language."

Inelegantly dunking a wedge of bagel into her coffee, Pamela was startled by Mai's words. "But the Universal Declaration of Human Rights is the best tool we have to effect change. I think Eleanor Roosevelt was inspiring. She convinced heads of state that putting nations and territory first kept leading us into world wars, and that we need most to protect the dignity of each individual human being."

"Yes," agreed Florence. "War and land are not so important as people."

Pamela continued, "I love how she spoke of the importance of human rights 'in small places, close to home.'"

"'Small places close to home.'" Mai echoed. "Yes, I love those words too. But human rights crusaders often forget that it is not *only* individuals who are important in those small places, it is entire communities that have a history of trying to look out for one another. Where are the rights of the community when some big multi-national company comes to overturn their way of life for a profit?"

"You said," Florence tried to remember the turn of phrase, "the human rights hypocrisy. And that is what you mean?"

"Yes, but it's not only that. It's also the way that certain countries speak as though they had a monopoly on human rights."

"I guess you mean countries like mine?" Pamela asked.

"You are from England?" Seeing Pamela nod, Mai continued, "Well then, yes. England, the US, France, and some other countries proclaim democracy as the most important human right — but ending hunger and homelessness are human rights too. And your countries are rich. Look how much wealth they squander without ending poverty."

Remembering her experience in Hungary, Pamela was thoughtful. "So you mean that maybe a country without democracy is still working hard to defend human rights by making a strong commitment to ensure that no one is left alone in the streets to starve?"

"Yes," Mai confirmed. "I didn't mean that I'm *against* human rights, but I do get tired of hearing 'human-rights language' from people who think that all the answers are in a single approach." Mai paused to sip her tea. "Now, may I ask you both some questions?"

"Oh, of course. Sorry if I was peppering you with too many of my own. Go ahead."

"Well, Florence, in your talk when you mentioned All Together in Dignity, I couldn't tell what your main programmes are. You mentioned art workshops and housing and street libraries and job training. Do you do all of that in every country?"

Florence laughed. "No, we do not. And you are right. It is not so easy to explain how we work. Pamela, you talk."

"Sure. Our starting point is getting to know people who have been left out of development projects and community centers, people whose extreme poverty has really isolated them from others. Then together, we try to agree on priorities for our work, depending on the context in each place —"

"Speak more slowly," Florence protested. "I want to be sure you are telling what we really do."

Abashed, Pamela admitted, "I get asked this question a lot. So I guess I've got into the habit of reeling off a speech. But the main starting point, wherever we are, is simple. It's human relationships: looking into one another's eyes. We want to see the humanity in people of all walks of life, and we want to develop mutual respect."

Mai tried to understand. "So your main focus isn't designing programmes or advocating on policy issues?"

Florence clarified, "We do run programmes, but we change them depending on what's happening in the lives of people in very deep poverty."

"Yes," agreed Pamela. "What we aim for is that people live their lives fully. We want all people to be able to contribute their intelligence to the world."

"You mean sending people to university?" Mai asked.

"Maybe sometimes," Pamela said, "but a lot of our work is with young children. So it could mean exploring beauty, music, and art. Or it could mean learning to use a computer or studying science."

"In Canada," Florence said, "Our members are mostly adults. We have meetings we call 'People's University.' And often we meet with people from our government or with university professors."

Pamela added, "As Florence said before, we often struggle to explain. Last year, one of our members from Madagascar was here for an event. One of the questions after her speech was, 'You keep talking about extreme poverty, but you don't do anything about hunger. How can you pretend to care about the poorest if you don't feed them?'"

"Good question," Mai said.

"Yes, it would have thrown me off course, but she had an answer ready to shoot right back. She asked, 'How can anyone else pretend to care about the poorest people without trying to shape the future with them?' That's much too tall an order for any one organization, but it's what we want to convince people to do."

"That sounds demanding — but you also sound positive," Mai observed. "What about burn-out? It seems that I keep meeting people who begin by doing work they care deeply about, but eventually it consumes them and so they look for less draining work — and then someone with no experience starts from scratch in their old job. Is that an issue for your organization too?"

"It's certainly a risk," Pamela admitted. "One of my teammates has been so fed up lately that she's wondering if she should quit and go work for her uncle instead. But one of the things about our work that keeps me from feeling burnt out is an annual event that took place about ten days ago in the UN garden."

"Oh, I went to an outdoor event," Mai recalled. "Soon after I arrived in New York, Varag Vosgrichian suggested I attend it."

"Did you hear Tanita Brown? She was the young woman who shared a message together with Ahmed Kapesa, just before the children went onstage?"

Mai smiled, "The pair who were doing rap with a drum? Yes, I liked what they said very much."

"Well, I find coming together in that way very motivating. It's just not often that people from such different backgrounds get a chance to speak to one another so frankly and to start getting to know one another. But when people want it to happen, it can be done anywhere. How did you mark the World Day in Canada, Florence?"

"Some of us traveled to Edmonton, out in Alberta. A small group there had an idea. First they made blank posters. Each poster showed only the silhouette of a person. They put the posters up around the city before 17 October. Then on that date, they changed the posters. They put other posters, with the same silhouettes, but this time the posters also showed words from people in poverty."

"How interesting," Mai said.

"Yes. Their idea was: people in poverty may be silent, but also they have something to say."

"I bet Tanita would like to see that," Pamela said. "She and her grandmother have been involved in our work here in New York since Tanita was a child. I sometimes wonder how she manages not to burn out."

"Tanita looked quite young to burn out already."

"She's 19 — but I think she's already coped with an awful lot on her own."

Blandine

While Pamela, Florence, and Mai were getting to know one another, Blandine found herself cornered by Jean-Christian who wanted to talk about the panel. "If I do say so myself, I think I put the points across rather well. I only wish the ambassador could have heard me —"

"But had he been here, *he* would have been the one to speak," Blandine commented softly. Jean-Christian, who had not stopped speaking, didn't seem to have heard her.

"— so I was thinking that he would probably appreciate hearing your feedback on the panel."

"My feedback is that I rather liked what Florence had to say."

"You can't be serious. Wasn't that her NGO that staged that outdoor ceremony last week? What a waste of time!"

"I don't know about that.... When you think of how hard it is to fight poverty, whether you're in the field like Mai Trong Pham, or whether you're trying to convince a minister or a business leader to cough up some funding or to try a new approach — well, don't you think it can be draining? I think the October 17 event was about trying to make sure that no one gives up, to keep our courage up."

"Do you even hear yourself? Didn't you see those people on Friday? Half of them looked like gang members or drug addicts. And giving them free rein to come to the UN keeps your courage up?"

Jean-Christian's bluster reminded Blandine of Alejo. They both intimidated her. But feeling emboldened to thwart Jean-Christian, she objected, "That's not how I saw them at all. I heard one of the men there telling Pamela how much he wants to find a place where no one will chase him away. Shouldn't the United Nations be exactly that kind of place? A place where a person with nowhere to belong isn't chased away by security guards?"

"You're assuming he's not armed. I think you're being very naïve. Anyway, I'm late for an important appointment." And with that, Jean-Christian strode away.

Varag and Blandine

That evening, Pamela's dinner party for Florence was to be held in Lower Manhattan, at All Together in Dignity's centre. As Varag rode downtown with Blandine in a taxi, he took note of her discreet smile. "You're looking rather pleased about something tonight."

"I had a talk with Jean-Christian after the panel discussion."

"Usually he leaves you seething."

"You're right, he does. But that's because usually I don't say very much to him. Today, I actually contradicted him — and he didn't like it at all."

"Quite a change indeed. You mean you didn't just nod and tell him that his speech had been even more brilliant than he thought?"

Blandine laughed. "Come off it. Even I have never told him any such thing. But I do seem to nod a lot, don't I? I always think that nodding will make people like him stop talking more quickly, but it doesn't seem to work that way."

When they arrived, Helen Jansky opened the door to usher them inside. Since it was Varag's first visit, she made sure to point out the photos displayed in the front room. "You know Tanita, so maybe you'll recognize her here, although she was just a child at the time." They saw her with several other children proudly showing off a brightly coloured wooden box on a sidewalk filled with dirt and a few shoots of young plants. "They had just painted all the flower designs on the box."

"Hey, we did more than paint — we made all the boxes from scratch," said a teenage boy joining them.

"This is Dauntay Walker," Helen made the introductions.

As Varag and Blandine followed Helen toward the room in the back where a table had been set for ten, they passed a small kitchen. Sticking his head in, Varag said, "Something smells good."

"Sure hope so," Jesse responded. "The menu is vegetarian lasagna with chicken on the side."

"Trying to please both vegetarians and carnivores?"

"That's the idea," Yun Hee answered.

"Where is Pamela?" Blandine wanted to know.

"Be right there," called a muffled voice. A moment later, Pamela appeared, with a large wet stain on the shoulder of her dress. Indicating it, she explained, "Of course, I had to spill tomato sauce on myself. But I *think* I've scrubbed it out pretty well."

"So all three of you have been cooking?" Varag asked.

"That depends on what you call cooking," Jesse teased. "Keep Pamela out there. We're better off without her."

"How nice to see that it's not only women doing the cooking," Blandine commented. "Here, Pamela, we brought you some wine and chocolates."

"Oh, thank you so much." Placing the gifts on a table, Pamela led the couple into the back room where Florence was just hanging up the telephone. "Did you reach your husband?"

"Yes, he is fine."

Hearing the doorbell, Helen returned to the front door and came back with Tanita and Sharmaine.

"This is all of us, so let's have a seat while Yun Hee and Jesse finish cooking. I think everyone has met already, right?"

Blandine greeted Tanita and Sharmaine while trying very hard to keep her expression neutral. Once again, she felt that Pamela had trapped her in an awkward situation. The girl clearly did not even have a seating plan and was just waving everyone randomly into whatever chair was at hand. Perhaps Pamela had actually never been taught the art of hostessing? Blandine remembered how carefully her own mother had tried to anticipate and prevent every possible faux pas among her guests. Maybe there was a self-help book she could offer to Pamela? Smiling to herself, Blandine wondered whether such a book as *Hostessing for Dummies* existed yet.

Varag, guessing that Sharmaine's presence disconcerted his wife, wondered at her smile, but was glad to see her relaxing. Accepting a glass of lemonade from Pamela, he raised it toward Florence. "Let's toast your panel of this morning. I was glad to hear you stir things up a bit."

"Yes," Blandine agreed. "It did go well. And shall we also toast Tanita for last week's eloquence? I must say, I was particularly touched by the children's performance with the lantern of hope."

Carrying a steaming tray of lasagna to the table, Jesse grinned. "We'll be sure to tell them."

As Yun Hee arrived with a platter of roasted chicken, Pamela smiled at them. "You both should take credit for that too." Then she turned back to Blandine. "And actually, I wanted to thank you for having made the effort to come. That meeting of ours in

September was so chaotic that I would have understood if you hadn't bothered."

Blandine made a slight grimace. "Perhaps I should have stayed until the end of that meeting, but I think I was rather out of place."

Tanita spoke up, "That's just how Ahmed and I felt about speaking at the UN — out of place. We just didn't know who might be listening."

Slowly, Blandine nodded. "I suppose that makes sense. We can in fact be a ruthless bunch at the UN." Turning back toward Pamela, she said, "You know Jean-Christian? Just after the panel this morning, he more or less told me that security should have been chasing some of your group away, as they were probably dangerous."

"Dangerous?" Helen asked. "It takes a small mind to be afraid of words."

"But you told me you contradicted him," Varag recalled. "What did you say?"

"Well, he was going on and on about how useless the October 17 event was. He went only because his ambassador insisted he go. I don't think he even listened to what was going on. So I told him that I thought it was important for people with nowhere to go to be able to come to the UN. Isn't that what the UN is for?"

"You'll get no argument from me," Varag declared. "But it's true that the Jean-Christians of the world are always ready to cast suspicion on others."

"Exactly! He called the whole group gang members or drug addicts." Hearing Sharmaine gasp, Blandine immediately regretted her bluntness.

But Varag was laughing. "Little did he suspect, it was our well-tailored guest, Alejo, who might have been the one there most likely to be high."

Helen arched her eyebrows. "Good point. Wasn't that what he said when we were having coffee after the event?"

"With all the talk about racial profiling," Varag said, "We ought to talk more about economic profiling. People make so many assumptions about one another."

The evening passed pleasantly. When Blandine and Varag got home that night, she decided to make a confession of sorts. "You know, I was quite annoyed with you for sending me to that meeting of Pamela's in September."

"Yes, so I'd noticed."

"But I think now that perhaps you had a point. I was rereading the programme from October 17. It explains why the commemorative stone in honour of the victims of poverty was first placed in the UN garden. I don't want to forget what it says." Blandine took the programme from the coffee table and read aloud:

> *"Over centuries, remembrance has contributed to the progress of humanity. Through monuments to suffering and death, we remind ourselves of the horrors of wars, slavery, and genocide. Why, then, are our landscapes not marked by monuments to recall the victims of the hunger, ignorance, and violence inflicted on people in extreme poverty? These people leave no trace upon the earth. They are buried in unmarked potter's fields. Their slums are erased from our maps. They are not the authors recording their history in our books.*
>
> *"The Commemorative Stone in their honour is a monument signifying that in extreme poverty, people often live and die in shame and humiliation. The stone's permanence is a sign that these people are important to our communities and our nations. It means that others want to end the shame, and that we want to engrave in our common history the lives of the most vulnerable people.*
>
> *"Joseph Wresinski, who inaugurated the first Commemorative Stone in 1987, said, 'I bear witness to you, the poor of all times, despised and disgraced. I bear witness to you, so that humanity may at last fulfil its true destiny, refusing forever that misery prevail.'"*

When she had finished reading, Varag said, "Beautiful. I'd like to remember that too. But do you think you might ever convince even Jean-Christian to begin listening to people living in poverty?"

Blandine gazed out the window at the darkened sky. "What was it Ahmed said? 'Until the sky turns silver'? We might have to talk until the sky *does* turn silver, but who knows? Perhaps one day I will."

The End

AFTERWORD ABOUT ATD FOURTH WORLD AND THE EXPERIENCES BEHIND THIS BOOK

Diana Skelton: I grew up in Washington, DC, where I knew people who lived in poverty and also diplomatic families based there to work with embassies or the World Bank. Since I joined the ATD Fourth World Volunteer Corps in 1986, it's been a revelation to me that people from these very different situations can get to know one another in a meaningful way. That's what gives me hope for the future: the enormous potential that society has when each of us finds a way to listen to and learn from someone whose life experience has been vastly different from our own.

My work with ATD (represented in this book by All Together in Dignity) began when I was 19 and helped with its Street Library workshops in the South Bronx. In my 20s, when I was married (to a fellow ATD Volunteer Corps member) and having children, we were based in Europe with an ATD team that connected teenagers in poverty from across Western and Eastern Europe, just after the Iron Curtain opened up. Back in the US, I spent nine years as ATD's main representative to the United Nations, which included meeting with UN Secretary-General Boutros Boutros-Ghali and with Her Majesty Queen Rania Al Abdullah of Jordan. Shortly after our third child was born, our family moved to the capital of Madagascar, where the government was evicting families living at the city garbage dump who were only trying to eke out a living by recycling whatever they could scavenge. Then in 2008-2016, I was part of ATD's International Leadership Team, which means that I had the chance to visit our members throughout Asia, Africa, Europe, and the Americas. Our role was to consult people in deep poverty, to coordinate our worldwide planning, and to make sure we could all sustain our motivation to continue. One of our key participatory research projects over those years was about the violence of poverty and the roles played by people in poverty in building peace. More than a thousand people from twenty-five countries participated.

I used this research to write a three-volume non-fiction book called *Artisans of Peace Overcoming Poverty*.

As Jean and I wrote this book, we relied greatly on Marie-Elisabeth Ayassamy for support, guidance, and inspiration. She first joined ATD Fourth World as a teenager. From 1980 to 2001, she was part of the ATD full time Volunteer Corps. Ten of those years were spent in New York City running Street Libraries for children in Harlem and Brooklyn and also working with adults in poverty to prepare for meetings at the Fourth World House. In 1996-2001, she was my teammate. She and I collaborated to prepare public events where people living in poverty met with United Nations staff and diplomats. We are very different people, and we were often on two different wavelengths during those years. But I found learning from her through our daily teamwork to be very rewarding, which is why I turned to her for support with this book.

Marie-Elisabeth Ayassamy: I joined the ATD Fourth World Volunteer Corps because its work was important for me. I grew up in a ghetto area, southeast of Paris. When I was a teenager, the volunteers of ATD came to my neighbourhood and opened new doors to me. They introduced me to other non-profit organisations. Meeting ATD was the first time I ever had the chance to go to the movies, or even just to sit around and really talk about life. In my family, my mother was too busy working hard to have much time to talk. She could not read, and she was working very long hours in a hospital kitchen just to scrape by. She went through a lot of difficulties in life having five children on her own.

I wanted to help other people like my mom. At the time I was already very involved in ATD's youth movement. For my job, though, I had been working for two years with the postal service, on the night shift. It was a civil service position with lifetime job security. But even though it represented stability, I didn't find it interesting; so I quit in order to join ATD's full-time Volunteer Corps, where I spent more than twenty-five years. In France, I was part of ATD's teams in Marseille, Sartrouville, Noisy-le-Grand, and Champeaux. I was also part of the team on Reunion Island, off the coast of Madagascar. Then in 1990, I joined ATD's team in New York City where I still live.

I stopped working with ATD in 2001, and now I am a teacher at the International Preschools, where the context is completely different. In this job, my regard for young children has grown stronger. My hope is for all children to get the social and emotional support they need as early as possible so that they will have the foundation to develop their own education. And of course, children also need to play and sing and laugh.

Early Childhood

When poverty makes your childhood chaotic, your home is full of worries. Before you even know the words to speak about it, you witness things that little children should not have to see. That damages children. Their lives lack structured routine, so it's very hard for them to begin structuring their thoughts, or to situate themselves in the physical world and develop fine and gross motor skills. If you don't have time to learn the basics by age 4 or 5, it's still possible for you to succeed — but it's not the same. There are barriers. It takes so much work to catch up later.

My mother, Ignace Jeanne Ayassamy, never went to school as a child in Guadeloupe. She was working so that her younger brothers and sisters could go to school. When she grew up, she left her native island. She was ambitious and hoped that in France she would find work. The first time she ever became a student was when she was 40 years old. She took literacy classes with a member of ATD who visited her every week, and she learned to read. But it cost her an enormous effort. She can spell phonetically now, but it's still hard for her to understand a written text. That's a handicap in life. She never caught up with everything she could have learned if her life had been different. But after she learned to read, she took on another challenge. She was very motivated to be more independent, so she took driving lessons. It took her many years to pass the exam, but she invested the time and money, and she finally got her license. She also finally got a stable job, doing maintenance for the post office. She is a strong woman. The strength people say they see in me comes from her. She could not give us all the comforts and support that we needed, but she always sent us to school. We practically never missed a day of class.

I went through many things in my childhood that were hard to understand and that I still don't understand. The only thing I can say is that my mother lived the life she did because she didn't have people around her who understood her. She wasn't perfect. But the people around her were too judgmental. For my part, I'm determined to try to understand the history of my family and of so many other dislocated families. Why did we end up in these situations? I have two brothers and two sisters; but my mother raised only three of us. That suffering marks you for life. You lose trust in society.

When I began working with ATD, I was living out my trust in society, in a way. What has always drawn me to ATD is the close attention it pays to the people who have been the most rejected by society.

When my mother moved to France, she was alone with us children and had no one she could count on. She did a thousand and one odd jobs in order to raise us. Things were very hard for her. Then, when I was 3, we fell into miserable poverty. All of us children were temporarily removed from her custody. That period in her life is a mystery to us. The only thing she tells us is that more than once she had nowhere to sleep but in subway stations. My 4-year-old brother and I spent four years living in an institution before she got us back. For my other brother, the removal from our family lasted his entire childhood. He didn't come home for good until he was 14. He had been sent further away than us because his health was fragile. My mother couldn't afford the train fare to visit him, but she never abandoned him.

We were so young when we were sent to the institution. I

remember being moved from one centre to another, but none of the moves were ever explained to me. Now that I am working professionally with toddlers, I realise how crucial it is at that age to have the right context for learning. It's not that my brothers and I haven't coped and succeeded in life, because we have. But if our childhoods had been different, who knows if we could have gone further? Society really needs to invest more in early childhood because of the effect it has throughout your life.

The Methodology Behind Cooking Together

One of the things I did with ATD was to bring people together, not only to meet one another informally and eat meals but also to cook as a team. I am a firm believer in the importance of getting to know one another by doing a concrete job together. It's a methodology for building community. When people introduce themselves by talking, it can end up being about who has studied more. People tend to see others in categories depending on how comfortable each person is at presenting themselves. So getting to know one another through a project like cooking can help us to go beyond categories.

Cooking projects can be fantastic fun with children. But the challenge is bigger with adults. For big celebrations, we'd often have ten of us adults in a kitchen. Some were people living in deep poverty; others were middle-class or rich people who wanted to help out. Everyone has a different idea of how things should be done in the kitchen. My rule was that we avoid having long discussions and disagreements about the menu. So to prepare a special meal every Christmas, together with the parents living in poverty we would decide in advance on the menu that would make our children the happiest. The holidays are not the time to worry about diet and nutrition. We just wanted the kids to have a joyful celebration. Usually we cooked traditional southern American recipes, because so many of the families in poverty in New York came from the south. Then on the big day, our cooking team would be a mixture of parents in poverty and people who wanted to support them so the project would succeed. And we were really very diverse. Some of the people drove each other crazy just because of their ways of expressing themselves. It was never easy, and we were always exhausted. But every time, all of us knew that the children were really looking forward to enjoying a big festive meal. So we had to make it work.

People in the Depths of Poverty

Whether it's for cooking or attending a meeting, whenever you bring people together in a group, some people are more outgoing and comfortable expressing their ideas. But our priority with ATD was to involve people in the depths of poverty, like one mother who always used to say, 'Why are you asking me to talk at the meeting? Ask my neighbour instead. She's the one who's smart.' For people like her to become comfortable in groups, I spent a lot of time making individual visits. I don't mean the kind of "home visit" that social workers make. It was more a question of being available for whatever made sense for each person. For instance, there was one mother whose son took part in the weekly Street Library we ran as a time to read books aloud and do creative activities together. When this mother was summoned to her son's school because he'd been acting up, she asked me to go with her. It wasn't in any kind of formal role, but just as moral support for her. She knew that in the Street Library, I had seen a positive side of her son and how he behaves outside the structured context of school. Our relationship helped her to stay calm while the principal criticised her son. Without that kind of individual support and really getting to know people one-on-one, the people going through the most difficult situations wouldn't have come to our group meetings or events.

Another priority with ATD is not to separate people by considering some "good" and others "bad." Middle-class people who want to do something about poverty often want to help "the good poor." But when people feel miserable and judged by others, that often forces them to protect themselves first of all. And I believe that everyone can change. There was a social worker in the neighbourhood where we ran the Street Library.

After he visited the parents of some children we knew very well, he told us, "After spending time with a difficult family like this, you need a vacation. I can introduce you to an easier family." He could not understand that it was part of our goal to see something positive in all people. Some of the families we supported had a teenager in jail, so going with the parents to visit the young people in jail was another way to show that everyone has something positive inside them.

People in Poverty as Activists

We live in a society of expectations that grow higher and higher. Someone who does not fulfill those high expectations is judged harshly. But I think we should look for the success that Bessie Stanley describes:

> 'What is success? To laugh often and much; to win the respect of intelligent people and the affection of children; to earn the appreciation of honest critics and endure the betrayal of false friends; to appreciate the beauty; to find the best in others; to leave the world a bit better, whether by a healthy child, a garden patch or a redeemed social condition; to know even one life has breathed easier because you have lived. This is to have succeeded!'

Some of the people in poverty we supported eventually succeeded by becoming activists who could take the lead to defend others. One mother never set foot in any of our meetings for a long time, but she would say, 'I'll join you one of these days.' Even when she did not join our gatherings, she was already a strong leader. When her building was infested with rats and the landlord refused to do anything, she called up a TV station and got them to come report on it. Then the landlord had no choice but to get rid of the rats. And finally, one day, she started coming to our meetings. She said, 'Now I can come because I've kicked my drug habit and gotten my life together.'

Another example of activism came from the woman who used to say, 'Why are you asking me to talk at the meeting?' Even though she wasn't comfortable speaking in public, she's the one who asked us to bring the Street Library to her block. She said, 'The only thing happening on our black is drug deals. We need to do something for the kids.' She couldn't accept that there was nothing for the children; she had to act. Another woman in poverty decided to help us get discounts or donations from stores for the food we served at events. She was used to fighting to feed her own family, and she would insist to store managers, 'You have to donate this food. It's what you owe to the community.' Several of the parents would make a point of sitting down to watch the Street Library whenever we came. They might not have been comfortable joining in, but for them, watching us from a stoop showed their children that this project mattered to them and showed the neighbourhood that they were protecting us.

All of them, and many other activists living in poverty eventually helped us to prepare a seminar together with teachers and academics. Our goal was to show why poverty can make it hard for children to learn in school, and also to show the conditions that make it possible for the same children who are struggling in school to succeed at learning and creating in a Street Library. This content of this seminar has been published as a curriculum for educators or anyone working with low-income children: *Unleashing Hidden Potential: How Parents, Teachers, Community Workers, and Activists Came Together to Improve Learning for Children in Poverty*. It was possible for us to do that intellectual work together because of everything we did beforehand: not only running the Street Library, but also supporting people individually and bringing them together for concrete projects like cooking or times of celebration before having meetings and seminars.

Joseph Wresinski, who founded ATD, saw the importance of activists living in poverty working in pairs with members of the Volunteer Corps. My understanding of his approach was that you have to have at least two people who see things differently and who are on an equal footing. It is easy for someone who is educated to lead the word of someone with less educated; but the reverse does not happen easily. For pairing people up as teammates to work, both people have to want to learn from each other. If your goal is to meet people individually, and also to change conditions of poverty, you need both points of view and both approaches.

My own work as an activist includes helping with this book. The writing was done by Diana and Jean, but I've contributed what I can so that readers can understand why certain actions to overcome poverty are worthwhile. Since I began working at the International Preschools, I've begun concentrating on young children, wherever I go. The question of early childhood brings me back to the roots of what Joseph Wresinski wanted in founding ATD Fourth World. He started by opening a preschool for children in an emergency housing camp. It's important to me that our society be able to help all children at that young age.

Drawing Courage from Moments of Joy

I have both good and bad memories from my childhood years in an institution; but the moments of true happiness that stand out are when we sang together. Even when I felt the loneliest, music made me happy. That's the feeling of joy and well-being that I want to give children today.

That's what ATD did with the flower boxes. The ones that Tanita and Dauntay made are based on ones that we made with children in East New York, Brooklyn. On Montauk Avenue, all the children there really looked forward to our Street Library. But the whole area looked so desolate. There were hardly any trees, and nothing pretty. There was just concrete, wherever you looked. I think that it matters to kids how things look around their home. They want to transform everything, even if they can't usually carry out everything they can imagine. So those of us who were running the Street Library saw potential in front of one of the children's apartment buildings, where there was a small patch of dirt. Our first idea was to plant a real garden there. But we couldn't get permission to do that. Even when there's a setback, though, there's always something you can manage to do.

So instead, we helped the kids to build four large boxes out of wood for planting flowers. We got sponsorship from the Green Guerrillas resource centre, but the children did all the work with us. To build the boxes, we worked right out on the sidewalk over several weeks, so the whole neighbourhood saw how hard the children were working. Some parents came to help us every day. We made the boxes three feet high by three feet wide, so you could see them from far away. When the woodwork was done, the children painted pretty nature scenes on the boxes in bright, beautiful colours. Then we filled the boxes with dirt, and we planted flowers. We put all the boxes along that block where we held the Street Library and it made the whole street more beautiful for everyone to enjoy. If you were feeling sad, I think that just looking at the boxes could inspire you with courage.

ATD Fourth World is a movement for human rights. As members of ATD, what we did most was to accompany and support mothers and fathers living in neighborhoods that are completely infested with violence and drugs. With these parents and other members of ATD, we created a community of respect and attention centered on children. One of the goals of the Street Library is to invite children to love books, a key tool for creating this sense of community. It was never easy to foster collaboration among people with different levels of education, all from different backgrounds, having different personal problems, and envisioning different kinds of solutions. What we did was not perfect; but I do think it made a difference in the hearts of the children who grew up in the Street Libraries.

Jean Stallings: My Journey to Activism and Writing

I'd like to share something about what writing means to me; about my own journey in life with Johnnie Tillmon, Dr. Martin Luther King, and Dick Gregory; about ATD Fourth World; and about people I know who helped inspire the characters of Tanita Brown, Ernestine Jones, Darleen Walker, her son Dauntay, and others in this book.

I come from a very hard childhood. Writing has been important to me since kindergarten. Because I was left handed, my teacher tried to take the pencil out of my left hand — because it was a no-no then in the 1940s — and put it in my right hand. And I kept insisting I couldn't do it. I couldn't do it and I would have to tolerate taps on my hand because I had to become right handed. At the same time, I was already able to read well. The teacher complimented me even while tapping my fingers and taking the pencil out of my left hand and putting it into the right. I guess giving a child a positive thought can block out negative thoughts? I held on to that. And when finally I could start writing on my own, I felt a connection with words. I've always been interested in reading.

Samantha Simpson is a long-time member of ATD Fourth World in New York City who went through many struggles in her family too. They lived in shelters. She lost her mother at a young age too. But she's come around. What a speaker! What a beautiful, intelligent woman she is — and she's such a beautiful writer of poetry. It's a good feeling when you can express yourself and give someone else a little bit of that seed for nurturing people with just an idea. There's also Kathleen Saint Amand. I was so honoured to hear her speak on October 17 a few years back. She spoke about her life and struggles. She spoke about humiliation that she had to go through when she lived in a shelter in Queens. When people found out she lived in a shelter, they insulted her family. The night before the event, when she showed us this testimony, it had us in tears. When she read it at the UN, the ambassadors applauded her and even stood up when she finished.

Zena Grimes is another member of ATD Fourth World who lives in poverty. She trains the ATD volunteers in many ways. She has lived in shelters and has had many volunteers support her through the process of getting out of the shelter to finally get into public housing. She had a couple sets of twins, twelve kids in all. She lost a son and carried on. Recently, her brother was killed and she carried on. She's gone through so many things; but this young lady had no high school diploma or GED.* The teachers in her children's school would tell her to help her children with their homework. So she asked them, 'What about us parents? We want to get an education too.' And they listened to her. I like to think that a lot of her courage and empowerment to confront them came from the many years that she was able to speak out to ambassadors for ATD Fourth World. Events at the UN gave her confidence to give the teachers a challenge. She initiated a project where those teachers organised a group to start classes for the GED. Today Zena Grimes has a GED diploma. I'm so thrilled that the group was able to go back at thirty-something years old, and then come looking to get a college degree. I'm so proud of Zena. When we first met, it took her years to begin to trust me. But today, she has amazing confidence.

When Someone Has Faith in You

I had to struggle to get educated myself. I had a troubled home life. I left high school at 16 years old to work as a house cleaner. Years later, my mother encouraged me very much to go back to school and supported me to get my college degree at age 40. That's why I told Zena, 'If I can do it at 40, you can do it now because you're so much younger.' I hope that one day she'll understand that she can go to college too.

It was a struggle for me. I had five children. My youngest had palsy, so studying was a struggle whenever she had to go to therapy. Every day, I felt overwhelmed. When no one pays attention to what you need for yourself, you can feel resentful

---

* The General Educational Diploma, designed for those without a high school diploma, is awarded based on a set of tests to certify aptitude, knowledge, and skills in language arts, social studies, science, and math.

and lost. But when someone has faith that you can do it and tells you, 'Just try to hang on,' that makes you feel that you can't disappoint them. They believe in me. Once, my textbook got ruined. I couldn't afford to replace it, but my mother found a way to buy me a new one. That belief she had in me is the same thing that I give to younger people with the ATD movement. I want to make them feel capable. Many things that people say that you can't do in life are actually the very things that you *can* do. You find out that you can do them all.

When my children were growing up, the National Welfare Rights Organisation was made up of mothers: some single, some married, most on welfare benefits. I identify myself as an African-American always; but I also feel that I belong to the whole world. I didn't consider myself part of the civil rights movement, although reflecting back I can see that we were. Many people don't realise that we mothers worked. The reputation was just 'single women having all these babies and getting on welfare'; but so many of us worked. The way I started with this organisation was that I heard there was going to be a thrift sale at the community centre. So I put my babies in the carriage and off we went to buy some things cheaply. I was walking around picking out things when I heard talking. Someone said, 'Do you want to get information about help for your kids? Come to this meeting.' I hesitated. I was terrified to walk through the door into that meeting with my babies in their stroller. But other women reached out to me that day. They planted a seed in my heart that began my journey to activism. I went into the room and here were these mothers like myself. That was it — forget the bargains! I was so taken aback. They were expressing their displeasure with the political system. It seemed to me that it was a place of safety, where mothers' voices could be heard. That's how I became a member of the national welfare organisation. Someone asked me to sit in on a meeting and it changed my life.

Wanting to Be Treated With Dignity

At that time, in the 1960s, there was great shame in being

unmarried and having children. Poverty and shame went together. There was no recognition for single mothers as human beings. You were outcast because of the colour of your skin, and also as a single mother. We were stigmatised and intimidated by caseworkers for the social service authorities. They would inspect our homes, unannounced, looking for a trace of a man under your bed, in your belongings. They were trying to prove we were lying about being single. They turned our homes upside-down in front of our children. They checked your food, they checked everything. It was terrible. They were disrespectful — as though your welfare payment was coming out of their pocket. They would say: 'You're going to do what I tell you, or else.' They would threaten you. As women on welfare, we were humiliated. We felt talked at, as though we had no part in the decisions in our lives.

Our goal was to let people know that we wanted to be treated with dignity. In the welfare rights movement, other women trained me. I found my own voice. And we cared for one another, even in hardship. In your worst moments, what you need most is someone who will look into your eyes without disgust.

I started going to the National Welfare Rights Organisation meetings. I felt so good going to the meetings. We had a meeting up in Albany one day. I didn't realise it was for preparation to go speak outside of New York State, but I went to this meeting and asked questions. They gave me confidence to speak: 'You have a voice, Jean!' That's how I felt. When the meeting in Albany was over they said to me: We want you to be a delegate for us. We want you to go to different places and speak out about the mothers you know. Wow! My mentor was Beulah Sanders, a woman still active in human rights. She taught me how to be an activist. And so I started going to different places. I had the opportunity to meet a congressman to talk about different issues. That's how I got involved. I didn't consider myself an activist. I considered myself a young mother who was struggling and who had the opportunity opened to her. People told me, 'Come join us. You're going to learn how to speak out for yourself.'

Teaching Dr. King

That's how I wound up going to a YMCA in Chicago to meet Dr. Martin Luther King in 1968. He was planning for the poor people's campaign but we women weren't being included in the thinking because of the myth that "welfare mothers" were lazy. At that time, women were not at the forefront of the civil rights movements. We were vocal, demanding mothers. We were not pleading. We said, 'We have a right!' Sometimes people were taken aback. Even Dr. King's movement wasn't always pleased with us. People today don't realise what we were up against.

The organisation wanted me to go to its national committee meeting in Chicago. That trip to Chicago was my first time taking an airplane. I travelled with Mabel and Abby, two other delegates from New York. I didn't know if I would be properly dressed. Someone gave me shoes — proper shoes — to wear when we would meet Dr. King. We were women from all over — Baltimore, Roxbury in Boston, California, all across the United States. Some people thought we were too aggressive, but it was what we had to do. We shouted our way in — 'Open the doors, open the doors for us mothers!' And they did.

When we got into the room with Dr. King, it was like talking to someone with an aura around him. It was all in his eyes. But did we hold our heads down? No! They didn't call national welfare rights activists "women"; they called us "warriors" — "warrior mothers." They called us that because we didn't "be," we "told." We didn't let them talk down to us. And we expressed our desire to be recognised by his movement. I asked, 'Why isn't Coretta talking to us as a mother?'

'Sister,' he replied, 'Coretta's not feeling well, but I will relay the message to her.'

We said to Dr. King: 'We want recognition and respect. And we want to be a part of your movement, but you will have to include us in your talks. You have to tell people the challenges we face, because mothers are the bearers of the next generation.' We talked for a long time.

Johnnie Tillmon was the head of our organisation. She said, 'You don't know very much about us do you?' At first, he didn't know what to say. She continued, 'Dr. King, if you don't know, just say so and we'll teach you.' He wanted to learn what our needs were and to find out more about us. And he wanted us to be included in planning the poor people's campaign. He was killed a few months later. But his poor people's movement was branching out — he was starting to oppose the war in Vietnam and to include women.

At the time, I didn't realise the historical context of it how important it would become to me and many other young mothers to have that connection to Dr. King. After he passed, it was just so hard. Part of your heart was gone. But we learned from that experience.

We also met Dick Gregory, who was a great actor and activist then and right up to his death. That was at Lake Forest College, where Hulbert James, a National Welfare Rights leader brought us. I and other mothers had the opportunity to get on stage to talk with Mr. Gregory. I was thinking, 'Oh my God, what am I doing on stage next to this great man?' He encouraged us to keep talking and helping ourselves in other ways. He also told us what he would do to advocate for things that we needed. So I had the opportunity to meet people that I never thought I would meet. They gave me a sense of self-worth to speak out and to write. I was invited to the caucus for child care, and they listened to us. We got the funding for child care that we needed. That kind of success for women in poverty was pretty rare in those days.

We had dignity. The War on Poverty in the early 1970s helped us women. I had the opportunity to advocate. They sent me to a congressman's house to discuss our issues. He was responsible for funding for many things. In the community at that time, we had no child care and no Head Start programme. He asked about my vision for my children. I said, "We need education and training to get off welfare. We want to work. But I'm not leaving my babies any place unsafe. I want them to be safe but I have nowhere for them to be while I learn and work." I couldn't afford to pay anybody then. And so he gave us funding for a Head Start programme in our community centre. My daughter was one of the first ones to go into that class. I was thrilled. Then they started training us in nutritional programmes. It sounds simple, but you need to learn to cook nutritional meals. They got funding for it and I was trained to manage the food pantry. I was working to feed my children without Food Stamps. Along with distributing cheese, butter, beans, and dried milk, I put up a bulletin board with notices to the community telling them what their rights were. I felt like I was part of something that was good. My mother was so proud.

The National Welfare Rights Organisation propelled me to go on to other things. I got my education and volunteered in different things. That voice for change was in me and I went on using it. It's so important to feel part of something. It doesn't have to be big. You don't have to be famous. You just have to give a part of yourself. I wasn't a leader but a little seed. I learned to speak without fear. I had a voice.

I meet young people who don't feel they can do anything. You just have to plant a seed of hope and listen to their pain. Their experience means more than anything. Once they start talking to others, once they meet others and listen, they see people who are suffering more or less than them, and they begin to feel the safety net opening up.

I want young people to know there are things they can do. In my day, it wasn't just the Freedom Riders or the leaders. Everyone played a part. Maybe it's just a small part, but what matters is that people change their own lives and someone else's life too.

Worry Can Swallow You Up

So many people in ATD Fourth World are doing the same thing: accomplishing something despite the difficulties. I've seen young mothers like Zena going to talk to ambassadors and also coming back into the community. Zena started speaking with the mothers in the projects. She encouraged them to come out and be a part of the ATD Fourth World Street Library. Other mothers started slowly coming outside with their children and learning with them. She brought many people to the Fourth World House. There's also a young man, Obie Donald. He came from a lot of struggles but he's doing very well and going to college now. I've seen him develop. He's shy sometimes but I've listened to him talking. I understand that he works hard and has a very strong mother. It's just something good to see.

You need support when you're home alone and you're overwhelmed with that feeling of worry. It can swallow you. You're worrying about food, clothing, your children, if they're getting the right education. Many schools and school systems are not for poor children the way they should be. The backing is not there. They expect certain children to fail because of their background. I remember many times raising my children, they were expected to fail. When my daughter who had cerebral palsy was in high school, she had to get extra help because of her walking. She had this gait where she dragged one of her feet. So she went to the school's special resource room for one hour each day. Putting her in the resource room was considered special education, and that gave the school extra funding. But the school also wanted to refuse her a high school diploma because of her being in 'special education.' She was really smart and her grades were up to par. But the district heads and the superintendents said, 'She takes an elevator, so she doesn't qualify for a regular diploma.'

I said, 'What? She takes the elevator, which means she's gonna get a diploma that's less than what she earned?' Unbelievable! I had to go to bat for her with all those supervisors. It worked, though. She not only got the diploma she earned, but went on to earn two masters degrees and become a registered family therapist.

When I can think of these things, the words just flow. I wish now that I had more time to just sit and write everything. But I feel overwhelmed sometimes with a lot of things that I want to put on paper. Writing releases me. It's like water, when you get into a shower and water pours down over you, you feel this sort of flooding release. Writing releases some feelings that I have. I still suffer from sadness from time to time. Before, I couldn't admit that I'm good enough to have a gift to write. But now when I write and I can look at these words, I can accept that writing is important to me.

School Was Denied to My Uncle

My mother gave me this book, printed in 1899. It was first given to my uncle, Willie Moses Bates. He could not read. He could not write. He was never able to attend school because he was placed in the cotton fields to help work for his family's wages. My uncle 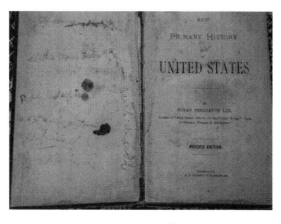 was longing to read. He was given this book by a white person, the plantation owner's son on the land where he picked cotton as a boy. School was denied to him.

This book has been in my family for nearly a hundred years and represents a time when education was not available to all children. My mother remembers all her brothers sharing this book to look at the pictures and to learn.

I told my mother years ago: 'Thank God that my uncle could not read the negative remarks about Native Americans and slaves in the book.' This American history book was written in 1899 by the daughter of a Confederate general. The way it speaks about people is not a way that anyone can feel proud to read. One passage describes life in the South of the United States by saying: 'People in the South were more lively than in the North. Plantation owners lived in large houses, with cabins for the slaves nearby. They were kind to strangers, always had their houses full of visitors, and did not feel they were committing a sin by having slaves. But many Northern people were holding them up to the world as great sinners.' The book is even harsher about Indians. It says, 'The savage and barbarous Indians were [...] idle, boastful, cruel, and torturous. They had no regard for the truth. The Indian was a tyrant over his wife whom he would often beat and drive away from home.' When I first read it, I couldn't believe that this was a schoolbook that they used to teach children in South Carolina. It's heartbreaking.

But my uncle never did learn to read. Instead, he would practice writing his name throughout the pages: 'Willy Moses Bates, Willy Moses Bates.' I think about the hardship that he and so many people in my family went through because they were in the south. I know that the perseverance and hope and faith that my uncle had is in families in poverty in every part of the world. I trust that the message of hope and strength continues. It's important to me to tell others about this book so that people think of my relatives, who could not read, but who inspired the next generation in our family to continue to strive toward higher education.

Tanita's Teacher

In Chapter 2 of *Until the Sky Turns Silver*, Tanita remembers that once she saw her teacher talking to a homeless man. We based this passage on a similar encounter that I had with someone who was homeless. One day, I was on my way home from a meeting at the Fourth World House. My granddaughter Brianna was with me. We were waiting for a train in Penn Station and this man was next to me. He was looking at my granddaughter, most likely because she was a teenager, 15 or 16 at the time. She is an attractive young girl. He was just looking at her up and down, and he said, 'Is that your daughter?'

I was thinking, 'Nope. Don't do that.' So I let him know right away that I thought he wanted to say something to her. Then I simply asked, 'How are you?' And he respected that. He didn't get nasty. He just stopped immediately. I don't think he even looked at her any more. He felt comfortable I think because I directly told him, 'No this is the limit. Don't do it.' He accepted it. Something was good in that man.

He answered me and it just flowed. He told me that he was in the train station because he was homeless. He didn't ask me for money. But he said that from time to time, people would give him a used train ticket. He needed to be able to show the police a ticket to stay in the station. Otherwise, they would make him leave. This was where he lived. He had a place to sleep in the train station and a place he could go to the bathroom (for there are bathrooms on each train at Penn Station). He was just roaming around the train station and getting on a different train each day, not knowing where it was going.

I then just started to ask him questions about himself: 'How are you? Can anyone help you? An agency?'

He started talking: 'No, no, no. It's unsafe.' He said that it wasn't something he could do. He tried but it didn't work for him. I asked him if he had any family close by. He just opened up then. This man had a well of hurt inside. He starting talking about rejection. Because of the way he lived, he couldn't have contact with his family. He had a family – a wife and a child. His eyes just shined when he talked about his daughter. I asked how old she was, and he told me. He said he can't see her.

I asked, 'You're not allowed?'

'No, I can't see her,' he said. 'I don't want her to see me like this.'

I asked whether he ever talked to her on the phone and whether he had her contact information.

He said, 'No, I don't want her to know about me. It's better like this.'

But I said, 'What about her?' I just started talking to him about the loss that she must feel not hearing from him.

He said that he knew she loved him, but that he didn't want to hurt her any more.

I talked to him for quite a while about the value of words. Even if she didn't answer him, he should still let her know where he is and how he feels about her. This is something she will carry with her for the rest of her life. I wanted him to let his daughter know that he cared about her and that he loved her.

Then, it was as if an idea came into his mind where he felt that maybe he could do it – maybe he really could after all. What a good feeling: to see that man's face and to see his eyes. It was planting that little seed. I wanted to nourish it a little more. I hope that one day he did write that letter. Can you imagine that little girl? I know what it feels like to have someone say that they love you when you haven't heard it before. I hope he gave that to her.

The World Day for Overcoming Poverty

Ever since I got involved with ATD Fourth World, on every October 17 I get to go to the United Nations and listen to families in poverty who have worked for months and months to prepare to express their feelings. They do this by going to meetings, by writing, or by having home visits from ATD's volunteers. They can tell the United Nations about their daily struggles of living and struggling to live; about their children; about dealing with the crisis of housing in New York City; about dealing with feelings of being isolated; about how they don't feel like they have a voice in the community; about politics.

On October 17, you get to hear them put all those feelings of hurt and despair aside to say, 'I am somebody. You've come here to listen to me and I am going to tell you how I feel and what I need from the UN as a governing body.' It is very important. It gives them a sense of dignity.

This World Day also empowers people like Blandine, Varag, or Helen who listen to the poor, because they get to hear people at a different level. People in poverty are not giving a list of complaints. They are saying, 'I am living in poverty, but I am still here and I am still determined to give my family and myself a better life.'

ATD Fourth World, which first started the October 17 commemoration, is a movement that I've been part of for eighteen years now. What has changed the most for me is to see young people grow within this movement. I first met many of them when they were very young — in elementary school — and they've grown and developed into advocates. They have helped and brought people into communities. They have brought people out of housing projects and into the meetings at the Fourth World House. They have told other young people: 'This is what we have done and you can come join us. You can learn to express your feelings without going to the streets, and without getting involved in crime. You can do something that is going to help you and your family and give you a sense of pride.' I've seen that, and I've seen them come in and bring young people with them that you maybe would not want to pass in the streets because of their attire. And all these young people turn out to have a heart of gold. They want the same thing as any other child in America. It's wonderful.

On October 17, even if you don't live anywhere near the United Nations, all of us can make it a special day to end the silence of people in poverty. It's a matter of getting the word out about it to different people. You can't stay in your own community and talk to the same people about October 17. If you want to enlighten a different class of people — people who can help you, people who have a network — you have to get out. One of the things about the young people that I have seen is that they get out into the community and go visit communities outside their own neighbourhood. They are meeting people from different levels of life, giving them a sense of what they have done. They talk about why they are engaging others to help create a ceremonial event for October 17. It is very important to teach these young people to go out into other communities and also to go out into the political world and tell government bodies what this day means to us.

I am part of the International Committee for October 17. In 2014, we held our meeting in Dublin, Ireland. We visited a rehabilitation centre for young people who had been caught up in drug addiction. I had the great pleasure of meeting a group of glorious young women. I told them about my own experiences and feelings. I think everybody has been touched in some way by a friend or family member who is caught up in the world of drugs — that world of despair. The young women poured their hearts out. Some of them have issues that are unpleasant to cope with. They wanted to know how I handled that as a mother, a grandmother, and now a great-grandmother. Some of them were very upfront with me and told me that I should have done something different for my own family. I learned from them. They were not criticising but saying, 'We needed a certain kind of help, but we needed it in a different way so that we could have felt we could do something for ourselves. If things had been different, we would have gotten help a long time ago.' Our conversation was a great chance to exchange ideas with them and to exchange respect. I care so much for them and still keep in touch.

ATD Fourth World has also connected me to young people in Palestine and Israel who want to connect and move forward in peace. I wrote a poem for them:

Children, oh our children.
We have pierced our hearts
with our history of unspoken pain,
turned the promised lands into dust bowls of steel,
crumbled bodies of souls, young and old,
into shattered ashes down into the ground
that will never bear seeds.

Children, oh our children.
Hear our cry, mothers of your womb,
we say to you there is justice and peace,
understanding and relief,
only with the courage of speech,
you must share your bonds of love,
no barriers in between.

Children, oh my children.
Past disagreements of wars we hold as lessons,
for we know to repeat is failure,
listen our children,
take the lead,
march together unafraid of rejection,
clothed in hope it is you who will make the dreams
and hope of peace be the promise of the lands.

In so many places and in so many ways, we're in trouble! But we can never give up. We have to cast away our doubt, and our fear, and our anger. I do get discouraged when I see evil. But will I let an evil spirit overtake mine? Can I let it make me lose the purpose of my life?

The answer is no. We can never let that happen, and we will never give up.

NOTES

During the years this story is set, the Prevention Assistance and Temporary Housing centre, first mentioned in Chapter 2, was called the Emergency Assistance Unit. The term EAU has been changed to PATH because it is more familiar to low-income residents of present-day New York City.

Tanita and Ahmed's speech at the United Nations in Chapter 9 includes excerpts from interviews to prepare the World Day for Overcoming Poverty (also called the International Day for the Eradication of Poverty and marked every October 17) conducted in 1992 with several of the above people, and from speeches written for October 17 in 1996-1999, 2001, and 2004.

Yun Hee's song in Chapter 9 is excerpted from "Every Child Should Have a Chance," a song written for October 17, 2000, by Estelle McKee and based on the words of children in New York from All Together in Dignity/ATD Fourth World.

The quote from Joseph Wresinski in Chapter 10 is an excerpt from his poem, "Verses to the Glory of the Poor of All Times," translated from the original French.

*

For more information about All Together in Dignity/
ATD Fourth World or the World Day for Overcoming Poverty, please
see www.atd-fourthworld.org.

35584467R00143

Printed in Poland
by Amazon Fulfillment
Poland Sp. z o.o., Wrocław